Robyn Mundy's writing speaks to her fascination with wild places and their sway on human lives. In the preliminary stage of writing *Wildlight*, she and her partner spent four months living and working alone on Maatsuyker Island as volunteer caretakers and weather observers. Robyn has summered and over-wintered at Australian Antarctic stations, working as a field assistant on science research projects. She works seasonally as an Assistant Expedition Leader on ship-based tours to the Antarctic, Arctic and other remote locales. At home in Tasmania, Robyn writes and teaches writing. Visit her website at: writingthewild.net

Also by Robyn Mundy
The Nature of Ice
Epic Adventure: Epic Voyages
(co-author with Nigel Rigby)

WILD LIGHT

Robyn Mundy

PICADOR
Pan Macmillan Australia

First published 2016 in Picador by Pan Macmillan Australia Pty Ltd
1 Market Street, Sydney, New South Wales, Australia, 2000

Cataloguing-in-Publication entry is available
from the National Library of Australia
http://catalogue.nla.gov.au

Typeset in 12/17.5 Bembo by Midland Typesetters, Australia
Printed by McPherson's Printing Group

Lighthouse sketch on page 289 reproduced with kind permission
of Ailsa Fergusson.

Australian Government | **Australia** **Council** for the Arts

This project has been assisted by the Australian Government through the
Australia Council, its arts funding and advisory body.

MIX
Paper from
responsible sources
FSC® C001695

The paper in this book is FSC® certified.
FSC® promotes environmentally responsible,
socially beneficial and economically viable
management of the world's forests.

For Ian Templeman, mentor and friend
1938 – 2015

Note on pronunciation

Maatsuyker Island was named in 1642 by Dutch navigator Abel Janszoon Tasman during his exploratory voyage of Australian waters. 'Mat<u>sy</u>ker' is the common Australian pronunciation.

PROLOGUE

2015

Stephanie's focus slides from the sliver of moon to the beacon at the tip of the wing, distant enough to appear as a star. She looks down through the night at a twinkling of lights from some tiny tropical island, barely discernible from this great height. Ferdinand Magellan's wayward course across the Pacific missed all but two of this ocean's thousands of islands. Perhaps we navigate life in such a way, alter course at just the wrong moment, blink and miss landfall, pass by unseen.

Steph reclines her seat, tucks the doona around her feet and pledges eternal devotion to Qantas for the upgrade. Behind her the first dusting of snow on the Sangre de Cristos, the wool coat she shrugged off and left on a plaza bench at Santa Fe.

On the far side of the dateline floats an image of Sydney Airport, bittersweet with homecomings, a crowd of expectant eyes searching through and beyond her while those incoming, weary from the long haul home, peel away to waiting arms. The cover of the inflight magazine reins her in: a culinary smorgasbord too glossy for melancholy. Stephanie homes in on the cover's lavish table setting: glass vessels, ultramarines and aquamarines, the sea greens of the ocean. Blown glass, artworks in themselves.

She raises her seat, riffles through the pages. *Harvest from the Haven.* She halts at the photo of a man, jeans and jacket, his arm resting on a wooden crate of produce. The likeness is uncanny. Mid thirties, three years older than her—even the age would be right. The face seems oddly set, perhaps self-conscious before the camera; oceans more worldly than the boy she once knew. Stephanie studies his hands. She skims the text. *Organic dressings and condiments served in our first-class cabins and Qantas lounges.* A name shimmies off the page, her chest held tight by the words. *Tom Forrest.*

Her first lover.

The boy that drowned at nineteen off Maatsuyker Island.

1

1999

Steph wheeled through the sky, willing herself to be fearless and free. Then the helicopter lurched and courage dumped her with a reminder that only a shuddering bubble of tempered plastic separated her from the wilderness below.

Before the helicopter had left Hobart she'd been reduced from a sixteen year old to a needy child—*Let's get you sorted*: the pilot, aftershave overload, threading the seat harness and fastening the convoluted buckle which now Steph wasn't sure she could undo In The Unlikely Event That The Helicopter Should Be Required To Ditch.

Under an hour, the pilot said the flight would take. Not even halfway there. She'd kept the swirling in her stomach under control, but civilisation was now a light-year behind and they were passing so near the mountainside you could practically reach out and brush the trees. The pilot turned to her and winked and Steph wondered if he'd wangled things so she scored the front seat. She wanted to motion ahead the way her father did when her mother was driving and talking and pointing out things all at the same time, as if to say, *For God's sake, Gretchen, keep your focus on the road.*

They were lower than both peaks now, weaving around pockets of mist through which the pilot, unless he had radar vision, and Steph hoped beyond hope that he did, could see nothing at all. She wrapped her arms around her stomach which sloshed like a water-filled balloon. Callam would have revelled in this. But her brother was gone, and if anyone remembered the bad things, they didn't dare talk about them now. Saint Callam, she sometimes felt like saying when her mother went on. If her twin brother really was up there looking down, he'd be laughing his testicles off and going, *Scaredy cat chicken shit you're gonna crash you're gonna die*, and plenty more where that came from. Steph's head throbbed with the glare. Her stomach pitched and rolled.

She glanced back at her father wedged in the far corner, gazing out through the helicopter window as if he hadn't a care. You'd never guess he was as scared of heights as she was. Perhaps that was the definition of adulthood: you just got better at hiding how you felt.

Why were they dropping? Steph gripped the seat and willed herself to sit statue still, to focus on the waterway below. River? Rivulet? Or a glistening black serpent winding its way to sea? No roads, glimpses of a track; chances were there was nothing down there among those acres of button grass but a wilderness writhing with tiger snakes. And by God, Steph had let it be known, if the island they were destined for harboured a single such creature, her mother would be embarking on this certifiable pilgrimage ALONE.

Her eyes sharpened on the helicopter door, processing upside-down instructions, trying to make sense of the arrows: one of those levers, she remembered, unlatched the door from its hinges and sent it spinning off into the cosmos In The Unlikely Event That

The Helicopter Should Be Required To Ditch. The pilot had acted out each step of the safety briefing, bracing as they prepared to crash, beating his arms above his head like a lunatic as the rotors sliced through water. Steph had an image of herself hurled like a plum through blind darkness, the slam of the Southern Ocean smashing her apart. She had nodded nonchalantly when the pilot explained that she would lose all sense of up and down, water flooding the cabin, her survival dependent on holding her breath and keeping her wits intact to unbuckle the seatbelt. Wait for the rotors to stop, follow the lifeline of bubbles from your lungs that lead to the surface. *What then?* she would liked to have asked. The one hundred k medley back to Hobart? A bright September morning deflated into grisly ways to perish in Tasmania's wilderness. They weren't even over water yet.

The helicopter veered, the tinny muffle of the pilot's voice crackled through her headset. 'Precipitous Bluff.' Steph opened her eyes to a piercing blue and the glare of morning sun. A jackhammer pounded at her skull. The pulsing silhouette of the pilot's arm gestured to the right. 'Ironbound Ranges.'

Her mother, seated directly behind, tapped Steph's shoulder. 'Look. Down there.' Her excitement carried through the head-phones. 'Louisa Bay. We're close.'

Her father reached from the back corner, tapped her shoulder. *You okay?* he mouthed.

Steph shrugged. She felt awful. God, now her mother had the video camera pointed in her face. 'No,' she said too sharply. The pilot turned at the commotion. Steph scrambled through the side pocket for a sick bag, a tissue, a cloth—please, anything!—but the projection of vomit filled her cupped hands. Her stomach purged a second round. The smoothie her mother had warned her against ordering for breakfast ran curdled over her jeans and inside her new red gumboots. She felt agitated movements from behind; her mother slid an emergency card beneath her chin to act as a drip tray. Steph pushed her arm away. The rank smell permeated the cabin along with the pilot's disgust. Steph withered.

From somewhere a towel and water bottle was thrust in her lap. She wiped her mouth and hands, swished water around her mouth, gagged at the prospect of swallowing and drained the putrid mess back into the towel.

If you've had enough practice you can stop yourself from crying, but inside this whirring capsule there was no escaping humiliation. She turned to the window to block out the world, her parents' reassurances, *Almost there, sweetheart. Not long now.*

They were over ocean, skirting a large island. 'Big Witch,' the pilot called it. Another ahead. Steph squinted at a cove marked with a gantry, a broken line of railway sleepers carved a scar up the slope. The Gulch, the haulage way: she knew those landmarks from her mother's old photos. The canopy of green was one of those optical illusions that your eyes struggled to make sense of: you might be peering down at treetops, or you might be looking down at barren coastal scrub that barely reached your knees. Her hands felt sticky. They stank. Steph wanted to brush her teeth. She needed to pee. She took another gulp: the water tasted stale.

The helicopter rounded a ridge to where two white cottages nestled side by side on the hill, all country garden with painted fences, their perimeters of lawn keeping the bush at bay. A grass road meandered past the cottages then disappeared into bush. 'Second and Third Keepers' Quarters,' her mother said through the headphones, as if the old lighthouse was still manned. Her voice carried a reminder of whose rightful domain this was. Steph and Dad were the newbies. The helicopter tilted at such an angle Steph had to pull back from the door in case it inadvertently opened and flung her out like a Red Cross rations drop. They passed over the old Head Keeper's Quarters, a solitary cottage flanked by a paddock that abruptly dropped away. Steph saw where grass met cliff, sheer to the ocean below. She craned to look back at a second roof as tiny as a doll's house, at a path that led from it to a weather screen. The grass road reappeared, arcing downhill toward the southern tip of the island, indigo lapping cliffs on either side. The ocean looked motionless, tiger-striped with foam, still as a dead boy's breath.

Beyond the furthest point they circled back beside an ellipsis of rocks: shark's teeth foaming at the gums where they pierced the blue. The Needles. If Steph hadn't felt so bad she could have sung the name of those rocks before her mother announced them. They looked like the tail vertebrae of some prehistoric animal. Her mother pointed to the lighthouse perched high above the ocean, shiny, shiny white.

The cleared areas claimed by the cottages and lawns amounted to a tiny skin graft of civilisation upon a great humpback of wilderness. It was none of the quaint scenes from her mother's old photo album, the stories Steph grew up with. Devoid of beaches, the place was a fortress, walled by cliffs and a moat choked with kelp.

Below, a limp windsock gave way to a clearing in the bush that looked too small for a landing pad. The blue nose of a vehicle peeked through the trees. The helicopter hovered, swayed its hips. They inched lower, the pilot peering down through the side window. He manoeuvred the throttle as lightly as a computer mouse. They were even with the treetops, now they were below them. Steph read a painted sign: *MAATSUYKER ISLAND.* A soft thud, a bounce, the kiss of solid earth, an exhalation as the rotors lowered pitch. They were down. They were safe.

2

Steph mistook Lindsay, the outgoing caretaker, for a ranger in her green brimmed hat, a Parks emblem embroidered on the front. Lindsay stood at the door of the Head Keeper's cottage with her feet set apart. She handed over the contents of the pile one by one and Steph tried to be grateful, truly she did: a threadbare towel, a frayed shirt crumpled and stained, a pair of lilac trackpants that could— that should—have been a Vinnies reject. Steph tried to smile. She tried to be polite.

Lindsay knew. 'Best I could find in the emergency drawer. They'll have to do until we bring down your bags.'

'Do you know where Mum and Dad are?'

'Brian's taken them up to do the nine o'clock obs. Plenty of time for a shower, get yourself cleaned up. Tummy all settled?'

Steph closed the bathroom door. The weather observations were *her* job. She'd done the training in Hobart. They'd all agreed.

An old-fashioned bath was set beneath a full-length window. Anyone could walk by and look straight in. Away in the distance a spear of land stretched across the blue. Steph huffed. All her mother's talk of the roaring forties: the ocean glistened, barely a breeze. From where Callam was looking down, Maatsuyker and its surrounds must resemble a smattering of biscuit crumbs brushed off Tasmania's south-west rim.

It took an age for the hot water to coat the window with steam and give her privacy. Steph was down to underwear and socks when the door banged. Lindsay's form filled the scalloped glass. 'Don't be too long, pet. We need to conserve our resources.'

Water? It rained two hundred days a year at Maatsuyker Island.

The textured glass of the shower cubicle was webbed with cracks, the caddy's rubber coating flaked off and encrusted with rust. Everything in this house—their house now—looked fit for the tip. Steph picked up a block of grey soap as coarse as sandpaper; it smelled of sweaty socks. She opted for a dried sliver of green that slipped through her fingers the moment it was wet. She placed her foot across the drain to stop it disappearing altogether. Another rap on the door.

'Almost done, Stephanie?' Lindsay sounded cross.

'Nearly.' You could never tell with people. Lindsay had seemed kind—grandmotherly—when they'd met at the helipad. *Let's get you cleaned up, poppet.* She'd marched Steph and her parents down the grass road, nodding to landmarks as if it were Mum's first time on Maatsuyker Island. Steph felt for her mother. She looked vulnerable again, her big moment that should have been just the three of them dawdling and detouring, Mum showing Steph every little thing and sighing and saying, *That's the track that goes up to the Light Keeper's Tree* and *That's where we kept the chooks* and *We even had a pig here for a while* and *That's where I used to run down the path through the arbour to get to the lighthouse and meet my dad at the finish of his shift.* From ground level the cottages didn't look as cheery—white walls scabbed with red where brickwork showed through, the paintwork flaking and dribbled with rust. The palings of one fence were gone altogether, the other hung at a lean, patched with fibro sheets.

'Someone's put some work into that vege patch.' Her father's voice sounded hoarse. His halting speech reminded Steph of a light globe on the blink. Dad brushed away Lindsay's look of concern with a wave of a hand toward the terraced beds. Patch? Plantation. The vegetable garden took up more space than their front and back yards at home.

'We arrived to a beautiful crop, James. Fresh veges all the way through.' Lindsay was taken with Dad, you could tell. She would have heard him on the radio. 'Our turn to do the same for you two.'

Three, if anyone should bother to count.

Now, hovering there outside the bathroom, Lindsay had transmuted into the Water Police. Steph imagined her stopwatch running. She reminded herself that by this afternoon Lindsay and Brian would be gone, on their way to Hobart in the helicopter. *Whoo hoo*, the ghost of a voice butted in. *Bet you can't wait to be on your ownsome with Mum and Dad.*

Shut up, Callam. But her brother was right. Sixteen, the biggest year of her life. To be dragged out of school as if a Higher School Certificate didn't count. Five months stuck on an island with no one but her parents. Steph mashed the soap through the grate, she drew a stricken face upon the misted glass, the hair a swirl of kelp. Who would be around to help her with the afternoon weather? She needed Brian. She turned off the taps. She needed Brian now.

*

Steph followed the path uphill from the house. A posse of green birds flashed by. The whine of the helicopter escalated to a squeal, the air pulsing as it lifted from the helipad. Beneath the fuselage a rope spun ever-widening circles like a carousel ride, its sling load of netting bulging with Brian and Lindsay's outbound gear.

The empty weather office reeked of mould. Mum's sunglasses sat folded on the desk. Steph put them on, studied her reflection in the window. She'd never be as elegant as her mother. Why hadn't they waited for her? Alongside a computer, the weather logbook lay open. Steph ran her finger along the numbers and codes. She couldn't remember what they all meant. Another desk was littered with dead blowflies and info sheets about clouds and weather and measuring the ocean swell, the print bleached from sun. The desk would be big enough to spread out her art. Steph opened the locker to a fug of mustiness, to forms and wicks, barograph charts, a pile of old logbooks stippled with mould and warped from damp, the bindings a loom of cotton thread. Somewhere in the collection was the imprint of her grandfather. She tried to conjure an image of him living and working at this place. Zip.

Keeping up her grandfather's tradition, her mother had sounded so proud when she'd taken Steph in for training at Hobart's weather bureau. This sky was nothing like Hobart. This was supersized, urgent, layers of clouds in too great a rush to ever stop. The cirrus was easy to recognise, opalescent, crimped as sheep's wool, like the photo on the poster of cloud types stuck to the wall. A low bank of powder puffs marched overhead, as sprightly as a chorus line. Across the ocean to the mainland, a steely billow rose to an anvil behind the mountain range. Down low, a band of sea salt hazed the coast.

Steph paced the short path to the weather screen and looked down across a paddock that angled past the house. Beyond was a wall of green that obscured all but the dome of the lighthouse. The air felt cold. The sun burned her skin.

She heard voices and saw Brian in his fluoro vest peel away from her parents and race back along the road. She stopped herself from chasing him down.

'There you are,' Dad called to her.

Her mother's gaze shifted to the lilac track pants. 'Lordy.'

'When's Brian coming back? Why didn't you wait? Do you have my clothes?'

'Chill out, Steph. Brian's gone to get the bags now. Dad's all up on the weather. He'll do the handover.'

'Dad?'

'Yes. Dad.' His voice rose with indignation. 'Many thanks for the vote of confidence.'

Steph trailed her parents to the house. Dad held open the flywire door. 'Care to do the honours, milady?' He swept his arm for Mum. 'Hallowed ground that it is.'

Beyond fickle, the pair of them. *You can't turn back the clock*, her father spouted before they left Sydney. Now, as Mum stepped inside and looked down the hallway, her smile pursed as it had back then.

Fire extinguishers and safety signs lined the formal entryway. You could bet there had been no OH&S in the seventies. They stepped over loose carpet squares patterned with swirls. Steph could recite a list of her father's trusty sayings: *Nothing stays the same* at custard-coloured walls bare except for rusted nails and hooks. *You can never relive the past* at the crumbling Victorian archway her mother had raved about. Those two 'chandeliers': clouded plastic pendants as tacky as toys.

'How do they keep the place warm?' Her mother's voice sounded meek. Each room had a chimney and mantlepiece, each fireplace boarded up. Dad gave a theatrical, 'Ugh' at the double mattress covered in brown vinyl, the sort you'd have for kids who wet the bed. They followed her mother down the hall.

'Steph, you'll sleep in my old . . .' Her mother's voice trailed. Steph looked in the room. Callam. The last months he was alive you could never pin him down; now he sprang up all the time. A window that looked out at the water, the same as her brother's room; another that faced the sky. Glossy white bunks like those they had shared as little kids, before Steph had got her own room. Even the ladder on the bunks was a matching shade of blue. *Home away from home*, Steph might have spouted if it hadn't felt so raw. Back at home she'd felt invisible, her mother's focus intent on turning Callam's room into a shrine. The only thing missing was a donation box for entry. Her mother gripped her sides as though her innards might spill. Dad stood silent and still. *A break from all the memories,* her mother had said about coming here. *A chance to move on.* She hadn't counted on Callam West sneaking in ahead of them.

No one dared speak as they followed her through the glassed-in porch. She led them to a room piled with junk, the label on the door: *Museum.*

'My father's old office.' Her mother's voice was flat. Dad picked up a set of signal flags then set them down. The room felt cold and damp. No one's heart was in it. Steph's hair hung wet and heavy on the shoulders of an old lady's shirt that smelled of mothballs. Mum propped herself against the wall like a bird too feeble to hold itself up.

'Twenty-five years, Gretchen. Time marches on.' Steph caught Dad's blink of irritation. Her father didn't want to be here any more than she did. Hallowed ground? The house was as skanky as a Kings Cross backpackers.

★

'In here, good people,' Lindsay chirped. The kitchen smelled as good as Gran's. Lindsay scooped powder into a jug and whisked it into milk. Steph's stomach grumbled at the tray of scones hot from the oven. 'Don't wait to be asked.' Lindsay slid the tray her way. 'You'd never have survived growing up in our house. The hoovers, Brian called our two.' Lindsay began performing Gran's ritual with the teapot, three turns this way, three the other. Steph felt too hungry to eat slowly. Another failed New Year's resolution.

Mum opened cupboard doors. 'Shall I get the mugs?'

Lindsay offered a sad half-smile. 'It's your kitchen now.' Steph looked at the dinged furniture, the cracked linoleum. It was hardly worth getting sentimental over.

Steph took a second scone and followed her father out to a bright sunny room with a washing machine; more plant nursery than laundry. Trays of seedlings topped the chests of drawers. The air smelled earthy.

Dad inspected the labels. 'Brussels sprouts. Cauliflower. Cabbage. All Steph's faves,' he whispered.

'Hilarious, James.'

'We use those drawers for clothes storage,' Lindsay called from the kitchen. 'Only place in the house where things don't go mouldy.'

Her mother joined them and stroked the washing machine as if old Casper were stretched out on top, not shipped off to Canberra with his electric blanket to board at Gran's. 'Remember, love? We had a twin tub when we first married.'

Lindsay joined them. 'Hope you brought a good supply of pegs. I'm down to the last handful. Socks and hankies blown to Kingdom Come, till we knew better. There's at least two seabirds between here and Hobart wearing Brian's jocks.' She turned to Dad. 'Bri take you through the weather? All clear as mud?'

'Brian will show me, won't he? It's me, not James, responsible for the weather.'

Lindsay raised her eyebrows with a *kids these days* look. 'Bri has his work cut out at the helipad. Your food and boxes to shuttle over from the mainland. Our things to go back.' She turned her attention to Dad. 'They're expecting a front later in the day. They want us off ASAP.'

'*You* could show me,' Steph tried again, full of encouragement. She didn't want Lindsay to feel second best.

'We'll wait and see, eh.'

Adult code for *Fat Chance*.

'Heck, I forgot the jam.' Lindsay raced away. 'I've been saving the last jar.'

Steph helped herself to a third scone. The rusted fridge was small, decrepit, an inside freezer crusted with ice. 'How did you survive, Mother?'

'What do you mean?'

'Everything's—'

'Primitive?' Her father filled the gap.

'We were entirely comfortable. And happy.' Mum looked cross. 'The house was always toasty warm. Not like now.'

Steph spotted the phone-fax at the end of the bench. Her mother's voice distanced to a blur. Steph fired up her mobile. Tessa or Sammie: who to text first? Her mother droned on.

'Dad baked bread. We had plenty of fresh eggs and vegetables, sometimes we caught fish—he'd throw out crayfish rings when the weather was kind.'

Steph moved to the lounge room, punching the keys of her mobile. *OMG. We're talking Detention Cntr!!!!* She waited for the signal bars. She marched down the hallway and out the flywire door, past a large pantry off the wet porch where Lindsay wobbled on a stepladder, a jam jar in one hand, her free arm wiping dust from the shelf. Steph followed the grassed perimeter of the house, ignoring ocean and lighthouse, holding her mobile above her head and willing God Almighty Or Whoever Else Is Up There to grant her a signal. She angled up the paddock and aimed the phone directly at the tower. 'Take that.' A full minute. Nada.

Steph stormed into the kitchen. 'Can anyone get a signal?'

'You can chuck that thing in the deep blue yonder, the good it will do you.' Steam fogged Lindsay's glasses as she topped up the teapot.

'You didn't tell her?' her father said to her mother.

Mum shot him a look.

'Tell me what?' Steph said. 'Mum?'

Lindsay beamed. 'Ain't no curv'rage in this purta town.' She chortled at her own lame performance. Even Dad flared his nostrils with disdain.

Steph took a breath. 'The mobile tower is at the top of the hill.'

'Telstra repeater, lovie, for the so-called landline, when it behaves itself. Tasmar Radio repeater at the north end of the island. That won't help you, neither.' She looked triumphant.

'Telstra told us that there is mobile coverage. Didn't they, Mum?'

'I thought that's what they said.'

Lindsay motioned to the landline. She had an annoying habit of turning to Dad when it was something important. 'Linked to mainland Tassie by a series of VHF repeaters. Bri says the signal won't even support a modem.'

Steph felt ill.

'Steph, I know it's going to be different at first.' Her mother sounded earnest, wanting to avert a scene. Confirmation that it was true. She'd known all along. 'There's a lot to get used to. You can ask your friends to phone if it's important. They can fax you a letter. When I was growing up here we didn't have—'

'A letter!' Steph slumped into a chair. 'No one phones a landline from their mobile. You said it wouldn't be an issue. You said I'd be able to stay in touch. That's what you said, Mum. You promised. You swore.' Next thing she'd be blubbering in front of Lindsay. She wasn't having that.

'The landline is paid for by Parks,' Lindsay said. 'For business and emergency.'

Her mother looked embarrassed. 'We have to respect that. We can't go calling Sydney every other day just to chat with friends.'

'Respect, Mother? How about honesty?' Mum's face coloured scarlet. Lindsay looked away. 'I won't have any friends by the time I get back.'

'It won't be so bad,' Dad chimed in. 'What with the weather observations, Year 11 studies—'

'Year 12,' she reminded him.

'You'll have the island to explore, walking tracks, a bit of brush-cutting, your art always keeps you busy—island time will fly by.'

Steph flinched when he touched her shoulder. 'Trying to convince yourself?'

'Come on, Stephie,' Lindsay said. 'Not many teeny-boppers can claim their own lighthouse. I bet in your mother's day—'

Steph clasped her skull. Teeny-bopper? She was almost seventeen. She checked her mobile for a signal. She was on her own, cut off from the world. She turned to her mother. 'I've given up my life for you. Everything.'

Her mother sighed.

'My friends, my social life, Lydia's eighteenth, the most important term of school.' Steph couldn't stop. 'And why? To support my *mother* on an island that no one's ever heard of, where there's no one but my parents to talk to, no email, no TV, no internet. NO MOBILE COVERAGE.' She glowered long and hard. The flywire door banged. Lindsay paced along the driveway, intent on whatever food scraps she was ferrying to the compost bin. 'You never once asked if I wanted to come. What I thought. Did you ask Dad before you signed our lives away?' Her mother turned her back. She stared out through the window. 'This is all about you, Mum. Pretending you're still a girl living at a lighthouse, everything sparkly, as if nothing's changed, as if Callam were right here, squeaky clean and perfect.' Her mother bristled—Steph pounced on it: 'Boys' pranks. Right.' The stack of money Steph found in her brother's bookshelf. Every option Steph had conjured to explain that cash was bad. Dad's look of bewilderment at the sight of it had slumped to resignation. *Let's not say anything to Mum.* Everyone tiptoeing around the problem when her brother was unravelling before them. 'Callam might still be here if we'd dealt with it instead of wishing it would go away.' The window framed her mother's back. No response. 'You got your way, Mum. Five months together in this . . . hovel, so we can all,' Steph's fingers marked the air, '"move on".'

Her father's focus stayed fixed upon the floor. The heel of a hand struck Steph's cheekbone. It was as much the shock as the strength of her mother's fury. Steph cradled her jaw. 'Tenth birthday. Replay.'

'Fuck you.' Her mother drew a ragged breath. She never swore. As quickly the savage deserted her, leaving her slack-jawed, her mouth quivering. She looked like a person who'd suffered a stroke. Her father went to comfort her but her mother shoved his arm away. 'Leave me be, the pair of you.'

3

Where do you go when you're marooned by ocean, cut off from help? Steph reached the road, looked in the direction of the helipad, relived the pilot's disgust and turned the other way. Her face stung from her mother's slap.

She walked the road between vehicle furrows worn through the grass. All around, tea-trees and banksias were sheared to match the angle of the slope; they leaned in unison like swimmers at the starting blocks, stooped with outstretched arms. Bracken, reeds, creepers, ground covers, thickets of shrubs—everything about the bush looked sharp. You could be exiled in a place you'd soaked up through a lifetime of your mother's stories, hoodwinked into thinking you belonged. She tore off a twig and stripped it of its leaves.

The road led downhill around a bend, away from the house and the beady eyes of adults. Steph dropped her shoulders, slowed her step.

Her footsteps startled a tiny mouse that darted from the edge of the road and halted a metre away. There were no domestic animals on Maatsuyker Island. Everything was native. Steph lowered to her haunches, expecting the mouse to scatter. *Antechinus.* She ignored her mother's voice and watched the tiny swamp mouse snuffle through grass, its snout sweeping in staccato until it homed in on a spot just centimetres away. The antechinus burrowed at speed, its slender head disappearing into earth and pulling out the tail of a worm. It yanked, stretching the pulpy segment and reversing across Steph's gumboot, absorbed by the tug-of-war. The worm pulled free—glistening, beaded with soil; the antechinus swallowed it as swiftly as a string of spaghetti, then scurried to the undergrowth.

The hem of the awful trackpants dragged though wet grass. Steph hoicked them onto her hips and folded the waistband. The ditch on the uphill side of the road looked chiselled from rock. Water burbled along its course and collected in pools dammed by sticks and leaves. When the water broke through she saw it rush downhill, a small raft of debris spinning and toppling. It disappeared into a culvert that ran beneath the road. Steph crossed to where water spilled from its lip to a bank of wet mulch. Darkness threatened to fold around her. She pulled back, tugged at the sleeves of the shirt and wedged her hands in the pit of her arms.

A row of fuel tanks; a damaged wind turbine, one of the blades a broken wing. The roof of the shed was lined with solar panels. Steph opened the large door to generators, a bank of batteries, a workbench, checklists, logbooks, the smell of age and dust and engine oil.

This was the end of the road, the lighthouse all squatness and girth, a round of white bouncing in the sun. Steph shaded her eyes. The lower section of the painted brick remained in shadow, its door tied open with a heavy braid of rope that looked a hundred years old.

Steph circled to the side of the light tower concealed from the road, her back to the ocean so only the Needle Rocks would see her standing chest to mortar, pressed against the round of it, her arms extending across the belly of the lighthouse that felt as solid and unerring as a grandmother. If Callam were looking down he'd say she was acting like some hippie greenie—the kind who'd join a circle to hug some tree in an old-growth forest and sing mournful folksy songs. This was too raw for that. Beneath the flat of her hands, through the texture of brick and mortar, Steph conjured a matriarchy layered with grandmothers and great-grandmothers and all the great-greats before those. She closed her eyes and felt the protrusion of her hipbones, a press of ribs against the structure's permanence. A flow of air curled around the tower, soughing, lifting wisps of hair and veiling her eyes. The whisper of the lighthouse carried Callam's voice: *It's not just Mum's fault.* She tilted her chin to an expanse as white as an apron. She'd never forgive her mother. Not for hitting her again.

Steph stepped in through the heavy doors. A cylindrical shaft filled the centre of the tower like the funnel of a ship. She turned to a cabinet shaped to fit the circular wall. Each compartment housed a canister, each lid printed with a letter from the alphabet. She shook each one in turn, empty but for Z. She extracted a flag so frail from age that Steph could have ripped the cotton threads. Could have wrecked it there and then. Black, yellow, blue, red: four triangles meeting at the centre. Each signal flag depicted a letter of the phonetic alphabet, each stood for a message in itself that the old light keepers signalled in communication with passing ships. Z for Zulu. The semaphore set they were given years ago. *You Are Coming into Danger,* Steph would signal Callam from the house. He, on the railing of the swimming enclosure: *Altering Course to Starboard,* or whatever other flag he had on hand. Why did he have to change? Steph returned Zulu to its canister.

She climbed the spiral staircase—latticed iron steps that wound around the wall. She didn't feel fearful of the height because this tower was divided into floors. At the second storey was a table set with three polished lanterns, a visitors' book waiting to be signed. Each floor felt brighter than the one below, the natural light given by narrow casement windows set deep into the brickwork, by a shaft of light filtering down. Through the pitting and scratches of the glass, Steph spied a band of colour: a red fishing boat moving on the water.

The top steps led to a structure twice her height—the lens rested on an enormous iron cog. Steph ran her fingers over prisms. She pulled back at the disconnect, the moment before your brain makes sense of something, the way you sometimes can't distinguish hot from cold. It was the contradiction of each rib: the feel of sharp angles against a sweep of soft bowed curves. Steph saw where bubbles had been trapped in the glass. The sensation was electric; she felt it grip her gut; a shard of something vital and prophetic. Steph picked up a cloth. She rubbed at the glass until it gleamed. The keepers—her grandfather—would have taken turns at polishing the glass. The ribs shimmered with rainbow edges. Her mother's parents were long gone before she and Callam came along. She imagined them as carnies at a fair, packing their belongings and trundling to the next stop. Maatsuyker Light Station had been their final posting before Grandfather died. The single physical link Steph could claim was the ink bottle her mother gifted her when she and Callam turned ten. Callam's lip had stuck out at the nautilus shell Mum had saved for him. Her brother had no time for shells.

The ink bottle came from Deal Island in Bass Strait, the tiny glass vessel washed up in a storm—*still stoppered and filled with violet*

24

ink when your grandfather found it amongst the thrown weed. Perhaps it had come from a voyage in their *Great Explorers* book. Steph pictured an old wooden ship with Steph herself its figurehead, she and her vessel ploughing uncharted waters.

She'd relented, loaned Callam the ink bottle which he'd soon forgotten and shoved to the back of his desk amongst everything else. She'd gone into his room to reclaim it, lain on his bunk, tipped and tilted the tiny bottle before the light until he'd come in and demanded she get off his bed and grabbed the bottle from her. If she'd had another chance she would have let him keep it. Waited until he'd forgotten it again. Instead Steph fought him—*It's mine!*—yelling just as many names as Callam called her, he taunting her from the other side of the desk. The slow-motion replay of the bottle hurtling through air—perhaps he really hadn't meant to let it go. A shock of violet streaked across the doona, the wall, splattered across floorboards and patterned the rug like the tangled tentacles of some mythical jellyfish. Steph was on her knees and picking at glass as if desperation could reverse the outcome. She heard Callam race down the stairs: *Mum, it was her! It was her!*

Her mother's shock at the damage to the room turned to rage when she connected the violet with bits of broken glass. *Thirty years I take care of that bottle and you smash it in an instant with your selfish stupidity.*

If Mum had asked, Steph could have explained. But it was like trying to reason with Callam once he'd crossed a certain line. There was no space for anything but the force of her mother's hand that knocked Steph's head against the ladder of the bunk. Mum marched her by the arm to her room. The door slammed and Steph curled on her bed. When the light dimmed and she opened her eyes her father was beside her, stroking her hair, sitting her up and prising open her fist. *Why?* he asked. She shook her head. She hadn't realised she'd been gripping broken glass.

He bound the bloodied hand in a towel and put her in the car. At the hospital she buried her face in the weave of his jacket, tweezers nipping at a dartboard of glass. The pain of turning ten was indelible; Steph opened her hand to a crosshatch of tattooed violet scars.

She moved out to the lighthouse balcony and stepped back in fright. It hadn't seemed scary from inside. The lawn below edged against the cliff. A long way out to sea a single shark's tooth pierced up through the ocean, a lone pyramid of rock distant from the Needles. Directly below the lighthouse, Steph followed lines of foam to the red fishing boat. It manoeuvred so near the rocks it looked to nudge them. A figure on deck tossed a craypot overboard. She heard the engine rev and watched the boat swing away as lithely as a dolphin. Clusters of orange buoys trailed in an arc.

The figure looked up to the lighthouse. Steph lifted her arm to wave, grew self-conscious when the person continued looking her way without waving back. Wind ruffled the ocean surface. Beneath the thickening cloud shadows turned the ocean into something menacing. She moved to the sheltered side of the lighthouse.

Footsteps tolled on the iron stairs. 'You up there, Steph?'

Steph slid down to sitting. She drew her knees to her chest and fixed her focus on the ocean.

It took a sideways glance to see her mother's eyes puffy and red. Her mother placed a bag of clothes at the balcony door. 'Thought you could use these.' Her voice was soft and kind. Her mother was like an ocean wave, surging forward, building momentum until something—someone—in its path caused all that energy to break. Her mother leaned against the railing, as bold as Callam. 'The lighthouse was my special place.' Mum pointed to the single tooth of rock. 'The Mewstone. Shy albatross nest out there. On a clear day you can see all the way to Pedra Branca.'

Steph wouldn't be coaxed into conversation. She turned her head at the cry of birds, gulls circling the red boat below.

'Guess what? Brian's found some time. He asked if you'd like a run-through with the weather.'

Mum waited. Steph shrugged. 'It doesn't matter.'

'Of course it matters. Absolutely. The weather is *your* job. Dad and I are just the backup team in case you need our help.' Her mother motioned to the cray boat. 'Wasn't expecting fishing boats for another month.' Mum knelt down beside her. 'I overreacted. If I could take it back I would. I'm sorry. We'll work something out with the phone. We will.'

It might be years again of calm, swimming safely at the shore until you'd forgotten what it signalled when water sucked back from sand. She watched the red boat. Steph shook her head. She wouldn't let her mother off.

The figure on the deck disappeared into the wheelhouse. The boat motored out of sight beneath the headland.

Her mother went to go. 'They're leaving after lunch. What would you like me to tell him?'

Steph resisted.

'Yes? No?' Her mother waited. 'Steph?'

The weather. She needed Brian's help to get started. She didn't have the luxury of holding out. 'Where is he?'

'He's at the weather office. He's waiting for you.' The buoyancy in her mother's voice. Steph had traded her resolve for a few tips on weather and a decent pair of jeans.

4

The old sash window rattled loose and banged down in its frame. Steph hunched beneath the bedcovers, waiting to be showered with glass. Her shoulders ached. Her back felt stiff. Tension. This place was weird. The bunk had magically vanished, replaced with an old slat bed her parents must have carted down from one of the other cottages. Steph had scoffed at her mother's suggestion of an electric blanket. *It's not the South Pole, Mother.* Her mother let it pass without the usual argument, which made Steph wonder when and why resistance had become her default stance. She should feel grateful for the hot water bottle Mum had slipped beneath the flannel sheets. If it had been Tessa or Sammie's mother, Steph would have thanked them. You could talk to Sammie's mum. She never pushed. She didn't have issues. The only time Mum listened to anything Steph had to say was when they argued. That's all her mother knew. Not the real Steph. There was no point even trying.

Sheets of rain beat against the windows of the adjacent porch. When she looked through the old sash windows in the daylight, the ripples of glass blurred the world and turned it dreamy. Perhaps old glass held a memory of its molten self. Perhaps, ever so slowly, glass continued to flow.

The other window that faced the ocean took the brunt of the wind, a convoluted pull-up, push-out arrangement that thudded and wheezed like a punctured lung.

The rain had begun when the helicopter left. All that afternoon and evening. All day yesterday. All last night. Steph pulled her mobile from under the pillow and checked for a signal. *Dream on.* Beneath the covers, the light of the phone illuminated the cocoon of bedding, the nails of her hands gothic in the glow.

The wind shrilled like a castaway woman. According to her mother the island had a ghost. Steph saw her own hair tangled with baubles of kelp, her sea lettuce dress streaming and fluttering in the wind. She could feel that woman's suffering. She could hear it. Or was it seals bleating on the rocks below?

Allow yourself plenty of time before the observations. Brian had offered advice before he'd left. *The first few weeks everything takes twice as long.* Five-thirty. Steph pushed her head out from the covers. Cold air stung her nostrils. Black as midnight. She wanted to slide back down, stay in hibernation, emerge when the sentence was over and go home to sun and warmth and their house at Forty Baskets Beach within view of the Manly ferry. A reedy shaft of light arced the black. The darkness of its wake felt as thick as a newly tarred road. A Tupperware light, her mother called the automated lighthouse. *In my day, the real lighthouse, ships could see the light all the way from the horizon, forty ks away.*

'You awake, Stephanie?'

Steph groaned at her father's hoarse whisper from the opposite side of the door.

'Twenty to six,' he said. 'Like a hand with the weather?'

Who wouldn't huff at the intrusion? 'I can do it. I'm already up.' Steph pushed back the doona. Ventured a toe. Floorboards? Slabs of permafrost.

*

When the hood of her jacket blew back, she turned against the wind to draw it back on and tighten the toggles. The moment she faced forward the hood swept from her head and filled like a sail, its drawstring cutthroat at her chin. Hair whipped Steph's face. She couldn't see. She released her grip on the handrail and instantly realised her mistake. A gust punched her off her feet and skittled her hard into a woody bush. Steph felt her arm hooked beneath her body, her shoulder throbbed. Her headlamp lay loose on the ground, an icy spark of light glowering at the foliage, catching darts of rain. Her face felt wet and raw. She pushed to her knees. Retrieved the lamp. Crawled back to the handrail. She needed shelter. She needed to climb back into bed. Steph could hear her mother fretting: *What if it had happened at the cliff edge?* Steph did imagine, with a rush of vertigo, being carried off like an article of laundry.

Above the scream of wind, beyond the house, who would hear her cry for help? No admiring audience. It wouldn't be like Callam. No one would even know. *Drama queen*, her brother's voice mocked inside her head. Every dare, lies and deceit; what she'd let herself be party to those last few months. Hoping it would wash by and Callam would be Callam again. Steph clambered to her feet, ignored the flapping hood, wet hair thrashing at her face. 'You're still fourteen,' she shouted back. 'You'll always be a kid.' She gripped the rail but it hit her like a squall: Callam's face, the imprint of him fading to blue like a poster left out in the sun. Sometimes Steph could only conjure scrapings, just ugly chipped-off flakes—not good things, not the funny boy he was before he turned, whose belly laugh would make her laugh, who'd jig around the house and drive them all mental because he couldn't stay still. His voice would scrabble in her head, ridicule, then puff, he'd be gone, sometimes for days. Needles of rain stung her face. Steph wiped her eyes, adjusted her lamp. She leaned into the wind and continued up the path.

It took twenty minutes to even make out the clouds in the dark, and then Steph took a stab at their height. It was too dark to see the ocean, let alone measure its swell or gauge its state. And now the Stevenson Screen—the wooden box that held the thermometers. Steph braced against the slatted frame, feet set apart against the buffeting. At first sight of these white-painted slats you might expect the drone of bees, shelves glistening with honeycomb. She removed the nail that held the screen door. The frame was stuck fast. She tugged until the door jerked free; she almost lost her footing. She held the door steady against wind that tried to tear it backwards off its hinges then slam it down upon her head at each sudden lull. *Record the thermometers quick smart*, Brian had said. *Get the door shut before the wind affects the readings.* Five point five degrees Celsius. Steph dug in her pocket for the cheat sheet. Her fingers felt wooden. The pen refused to write. The paper was sodden. *Five-Five.* Steph recited the number as a mantra. She shone the headlamp upon the minimum thermometer. The early morning observations were supposed to be quickest, the easiest of the three. Steph closed the screen door, replaced the nail. Should she have reset the thermometers? There was no one to ask. Her brain ached with uncertainty, the sequence of tasks. She held the handrail and let herself be shunted by the wind, reciting her mantra, to the shelter of the weather office.

Steph could not recall a day of her life that had started in the dark. She wiped her face with a towel on the hook and checked for signs of blood. The windows warbled. The weather office felt ready to implode; she could feel the built-up pressure in her ears. She took up binoculars and traced the shape of the Needles, her focus shifting to the two low-lying rocks alongside. These two rocks, one small, one larger, were used as a reference to measure the swell. Steph set the stopwatch on her phone and timed the crests of waves—spindly lines of lace, froths of foam amid the gloom—cascading over rocks. She watched for minutes to be sure. She saw how the waves came in sets, nearly always washing over Moderate Rock and through the notch of Heavy Rock. Four metres, wave trough to crest. Twice her height. Could that be right? Steph checked back through recordings in the logbook: two metres, three metres—there: four point five. And on the next page, highlighted in fluoro, a recording of ten metres.

Beyond the Needles, way out to sea, a small light seesawed in the swell. The beam lit the waves then lurched skyward. Through binoculars Steph saw a spotlight positioned high upon a mast, a white wheelhouse and darker hull. Craypots were stacked upon the stern and bow—the red boat she'd seen on her first day.

She keyed the recordings into the computer. She pressed Send and logged the transmittal time. How was it that an electronic message could be zapped to Hobart in a nanosecond, while the same island was deprived of mobile coverage? Telstra had some serious explaining to do. Beads of rain dripped from her hair. Steph wiped the keyboard dry. Nine a.m. she'd be here to do it all again. Hardly worth the effort of going back to bed.

5

Tom gripped the new knife. Frank shouted from the wheelhouse. 'For fuck's sake, cut it!'

The steel blade caught the sunrise. In a single action Tom severed the nylon rope—a clean cut that parted float from craypot. The plastic buoy slid over the gunnel and plopped to the water, as carefree as a beachball. Carried inshore by current and swell, the buoy would turn and bob like a Sunday swimmer, its tail of cut rope slowly unravelling with the water's sway. By the time it reached shore—anywhere between the three southerly capes—its appearance on that rugged coast would seem no less an act of nature than other fishing flotsam washed up in a gale.

The longer end of rope belonged to a new craypot stripped of its first bounty for the season. The pot balanced on the gunnel awaiting the final letting go. Tom had spent the winter collecting tea-tree from the bush, stripping branches and steaming them into rounds. He'd grown quicker, thought himself adept at making stick craypots, but even his best could not compare to this, the craft that distinguished one of Bluey MacIntyre's pots.

'What's wrong with you?' Frank bellowed. 'Chuck it. Let's piss off out of here.'

It wasn't enough that they'd robbed Bluey of his catch: a score of new shellers too fragile for export but good enough for local market, extras undersized that any other fisherman would set free. The new quota system had split families, cast friendships adrift, had turned Tom's brother into the hardened nemesis of any fisherman around the state who had voted in the new order. Save the new orange-handled knife his brother had gifted him, inscribed *Tom Forrest* to mark Tom's second season on the boat, Frank had snubbed yesterday's official opening of the season. They'd been crayfishing against the law for weeks. Half the fleet must know it. The person he'd seen looking down from Maatsuyker's lighthouse would know it. Tom released the pot and watched it surrender its existence in a spiral of bubbles. His brother could as easily risk his life to finish you as save you. You were in or out with Frank.

Frank cranked the engine. Tom joined him in the wheelhouse, slid the door shut. They steamed away from Bluey's patch.

Trouble was, Tom liked Bluey MacIntyre, the old man of the fleet. He'd been fishing this coast for close to fifty years. This was Bluey's third term as association president—he'd made it his mission to champion the crayfishing quota. Bluey had called meetings around the state and gone on tour to convince the members that stock numbers were at a critical low. They could scoff all they liked at the Fisheries' report, call it bullshit government propaganda, but was there a fisherman in the room, Bluey had looked Tom in the eye and held his gaze, who could honestly claim they'd seen signs of larval settlement in the water these last seasons? They were decimating their stock, destroying their livelihood, wiping out their kids', their grandkiddies' future. *I'm not pointing the finger.* He'd thumped a freckled fist against his chest. *As much my doing as anybody's.*

What Bluey said, what Frank seemed deaf to, made basic sense to Tom, a logic that hadn't needed a mind-numbing semester of environmental science to see that a sustainable limit would ensure a fishing future; a limit, Bluey said, that would better protect lives by *doing away with this mad stupid pressure we all feel to go out in marginal conditions. Smaller boats are at the greatest risk.* Heads had bowed, feet scuffed at the unspoken reference to the Hadleys, father and son lost last season when their boat took a wave. But Frank no longer owned a small boat. He'd borrowed big to buy and refit the *Perlita Lee*. He had to catch more crayfish or he'd drown, regardless.

Frank's wife Cheryl had turned up at the boat launch with a salon tan that flouted Tassie's winter. When Cheryl had wobbled around the vessel to see the stern unveiled, Tom had guessed she would soon turn sour.

Tom's mother had stood beside him and he'd heard her gasp with surprise when the cloth was pulled away to reveal *her* name, *Perlita,* beside their father's, *Lee,* flourished in large white script across the boat's stern. *Perlita Lee.* Had it brought bad fortune, Tom would later wonder, to give a boat a dead man's name?

As thwarted as a beauty queen stripped of her rightful title, Cheryl had heaved that bottle of champagne against the timber bow with a force that caused the boaties at the boatyard to wince. Frank would have paid for his loyalties when he got home that night.

'If it isn't old Hab,' his brother spoke to the compact figure climbing up from the bunkroom. 'Did we disturb you with the motion, precious? Ready for a nice cup of tea?'

Habib checked his watch. 'Early time still.' His English still wasn't the best but Habib had been deckie long enough to withstand

Frank's deprecating humour. He pulled on bib and braces, stepped into rubber boots.

'We'll shoot the pots then anchor off Maat,' Frank said. 'I'll cook up a big greasy breakfast and Hab can brew his special coffee. How's that sound, me hearties?'

Tom and Habib grunted the obligatory approval. In different ways they both owed Frank. Each observed the other's indenture in silent resignation. Tom wondered what Habib might choose to eat at home, how much he shared with his new wife, in the privacy of language, about his work aboard *Perlita Lee*.

★

Frank's wife had equipped the cabin galley with a gleaming set of melamine plates and bowls, hardly touched when Frank was camp cook. Here they were in a swanky cabin—stainless steel oven and stovetop, microwave, fridge, DVD player, full-sized bunks— seated around the booth and eating straight from the pan. You might ingest a shock of saturated fat from one of Frank's fry- ups, but you could never complain about an excess of washing up. A congealment of chewed bones and bacon rind sat piled on newspaper.

Habib held up his coffee mug to Tom. 'You like?'

'Best yet.' Habib's coffee was brilliant. He blended and roasted his own beans at home; he'd shown Tom how. Tom poured himself and Hab the remains of the coffee pot. Frank was as happy drinking instant; as long as it was hot his brother didn't care. Cascade beer, the local Hobart brew, was the only drink Frank swore allegiance to. Offer him a Boags from the state's northern brewery and expect a clout around the ears.

'Time for a kip, eh, Tom-Tom? Hab, you get the new lines made up, those couta heads ready for afternoon.'

'When do you want to get away?' Tom asked.

'Three, four o'clock. Do an early pull while the new shellers are on the run, set them inshore before dinner. Two shots if the weather holds.'

Another long night. Tom assessed his brother's mood. 'All right if I go ashore for a while?'

'How many frigging potatoes you planning on digging up this time?' Frank's scowl eased. 'Go on, you daft idiot. Hab'll run you in. Take a radio and for fuck's sake turn it on. I want you back here pronto if the wind gets up. You understand?'

Tom did. It didn't pay to get it wrong.

6

The gully was delineated by tall trees: tallow wood, peppermints, the gnarly trunks of banksias. Somewhere here, Steph's mother said, had been a pigeon coop, years ago. They waded through chest-high bracken, avoiding stinging nettles. Their sleeves caught on the canes of wild blackberries. Without gloves the bush would have torn their hands to pieces. Her mother stopped to search. 'Everything looks different.'

The valley grew steep. Her mother almost slipped. Steph could hear a surge of waves being heaved against the rocks below. 'I think we should stop,' Steph said. Her mother agreed. They climbed the hill and picked up the track. Her mother was going on about the old days, homing pigeons flapping their way across the ocean. 'They say only one in three ever made it.'

'Isn't that exploitation? Cruelty to animals?' Steph said. 'How did they know to fly from here to some place in Hobart?'

'That's how they're bred. The keepers tied a message to their leg. To let Hobart know everything was fine—or not, as the case might be. Hobart would send a return message: sending medical assistance, when the supply boat would call, et cetera.'

'Why bother flying back here?'

Mum gave her an exasperated look. 'Birds know their way. They have an innate ability. Look at the mutton-birds.'

'Short-tailed shearwaters,' Steph corrected her. Again.

'Every year,' her mother ignored her, 'almost to the day, they come back all the way from Siberia. You wait. You won't credit it's the same place.'

Steph tried to picture a squadron of 800,000 pairs of migratory birds winging south. Crossing the equator. A pit stop at Papua New Guinea. A fly-by over Sydney Harbour Bridge. 'Do they stop to eat and drink?'

'They're seabirds. They can stop any time they like.'

They started back. Dad was hunched over the drain at the upper edge of the road, all gangly limbs, oblivious to Steph and her mother. The kneepads of his new work trousers were scoured black, the back of his shirt stamped with muddy handprints. He tugged at a handful of grass sprouting from the ditch, growling like a sea lion.

'James.' Steph saw her father jump.

'A little warning would be nice.'

'Darling,' her mother said. 'You're turning a basic clean-up into an archaeological dig.'

He dumped a handful of goo upon the road.

'It's just a drain.' Her mother looked tense. 'It only has to . . . drain.'

Dad thumped the rock with his fist. 'This drain, this entire length of road,' he swept his arm, 'is a monument to back-breaking labour and perseverance. Cut and fill.' Her father's halting voice was as bad as ever. 'A century ago some industrious team of workers sculpted it from bedrock with nothing more than picks and shovels. A stick or two of dynamite. It might have been good enough in your father's day, but you can bet the original vision wasn't a waterway clogged with all this rubbish.'

Hair blew around her mother's face like tulle. It didn't mask her irritation. 'It's going to take you months.'

He nodded. 'I have months, Gretchen.'

It wasn't like Dad to be snide. Steph couldn't tell if he was upset at being exiled to this island or at being banished from the ABC—enforced sick leave to sort out the problem with his voice. The change in her father's speech didn't faze Steph as it had the radio listeners who'd phoned in with complaints of the newsreader being three sheets to the wind, or on the verge of a nervous breakdown; some accused him of laughing at a private joke while covering important news headlines. Dad attacked the drain with a long-handled spade and scooped out a mound of fetid sludge. Steph held her nose. The change in his voice was neurological, her mother said, an intermittent wiring fault like a blinking fluoro light.

★

It was late morning, the sun shining through after days of rain, when Steph put away her schoolbooks and pulled on gumboots. She walked to the vegetable garden to collect spinach for her mother, the bush glistening with damp, Pearl Jam pumping through her earphones. *Last Kiss*, Steph sang along, which, depending on her loneliness scale, could work to make her cry.

Steph reached the terraced beds and shrieked at the movement: a figure crouched on haunches. A boy—man—fell back on his hands. 'What are you doing?' she cried. Anyone could see he'd been surveying the seedlings she and her mother had planted.

He stood and brushed dirt from his hands. He was tall, angular, and though it was still wintry, his face looked tanned from sun.

Steph's alarm seemed to trigger his. 'I wasn't taking anything.' Her eyes fell to the lumpy hessian sack bulging at his feet. She prickled. The sort you heard about, filled with unwanted kittens. Or snakes. Steph yanked out her earphones. 'Who *are* you?' She stood her ground.

'Tom.' He sounded meek, like someone who knew he was in trouble.

'Obviously.' She nodded at his coat.

He looked like a castaway in his grimy red coat with *Tom* printed in texta, patched jeans, his dark hair sticking out in all directions. He gestured toward the ocean. 'Tom Forrest. I'm off the *Perlita Lee*.'

'The what?'

'The cray boat.'

'The red boat?'

He nodded.

He looked older than her. 'We're the caretakers.' Steph spoke with an authority she didn't feel. 'Stephanie West.'

'Stephanie.' He picked up the sack and eased it behind his back. 'I met Lindsay and Brian a few times.'

She relaxed at the mention of their names. 'What's in there?' Steph nodded to the sack.

He glanced over her head like a cornered animal. She was blocking the exit between the garden beds. He opened the bag and reached down inside. Steph stepped back, pictured the headline: *Maatsuyker Massacre: Caretakers Bludgeoned.* He pulled a potato from the sack. 'They grow wild in the bush. I didn't think anyone would mind.'

A potato poacher. Steph laughed aloud. Tom Forrest's brow knotted, then he smiled. He had green eyes and perfect white teeth. 'They're all over the joint,' he said. 'From the old light-keeper days.'

'They're probably heritage-listed, like everything else around here.' She caught his look of concern. 'I'm kidding,' she said.

He offered her a handful. 'They're good roasted. Or cut into wedges. Chuck them if the flesh is green.'

He cocked his head at the rumble of a boat engine below the cliffs. Steph heard static from inside his jacket, three bursts of transmission, another three. He pulled out a handheld radio, the aerial bowed. She watched him give three clicks in return. 'Best get back to it.'

'Are you the cook?'

That made him smile. 'Deckhand. For my brother Frank. It's his boat.' Tom looked a bit whiskery, a sack on his shoulder, but he didn't strike Steph as being a fisherman. What would she know?

Tom had almost reached the road when Steph called to him. 'Are you coming back again?'

'Probably. When the weather's good.'

'I'll show you the lighthouse. Next time. If you want.'

He was the sort who thought on things. He nodded. 'I've only ever seen it from down there.'

'Hey.' Steph pulled her mobile from her pocket. 'Do you get a signal out there? On your boat?'

'Wouldn't know. Never needed one. I doubt it. Not down here.'

'You don't own a phone?'

He shrugged at her astonishment. 'You can get us on the VHF when we're in range. Channel seven two. I could radio you next time we're coming in.'

'Okay.'

She waited until he'd gone. Steph broke into a skip and ran back past the house. A congregation of tiny skinks basked amongst the rookery and on the concrete steps, feet set apart, heads tilted to the sun, their closed eyes adding to their yoga-like worship. Steph slowed as she passed but still they scattered into crevices. The path that led from their house to the lighthouse was encased by tea-tree, dappled with light.

She reached for her sunglasses. Sunlight glared off the lighthouse. The day was dry enough to wedge the doors open and slow the process by which mould populated every surface of every dwelling in this place. Steph wouldn't have altered a thing about the lighthouse but her mother liked to point out the rusting ironwork, paint flaking from the walls. *The way they've let it go.*

Rain had leaked in through the window frames. A line of buckets, with rags acting as wicks, drained much of the water. Steph emptied the buckets over the balcony. Tom Forrest would be on his way down to the Gulch, the island's singular landing site accessible only on days when the weather was calm. If the *Perlita Lee* passed by he might look up to the light.

Steph took out her sketchbook and traced a curve of glass. Her science and maths subjects she had to force herself to work at, but with art she could lose a whole day. Her parents had been called in to school to go over Steph's study plans for her time on the island. Steph had not expected to be lavished with praise when they got home. Her mother had mimicked Mrs Burrows's warbling voice. *Stephanie has the academic ability, and the discipline, to try for medicine, if she so chooses.* Medicine? It wasn't even on Steph's radar. Her mother looked so disappointed when Steph shook her head. *Why not?* Mum pleaded. *You're already a year ahead of other girls your age. Mrs Burrows says that if you study hard and do well in your HSC you could start a medical degree next year.* Later that night Steph overheard her father on the phone, praising her to Gran. *In the top ten per cent, Mum. Who knew?* Steph had gone to bed inflated with her parents' praise—since Callam she'd tried extra hard but they barely noticed anything she did. If it were Callam he'd only need to put the bins up on the road without being asked three times, or get a decent mark for an assignment that Steph had helped him with, and her mother would go into worship mode. Mum had seemed blind to the changes in her brother and the way he played her. On that parent-teacher night Steph had lain awake, weighed down by her parents' expectations. Who, at sixteen, knew sweet fuck all? All anyone wanted was to live life without the stress of planning it all away. Medicine. Steph had rolled the thought around for several days until all the rough edges smoothed into something she'd polished on her own. A decision could be agonising or could be clean-cut as glass. Steph phoned Gran in Canberra. *I've decided to try for medicine.* Normally Gran was so upbeat. *Medicine?* Gran said, nothing more.

Steph drew back at her sketch of the lens. She could recite the facts: Australia's most southerly lighthouse. Replaced by an automatic light in 1996. The last light station to be de-manned. But alongside statistics was a ton of things she'd never understand. The colossal weight of hundreds of glass ribs embedded in an iron frame. How had they hoisted it up here in the days of horse and cart, set it down with perfect precision? Ask Mrs B and she'd give you her trusty formula for every life achievement: *in breathtaking proportions of ambition, ingenuity and determination.*

Steph stepped inside the central mount. Looking out through the lens was like peering through a magnifying glass. The focus sharpened on individual threads from canvas curtains covering several of the windows. When Steph stepped back the focus blurred while the magnification increased. Another step and the rocks of the Needles inverted; they looked immense. She pulled on the heavy lens as you might to set a children's roundabout in motion. The surrounding prisms moved slowly. Steph scanned the empty ocean. Across the stretch of water she watched a coastline of headlands and cliffs, tantalising beaches, countless indentations. Fractured images streaming by.

She heard the rattle of the lower door. Her mother padded up the stairs as lightly as a cat. 'There you are.' She followed Steph out to the balcony. 'Taking a break from studies?' Her mother extended her arms and gave a curtsy to the ocean. She looked serene. She looked beautiful. 'My dad would sometimes send me down here. I even lit the light, when he was indisposed. I used to imagine being an actress, this balcony my stage.' Her mother tucked Steph's hair behind her ear. 'Coming back to Maat feels like rejoining the circle. Does that make sense, my darling?'

Steph saw a line of red moving on the water. Tom's boat. Her mother waited for an answer. She should reassure her, offer affirmation. She shrugged, willing Mum to leave, fighting her own meanness. Who'd been there to comfort her when Callam died? There were so many things about being a daughter—worse with Callam gone—that seemed upside down.

Mum spoke too brightly. 'Lunch is ready. I thought we could eat outside.'

Steph listened to her footsteps on the stairs, counted the seconds until her mother started up the road. Steph dashed in and looped binoculars around her neck. She returned to the balcony and focused on the boat. Two of them at the front beside the stack of craypots, Tom's red coat. The other man cuffed his head. Tom was looking this way, watching Steph watching him through his binoculars. He lifted his arm and gave a slow wave. Steph raised her arm until the boat disappeared from view. She circled the balcony to catch another glimpse. She slowed at the sight of her mother on the road looking back at her. Her mother turned and walked on. You didn't need binoculars to see she was upset.

7

The rusted gantry at the Gulch's landing looked set to collapse. Tom stepped over remnant wooden sleepers; the remains of the old haulage way extended as a scar up the slope, the bush slowly reclaiming it.

The sun had tracked above the island, a pale yellow orb spreading meagre warmth on and through him. A group of silver gulls patterned the rocks above the landing site, uniform bodies angled to the sun, feathers ruffling in the breeze. If you ignored the mindset that they were lowly seagulls squabbling about the boat for scraps, you might think them handsome, their red beaks brilliant, birds standing proud and sassy on those matchstick legs. A carpet of pigface fringed the rocks. The fleshy leaves were soft enough to squash between your fingers, yet the plant held its grip against six metre-swells that rollicked in to slap the coastline white with salt. In morning light, glossy flowers buttoned the succulent foliage, pleats of pink open to the sun.

Tom slowed at the terraces to search for ancient shards of abalone shell, opalescent, glinting in the dirt. It was the task of the aboriginal women, he'd read, to fish and feed their families when hunting was poor; women, centuries ago, who would paddle twelve kilometres from the mainland and dive all day in frigid water. How often were they stranded here? Or did bad weather wait until the paddle home to catch them at the point of no return? He pictured that line of women and girls in their rolled bark canoe, heads dropped, shoulders taut, arms on fire with the effort of reaching the safety of shore.

Tom climbed the narrow path, the vegetation thickening to bushy scrub. Crescent honeyeaters, silver eyes and scrub wrens flitted and bounced; the hillside was alive with tiny birds. Higher now, Tom moved through taller foliage. Wind rushed up the valley, the raucous shriek of cockatoos cascaded down.

He checked his watch. Early still. On a clear morning he'd be pulling pots in the dark, the first hint of dawn the eastern horizon purpling to a bruise. Before the sun tipped above the ocean, the promise of light would amplify the sky—a curtain turned blood orange, the Mewstone toy-like against its breadth. Tom might look up to the island to see a solitary light—a figure at work inside the weather station, or pacing to the weather screen. Below the main house stood the grand old lighthouse, regal in contrast to the automated light.

Tom relived the morning's stilted radio conversation. Every cray boat within range would have pricked their ears at a posh female voice. In the galley, Frank had stuck out his bum and pouted. *Maatsuyker returning to standby.* She made a change to the usual carry-on.

Tom-Tom has a sweetheart, Frank had smirked. There'd been no getting out of explaining Stephanie West to Frank and how they'd met. *So that's why you packed a set of good clothes this trip,* his brother said knowingly. You couldn't slip anything past him. *A looker, is she?*

Tom had done his best to sound casual. *She's all right.* He couldn't ignore Habib's grin. *What?* He'd felt himself colour, folded his arms. *I don't even know her.*

Have a shower, Tom-Tom. Get yourself spruced up. Can't go calling on your chickadee stinking of fish bait and seaweed.

They'd had a full month of fishing down here on their own, trying to stay under the radar. The grand sum of radio traffic had been the occasional yacht beating its way around South West Cape to Port Davey, a lonesome helmsman relaying his boat's coordinates to Tasmar Radio, or requesting updates on the weather. Now that the fishing season was officially underway, the volley of chatter between the cray boats seemed as boisterous as the furries sprawled across Seal Rock.

You mind what you say, Frank warned when Tom left the boat to come ashore. How easy it would be for Stephanie to let slip some innocent remark over the VHF, to confirm what half the fleet would already suspect: they'd been fishing illegally for weeks. There was no way Tom could think to caution her without implicating himself. He scuffed his boot across the track. Nineteen years old: he couldn't play the minor any more; he was every bit as liable as Frank. It would do their mother in to know the half of it.

A large iron wheel—the whim—sat rusted in the bush. It came from a time when horsepower meant just that. The light keeper's nag would have paced an endless circle whenever the supply ship called, turning the whim that drove the winch that wound the cable that inched the laden trolley up and down the slope. Worthless now; the horse retired when diesel power took over.

The track from the Gulch emerged at the northern extent of the road. Wet grass clippings coated Tom's boots. He crossed to an old shed and peered in through clouded glass at a large diesel engine and capstan. Even diesel proved a short-lived reign, a blink when you considered the human history of this place. Haulage way, trolleys and whim—the whole shebang shut down and engines left to seize and rust when helicopters superseded boats to resupply Tasmanian lights.

Tom recalled an old black and white photo of women seated in an open trolley being winched up the haulage way, scarves knotted beneath their chins, heavy skirts and pants, their shoes wedged against the backboard as casual as you please. Those lighthouse women entrusted their lives to the workings of the whim, the weight of their faith balanced on a single steel cable that held the trolley taut. One failure, one breakage—*snap!*—they'd all have toppled down. Tom's stomach turned at the prospect of mechanical failure, the thought of *Perlita Lee* pushing into heavy weather, her engine whining under strain.

Twice on the boat and once at home in Hobart Tom had had the same strange dream, had woken with bursting lungs from the sensation of swallowing the ocean. *Sleep apnoea*, his mother called it. *Bad dreams, cold sweats, Lee used to suffer the exact same thing.* Lee, she called his father, like the mention of a family friend.

It seemed to Tom that his enslavement to his brother Frank played out as a lesson he was yet to comprehend. Tom knew only what he didn't want, that the prospect of fishing all the days of his life—his only compensation a wallet full of cash and getting trashed the nights they were in port—was a form of living death. It wasn't the money that held him, not the way it had Frank by the throat. Tom felt rudderless. He had no wheel or sail or course to follow; he had no fucking clue. He wished someone as solid as Bluey MacIntyre would turn to him and say, *See there, son, that track along there? That's the way you're meant to go.*

Tom had been only a few days old when his father died, he had no sense of him at all. All Tom saw and felt, all he smelled and tasted when he squeezed his eyes shut, was Southern Ocean and salt-cracked lips and shreds of torn weed. His days rolling and pitching across its belly, his nightmares drowning in it. *Little-boy fear,* Frank's smirks said.

Those lighthouse women, sassy as seagulls. Tom envied their strength. It took rigid faith, or trust, or maybe it was bald-faced arrogance, to lean back in a wooden trolley and relish the view while being winched, near vertical in places, up four hundred metres of precipitous slope.

8

Tom looked taller. He'd brushed his hair. He waited at the flyscreen door, hands in pockets, trying not to appear as he did: tense and awkward. They'd spoken on the radio but all Steph could manage was a flaky, 'Hi there'. She chose to overlook his home-knitted jumper, the neatly pressed jeans. The girls from school would have carved him into pieces with their laughter.

'Mum wants to meet you. She's having a shower right now. We could take a look around.'

Tom followed her through each room of the house. Steph had to slow and wait. At each stop he gazed around, turned his eyes to the ceilings, soaked in the surrounds. 'This must have been top-notch in its day. A haven from the elements.'

Top-notch. No one said that. Steph tried to see it through his eyes. Fix up the cracks, ditch the carpet, new kitchen, appliances, laundry, bathroom, heat the place fifteen degrees—maybe. She'd tidied her room, made her bed, Blu-Tacked her illustrations to the wall. Tom studied the details of the lighthouse. 'You do these?' Gran was the only person who took an interest in her art.

'For a model I'm going to make.'

He studied each drawing in turn. 'They're good. Really good.'

He wasn't the kind to say things to be nice. An expression glanced through Steph's thoughts that reminded her of things not right about her school: the snobby girls who looked down on her, who whispered slurs behind her back. *Free ride*, they called Steph's tenure at the school that relied on a scholarship now that her father wasn't working. Those girls would know, the moment Tom uttered a word, would broadcast with looks amongst themselves, that Tom wasn't from a private school, that even if he was rich he wouldn't be the right kind of rich, that in his home-knitted jumper and carefully ironed jeans, Tom Forrest, gorgeous as he was, was *most definitely and categorically* not the kind that counted. Not long-term. *Flotsam* they'd call him to be kind; *Scum*, behind her back. Even the imagined voices of their disparagement, all these miles from home, held the power to subdue.

They walked around the outside of the house and stopped at the picket fence that overlooked the bay. The ocean shimmered in the sun. Steph saw the long band of cirrus cloud sailing in from the horizon. Soon the sunlight would be gone. A sea eagle glided overhead, criss-crossed high above them. 'Look at that,' Tom said. 'How good is this place?'

Steph nodded as you do before you've fully thought about the truth of things. 'You think?'

'All this?' He held his arms out to the view. 'I'd swap you.'

Steph avoided taking him past the bathroom—she could do without his first impression of her mother being one of a woman over forty parading naked before the window.

They angled up the grass behind the house. She showed him to the weather office and went through what she did each day. New Harbour. Mt Counsel. Louisa Bay. The Ironbounds. Tom knew all the landmarks along the coast that Steph used to measure visibility, the heights of cloud. They sat on the grass behind the office, sheltered in the sun.

'How did you learn about all this? The weather. Clouds.'

Steph confessed. 'I only know enough to get by. It's getting easier. You start to see a pattern.' She handed him binoculars and pointed to Moderate and Heavy Rocks, used to gauge the ocean swell.

'They look minuscule from up here.' He pointed across the bay. 'We'll be somewhere over there tonight. New Harbour, probably. You might be able to see our light.' Then he nudged her. 'We'll definitely see yours.'

A Dad joke but still it made her laugh. 'What's it like?'

'Over there? Cliffs, coves, beaches. You never see anyone. Creeks the colour of black tea.' He stopped. 'Maybe we can get you over there.'

'Serious?'

'I could check with Frank.'

Steph closed her eyes to the cry of birds, the dips in light, the rush of cold when clouds skidded across the sun.

'You like doing the weather?'

'Uh-huh,' she said, realising in that moment that she did. 'Other than getting up in the dark. Dad insists on setting his alarm, just in case.'

'Mum's the same.'

So he lived at home. 'How old are you?'

'Nineteen. You?'

'Seventeen. At the end of the year.'

'What does your father do?'

'He reads the news on Radio National.' Steph rested on her elbow. She didn't want to talk about her parents. 'You like crayfishing?'

'Has its moments. On a nice day, when it's calm and sunny. For the most part it's cold and wet and the wind's howling. You wouldn't want to be doing it forever.'

'What will you do? After this.'

He rose to his feet, brushed grass from his jeans. 'Million dollar question.'

Steph took him back to the house. Her mother gushed. 'Tom. I'm Gretchen.' It occurred to Steph that Tom was a novelty: they hadn't had boys in the house since Callam and his friends. She wore low-cut jeans, a wide belt. Her hair was loose. Everything looked shapely on her mother. Tom seemed entranced.

'I've put coffee on,' Mum said. 'Will you have some, Tom?'

'It smells great.'

'Actually,' Steph broke in, 'I was going to show Tom the lighthouse. He only has an hour or two.'

Tom's focus remained fixed on her mother. 'I was speaking to James on the road. He told me you grew up here.'

'You met Dad?' Tom didn't answer. Steph may as well have not been in the room.

'When I wasn't at school in Hobart I spent every second on Maat. My father was posted here close to four years.'

'Was the haulage way in use?'

'It most certainly was.' Mum's hands danced through the air. 'When I think about the supplies, the gear, the drums of fuel winched up that slope.' She turned to Steph. She was hatching a plan. 'The three of us could walk to the end of the road and open the old sheds, show Tom how the whim used to work.' She turned to Tom. 'Steph hasn't been there yet.'

Steph bristled. She'd been to the end of the road. She'd walked the track down to the Gulch.

'I—' Tom started. 'I'm not sure how . . . what are we doing?' He looked to Steph.

Steph huffed. 'It's totally up to you.'

'Maybe next time,' he said to Mum. Steph breathed.

'You two have fun then,' Mum said. 'I've shown Steph how to run the mechanism. You remember what to do?'

Steph knew better than her mother what to do.

She and Tom walked the road in silence. Cirrus cloud blanked out the sky. Steph couldn't think of anything to say. The wind felt chill. Tom stopped at the bend in the road to study the lighthouse. 'It's squat,' he said.

'It has four floors.' She didn't mean to be abrupt.

'Your parents are young.'

'How old are yours?'

'It's just Mum. She'd be pushing sixty. She sews and knits for a living. I've never seen her in a pair of jeans.'

'At least you're not expected to wear her cast-offs.'

'Worse,' he said.

Steph stopped in the middle of the road. 'What could possibly be worse?'

He lowered his head, turned out the collar of his jumper. Steph brushed his skin. *Thomas Lee Forrest*, read the old-fashioned script of the embroidered label.

'My mother's speciality. She still thinks I'll lose my clothes.' Steph readjusted his collar, conscious of the line of fine hair, her fingers on his neck. 'She would have added the phone number if there'd been room.' Steph's bad mood vanished with her laughter.

She led the way into the lighthouse and up the spiral steps. They moved out to the balcony. Wind and cloud had turned the ocean dark. They sat on the sheltered side, looking out at the Mewstone. 'How'd you get out of school for all this time?'

'No such luck,' Steph said. 'There's three boxes of work up there to get through. Weekly sessions on the radio with a tutor. I have to sit HSC exams at the end of the year. Back in Hobart.'

'And after that?'

'Uni. Medicine. If I do okay.'

'Smart and talented.'

'Demented.'

Steph showed Tom how to fit the large turn-handle and wind the heavy weights. She loosened the small screw to free the flywheel that set the cogs in motion. 'It's basically a large-scale grandfather clock.' The flywheel gathered speed, Steph waited as she'd been shown. She pulled the lever into gear and the pedestal began to turn.

They climbed the upper steps and Tom helped reach the hook to unclip the canvas curtains. Light and warmth poured in. Even with the thickening cloud, the lens magnified the sunlight and threw a strip of heat across Steph's jeans. She climbed in and stood on the turning pedestal. She beckoned Tom. The lens shimmered. The lighthouse hummed. Callam's voice. *Remember this.*

'Magic,' Tom said.

The light was more than function. It was ingenuity and art that harnessed light then threw it out across the ocean and far into the night. Steph ran her hand across the central spheres of glass. Concentric prisms fitted one against the other, a planet's shimmering rings orbiting as one. Every lighthouse lens was distinct, the character of the light a language of itself. 'I'd like to have seen it in action,' she said.

'You should ask Frank. He's been fishing down here for years.'

A gang of green rosellas landed on the outside railing. Steph watched their shapes dance and jitter through the glass. The rosellas squawked as if demanding to know what they were doing. Tom smiled. 'Busy body lot.' His eyes were brilliant green, not the green of the ocean but not the green of leaves either. A colour Steph could spend all her time trying to capture in paint or pastel, never quite succeeding.

They spent the morning talking, laughing. The presence of someone her own generation felt invigorating against a new sting of loneliness when he said he had to go. They walked along the road and rounded the bend to where Steph's father crouched over the lawnmower, tools spread across the grass. Dad stood up. 'Tom.'

'Mower giving you grief?'

'The usual coughing and spluttering,' Dad croaked. 'He's a piece of work, old Buster.'

'Buster?'

'His name, I was told, though right now I can think of others.'

Tom blinked, perhaps trying to make sense of her father's broken words. 'Can I take a look?' he finally said. Tom removed the cover from the lawnmower. 'Big job, the mowing. You can do without a breakdown.'

'I'm afraid mechanics aren't my strong suit.'

'Might be flooded,' Tom said. Steph watched as he undid a spark plug and wiped it clean. 'Leave it a while and see how it goes.'

Dad thanked him. 'How did you like the lighthouse?'

'A lot. I'd only ever seen it from the water.'

'You'll have to stop by and have dinner with us some time. Let Gretchen wax lyrical about the old days.' Dad winked at Steph. It was true that her mother went on, as though everything back then was perfect, but Steph didn't like it when her father spoke that way.

'I wish I could,' Tom said. 'Nights and early mornings we're shooting pots.'

'Shooting?'

'Setting them, pulling them.'

'Your family one of the local fishing dynasties?' Dad asked. 'Salt-water in your veins?'

'Not a drop. My brother Frank got into it when he left school. Boats aren't my thing. Not working boats.'

'Why fishing then?' Dad asked. Steph could sense Tom tighten. Dad's voice softened. 'Then again, how do any of us find ourselves on unmown roads, doing things we hadn't planned?' He closed the mower lid and gave Buster a friendly boot. 'Isn't that so, you big rust bucket?'

★

Tom stopped ahead of Steph on the way down to the Gulch. He took the VHF radio from his backpack. The aerial was missing. 'Shit,' he said, digging for it in the bottom of his pack then winding it back on. He called *Perlita Lee* which appeared briefly, then disappeared from view, beating back and forth across the waves. 'Frank's not happy.' Steph hurried down the track to keep up with him. 'They had to pull anchor, couldn't get hold of me.'

Waves rolled in as sets, the largest surging over the remains of the concrete landing. An aluminium dinghy rounded the corner, bobbing in the swell. It looked too rough for such a tiny boat. Tom hitched his backpack high up on his shoulders and clipped it tight. 'Stay there. No point both getting wet.'

The man in the boat waved. He wore a beanie, his face covered in dark stubble. 'That's Habib,' Tom said. He turned to leave, and then turned back. 'I wish I could have stayed.'

'Me too.'

His eyes moved across her face as though he were committing her to memory. 'Next time?'

'I'll be here.'

Tom waited for the set to pass and clambered over slippery rocks. The boat nudged close against the pylon. Tom climbed in and pushed the boat away. 'Say goodbye to your mother.' His clothes were drenched.

Steph watched him pull at the zip of his red coat. What was left of a buckle hung loose. She felt like a castaway, scrambling up rocks to watch them pull away. Habib's voice rose above the outboard, carrying into shore. Amongst the scraps of words Steph heard her name. 'Stuff him,' Tom called back to him. He looked to Steph and raised his arm to wave. 'She's worth it,' Steph heard him say.

9

For a week Steph's mother had woken in the night to scratching in the roof. Her father was apparently as deaf to the noise as he was to her mother's concern.

It was so long since Steph had dreamed of anything nice that the interruption to sleep felt all the more unfair. Her mother shook her awake and pulled the covers down below her shoulders. 'You were laughing,' her mother said quizzically. A *let me in to your world*.

Callam. They'd been together at Forty Baskets Beach, in front of the house. Callam was belly laughing—splashing a tall figure that could have been Tom who refused to come into the water. Steph grimaced at her mother's face inches from her own.

'Stephie, listen.' Steph blinked. 'There.' Mum gestured to a point on the ceiling. 'Hear it?'

Steph dragged herself to sitting. She checked the time on her phone, gave a throaty grumble. 'Middle of the night, Mother. Can we do this in the morning?'

Her mother kept her to her word. Steph returned from the nine o'clock weather to find her dressed in an asbestos hazard suit, a disposable bonnet and booties. Her mother had dragged the big ladder inside.

'What are you doing?'

Mum sighed, as if having to spell out the basics to a dolt. 'If a pregnant rat or mouse has found its way here, we're talking environmental disaster. This island has never known an introduced species, let alone a predator.'

Steph looked nonplussed.

'Think about the birds.' Mum snapped her fingers. 'They'd be wiped out!'

'What about Tinkerbell?'

'What?'

'Cats are predators. What about the sheep and goats and chooks and pigs that used to be here? They're introduced species. And the horses from the old days? And what about the blackberry bushes? And the Montbretia all the wives planted?'

'Tinks ate a handful of lizards. At the most.'

'How could a rat even get here?' Steph scoffed. 'We're in the Southern Ocean.'

'By helicopter,' her mother said haughtily.

'Wearing his personal flotation device?'

'Funny girl. A rodent could find its way into a packing box. There's myriad ways.'

'It could mouse paddle.'

'Go ahead and laugh.' She motioned to the window. 'We're just twelve kilometres from the mainland. A creature could easily hitch a ride on a log, a bit of flotsam.'

Steph went to laugh but the prickle charged through her before the thought had gelled. 'A snake.' Steph retreated to the lounge room and clambered from the chair to the tabletop.

'Honestly, for a smart girl you can be a trifle idiotic. Snakes don't scratch and squeak. I need your help, Stephanie.'

'You wouldn't be so brave if it was leeches. I'm not going up there.'

Mum clucked. 'No one's making you. All I need is for you to hold the ladder steady. Can you do that?'

'Where's Dad?'

'Working on the drain, I imagine.'

Steph's mother, cautioned by asbestos warning signs stickered to the wall, pulled on mask and gloves. She sounded as though she was talking through a snorkel. 'My dad used to scoot up here in his work clothes, sleeves rolled up. No one back then gave a thought to asbestos.' She switched on her headlamp. 'Wish me the best of British luck.'

'You're Australian.'

Her mother's booty tapped Steph's hand on the ladder. 'It's a saying. Sheesh. Lighten up.'

'That's rich,' Steph started but Mum disappeared through the manhole. Steph sat down to chemistry. The chapter was hard enough without the stomping going on above her head. 'Find anything?' she called. No answer.

The phone rang and Steph raced for it. It had taken all her powers to negotiate the use of the phone. And only if she contributed with the money she was earning from the weather observations. Two calls, hardly more than an hour each, and Steph had used up all her wages while Tessa and Sammie had done ninety-five per cent of the talking. Tessa and Sammie had promised—they'd given her their pledge—to call from their home phones the moment their parents went out. 'Stephanie speaking.'

'Stephanie West?' A woman's voice. Singsong.

'Yes.'

'Whose mother was Gretchen Cole?'

'Yes.'

'Cathy Innes here. Your mother would remember me as Cathy Smithies. We were on the lights together, many moons ago. Is Mum around?'

Mum had never talked about other children at Maatsuyker. 'She's not available at the moment.'

'Oh.' Cathy sounded disappointed. 'Another time, then.'

'Can I give her a message?'

'Just a big hello from Cathy. We saw your photo in the news-letter. What sort of day are you having down there?'

'Windy. It rained this morning.'

'My mother used to say we had a lean on us when we left Maat.' She wanted to chat. 'Makes me homesick for the old times. The old way of life.'

'Did you know my grandparents?' Steph asked her.

'We overlapped for three or four weeks when we were leaving, yes. In fact, your mum travelled back to Hobart with us on the boat.'

'You and Mum went to school?'

'No, dear. Hardly any of the lighthouse kids did. My brothers and I were homeschoolers. Dad had us work like navvies so we could get all our schoolwork finished and help out around the place.' Cathy had a chuckle that made Steph imagine a round-faced girl.

'Sounds better than boarding school.'

'I remember when we left, Mr Cole dressed up the lighthouse with signal flags, had the Union Jack flying. Looked a picture from the water. Made your mother bawl and just about set us all off crying, we were so sad to leave.' Cathy drew a big breath. 'All water under the bridge now.'

Steph went to say goodbye. 'I'm sorry you missed Mum.'

'A shame what happened with your grandfather,' Cathy said, still caught up in the old days. Steph thought she meant his heart attack. 'It was a hard, relentless job, the light keeping. None of them were angels. But you'd have heard it all from your mother.'

Steph prickled. Cathy started to tell her more. It felt like a betrayal. 'I have to go now. I'll tell Mum you called.'

★

Steph held the ladder. 'No rodents,' her mother sang. 'A welcome swallow's nest. Five sweet little eggs.' She was charged by the so-called treasures she had found in the roof. Her mother passed down a crate of old preserving jars thick with dust. 'My mother used these exact jars. I bet they were hers.' She handed Steph an assortment of empty flagons and bottles, one still full, unopened, stoppered with a cork. *Gull's Navy Rum.* The glass was filthy with grime. 'Who rang?' her mother asked.

Should she say? Her mother looked so happy. 'One of the pilots,' she lied. 'Checking the weather.'

'You'd have to pay me to fly today.'

Her mother hadn't registered that Steph had packed away her schoolbooks early. 'I'm going out for a walk.'

Steph ran along the road. The conversation with Cathy had thrown her. There was no way to ask about Grandfather and Grandmother without Mum claiming everything back then was perfect. Steph had figured out a long time ago that her mother didn't always tell the truth, not the full truth. It wasn't out-and-out lying.

Her mother didn't *see* things, especially when it came to Callam. Everything bold about her brother had altered shape. *Take a hike,* his new friend said to Steph when she'd joined them after school. She'd waited for Callam to tell the older boy she was his sister and to take a hike himself. *Piss off,* Callam hissed at her, annoyed and embarrassed by her presence.

According to Gran this second year should have felt easier than the first. By the second year, Gran said, you could no longer look back the way you had the first, thinking *this time last year we were all together, this time last Christmas, last birthday.* The last of everything, drifting from your reach. You medicated yourself on the distance of time—a sedative that dulled the sharpness then locked you in its murk. It was a kind of worn-out grief you couldn't easily share, not once the time allowed for sadness had lapsed. And not on a crackly phone with Tessa or Sammie whose jam-packed weeks danced down the line in sequinned colour. Tessa and Sammie had finally asked, *How are you, Steph? How are you really?*

What to answer? Tell the truth to friends whose lives had grown out toward the air while Steph's had turned its back to the wind, sheared to match the vegetation on this island. *You know,* she'd said to Tessa and Sammie. Neither did at all.

★

'What are the jars in the workroom?' Dad asked Steph when they sat down to dinner.

Steph pushed food around her plate. 'Mum found them in the roof.'

Mum called from the kitchen. 'I bet they were my mother's jars. The pantry used to be chock-a-block with her preserves and pickles.

I'm cleaning them up for the museum.' Her mother was a little drunk. Back in Sydney she would have wrinkled her nose at boxed wine. Here on Maatsuyker, home rules didn't always apply.

'Who was the Pimms drinker?' Dad said.

Mum put on a la-di-da accent. 'The ladies of the lights enjoyed a little tipple.'

'And the navy rum?' Dad asked. 'Your old man the soak?'

Mum didn't answer.

Her father took a second helping of chicken. He saw Steph's uneaten food. 'What's wrong?'

A shrug. 'Not that hungry.'

He lowered his voice. 'Are you all right?'

Mum squealed from the kitchen. 'Look! Look! Look!'

Steph and Dad followed her out through the laundry to the picket fence. The clouds had lifted to a blood-red sky. Against the sunset the Needles stood stark in silhouette. The ocean sat motionless, lush as coloured silk.

'The mutton-birds,' Mum cried.

Steph searched the sky.

Mum disappeared inside and returned with binoculars swinging from her arm. 'Take a look.' She pointed to the water.

What first had looked like slicks of oil were rafts of birds resting on the water. Thousands in a single group.

Colour bathed the lighthouse. The sun was mostly gone, bulging and heavy, the skyline a fruity haze streaked with painted cloud. In the dimming light Steph spied a needle of white, a spotlight, the movement of a distant vessel. She focused the binoculars: a red hull, a white wheelhouse. Tom.

A patch on the water ruffled as if stirred by breeze. In turn the next patch lifted, and then the next, expanding into wing. The sky was aflutter, a squall of wings rising and streaming their way. Birds swept up the cliff line, washed over the lighthouse, clouded the sky, rushed across their heads. A stream of birds poured past at eye level, darting, winding, tipping, changing tack to avoid colliding in the rush. Like novice parachutists, some thudded hard on the road then tumbled into furrows. Others careered into bushes, breaking branches as they fell. One came down upon the grassy slope, then tumbled downhill and landed in the ditch. A few glided in for a graceful landing on the pathway. Most crashed onto the lawn, or thudded against the rockery, picking themselves up and shaking off their arrival with an ungainly squawk. Immediately they set to, waddling off to find their nest, cooing and crowing to those in the air. The return of the mutton-birds. A sensory assault of chatter and industry, of clumsy flapping wings. No longer could they claim the island as theirs alone. Birds scrambled from the foliage and tore at overgrown branches, scratching at dirt to unearth a burrow. Steph sniffed at something medicinal, an acrid fume carried in the air. 'What's the smell?' It brought to mind sickly syrup laced with anaesthetic and a putrid trace of fish.

Mum looped her arm around Steph's shoulder. 'That, my sweet, is the real Maatsuyker Island.' She rested her head on Steph's shoulder, the air between them fumy with wine. Her mother sniffed back tears. 'My darling.' For a moment Steph thought her mother meant her. 'My beautiful boy won't ever be here to see this.'

'He is here.' In the light. All around. The realisation inflated Steph. Could no one else feel it? She spoke aloud. 'Can't we remember him without always being sad?' Dad studied her. Neither of them answered.

Steph left her parents, Dad's arm held around her mother's waist. 'There, there, love,' her father said.

Steph stood by her bedroom window staring at the night. The fishing fleet's cluster of lights sparked through the dark. She opened the window to the air. The moon had finally appeared, a broad silver blade pressed down on the water. Her mother would spend tomorrow maudlin. Her father would disappear after breakfast, another day of mowing or clearing out the drains. They'd been here a month and only Gran and cousin Lydia had found the time to call. Steph set her phone alarm for morning. The bleats and groans from seals carried through the night, mournful as a cattle yard. She inhaled the cloying smell of mutton-bird, air rancid with their oil. The endless chatter of birds. An orchestra of discord pulsating through the night.

10

The whiff of mutton-bird as Tom passed by a patch of newly excavated burrows. Beyond the smell of birds the fragrance swamped his senses. When the rain stopped and the air stood still, Maatsuyker's bush released an infusion of tea-tree, bracken fern, mountain pepper berry, freshly mown grass.

He heard a whistle. He looked to see Stephanie breezing down the road, arms flopping, hopscotch across the vehicle furrows, gumboots shiny as a fire truck. She raised her arm and waved, she broke into a run. He watched her smile. He heard her laugh. Tom could not remember anyone, ever, that pleased to see him. It didn't matter that he barely knew this girl racing down the hill. He felt giddy with feeling. A shadow reared up. *It could never be that easy, Tom-Tom.* As quickly it was gone.

She showed him the burrow in the wall of the ditch, a movement of grey feathers, a beak.

'One big rain,' Tom told her, 'the whole thing will wash away.' Brightness vanished from her face and he wished he'd kept his mouth shut. 'What would you like to do? Have you seen the Light Keeper's Tree?'

She shook her head.

'What have you been doing all this time?' Six weeks she'd been here.

'Plenty, believe you me.' She used her fingers to reel off the weather observations, her studies and assignments, her art, cleaning the old lighthouse, helping her mother in the vegetable garden. 'And my all-time favourite job?' She made a face. 'DEMOULDING WALLS. And then I'm in bed by nine-thirty because it's deathly cold inside the house and I have to wear thirty-seven layers and a beanie and a scarf just to stay alive.' She stopped to inhale. 'Then, *dring, dring*, and it's pitch black and freezing and I'm out of bed to do the six o'clock weather. And back up there at nine. And again at three and—what?' she stopped. 'What's so funny?'

He elbowed her. 'That's why they pay you the big bucks.'

She elbowed him back, tried to muscle him off the road, almost landing him in the ditch. He grabbed her. She squealed and broke free. Even in gumboots she was quick. She waited at the top of the hill, doubled over, laughing.

The light keeper's track started behind the cottages. A woven mat of clipped ferns crisscrossed the track.

'Dad's always doing some clearing or other.'

'How does he manage on the radio? His voice and all.'

'He's taking a break. He's hoping that will fix it.'

'What's wrong with it?'

'Spasmodic dysphonia. It's neurological. He says it's like having a vice around his neck.'

'Has he always had it?'

'Just the last year or so. There's some toxin they can inject in your vocal cords. It's supposed to make it better for a while.'

Tom swallowed. He felt his Adam's apple stick in his throat. It sounded bloody awful.

Across the surface of the water, close in to the rocks, pairs of white and yellow buoys arced toward the cliffs. Looking down on it, Tom felt safe. From here the ocean didn't look so mean.

Stephanie prattled in a way that made Tom think about his boyhood, waiting for his mother to come home from work so he had someone to talk to about his day. Stephanie was telling him about her school. A ski lodge in the snow they all went up to in the winter. She'd missed out on some trip to South America—because of coming here. Tom quietened. The contrast between them felt as stark as Maatsuyker's two lighthouses: one steeped in tradition, regal and grand; the other utilitarian, built for function. Tom's biggest school trip was a weekend to an old hydro village in the highlands and on to the dam, air white with fog and so cold it grazed his lungs.

She spoke about her two best friends, how the three of them wagged school and changed out of their uniforms on the ferry. They'd caught a train to Sydney's western suburbs.

'Get caught?' he asked.

'You'd never run into anyone out there. Tessa said she'd rather be infested by fleas from a thousand camels than be seen shopping at an outlet mall. She tends to be dramatic.'

'What's wrong with malls?' Tom asked. Not that shopping was his strong suit.

'That's how it is at our school, Tom. God, you'd never admit you paid twelve ninety-five for a top. It's bad enough having the other girls call us three *the poories*. Behind our backs. We told them we bought the tops at DJ's. *Oh, wow, they're gorgeous. How much?* Goes to show.'

They climbed the track until tea-tree and she-oak gave way to native cherries, tree ferns, stately things with feathered limbs that arched across the track. They arrived at a thicket of peppermints lofty enough to filter the light. It was the only place on the island Tom knew of where tall eucalypts grew. Underfoot the track grew spongy with moss and sodden leaf mulch. Tom stopped to tuck the hem of his jeans inside his socks.

She overtook him. 'Looking sharp.' She shrugged off her shirt to tie around her waist. He took in her bare arms, a pale strip of midriff. He thought to caution her about the leeches but this was her island. He didn't want to sound like anybody's parent.

She chatted as they walked, the trip to the States with her cousin and their family. Stephanie—even her name seemed assured in the way of someone whose world was infinitely large. She probably had a list of old boyfriends. She probably had one now. Ski lodges, America. Tom had been as far as Melbourne. A fifty-minute flight. *Tom's big night out*, Frank still referred to it with a knowing wink. You could never own up to any of that. Christ. The thought of it. He and Frank trashed, reeling down a street at who knew what time? *Happy eighteenth, little brother.*

★

The restaurant Frank chose for his birthday overlooked the river and Melbourne's city lights, each setting a parade of silverware and glasses, enough urban chic and posturing to make Tom tense, despite telling himself it didn't faze him. Next to Tom his mother looked as stiff as her shoulder-padded jacket that faintly ponged of mothballs. Only Tom was attuned to her discomfort, gaiety dutifully fixed upon her face. Melbourne was his mother's second home, she'd grown up there, but this wasn't her—she was happiest at home, overfeeding Tom on pasta.

The waitress with the accent tried telling them about the specials on the menu, the *rock lobster from Tazmeenia*. Frank cackled. *Probably caught the bastard m'self.*

People behind swapping weary looks.

It wasn't the fancy surrounds that made Tom wish the night away; it was a lifetime of Frank's benevolent dictatorship. *The whole weekend on me.* Tom would have opted to stay with his mother, on Aunt Fina's fold-out lounge, not stuck with Frank, two brothers padding about a shiny sterile apartment in Melbourne's CBD.

On the boat, at work, Tom accepted his brother's control. There it was the order of things. But in a fancy restaurant—if Frank could just turn the volume down, let other people be. Tom slugged down beer in a frosted glass. He switched to wine, despite his mother's frowns.

You never, Frankie, Aunt Fina shrieked on the drive home. *A hundred dollar tip on top!* Frank waited until their mother waved goodnight and closed the leadlight door. He drove back into town, parked in the underground lot around the corner. Two tablets rested in the flat of his hand. *The boys go out and play.* There was no opting out with Frank.

The wall of music in the nightclub turned porous, the bass thrumming inside his chest. Tom gave himself up to the press of overheated bodies, shooters lined up at the bar, floating on the dance floor with a girl whose name he never asked.

Reeling down a back street. They stopped to relieve themselves against an abandoned storefront, its roller shutters a stench of urine-stained graffiti.

Tom had never stepped inside a tattoo parlour, was too far gone to think straight. *Fuckin' blood brothers*, Frank told the artist, sketching a crudely drawn outline of two entwined anchors.

Tom sobered with the pain, at least enough to walk outside when it was done and draw in cold air. He guzzled water while the artist worked on Frank. His brother ranting about *Forrest Brothers*: the fleet of boats they'd own one day. Even trashed, Frank knew how to score a bargain. Matching shoulders, two for the price of one.

Where to, gents? The taxi driver's voice metallic through the speaker. At Frank's directions Tom dropped his head in his hands. *What? Eighteen, Tom-Tom. Your rite of passage.*

The house looked no different from his aunt's, no telltale light to guide the way.

Tom's preconception of a sex worker was scrubbed away at the line-up of women in the dimly lit lounge. The first, middle-aged and overweight, he assumed was the receptionist until she threw Frank a loaded smile. The face of the Asian girl, Willow, they called her, looked pitted and hard. But it was her shoe, tapping her disinterest beneath her cheongsam that made Tom wither. He wanted to escape that place, the mocking gaze of women. *Her*, Frank nudged Tom toward the strawberry blonde—a flouncy top, her makeup unable to conceal her freckles. Melody. Only now did it occur to Tom that they were made-up names. A hallway lit with naked pink lights, the air a cocktail of stale smoke and incense, a chaser of bleach.

She undressed herself without any of the clumsiness he felt in unbuttoning his own shirt. She had him pegged for the virgin he was, eased him down, straddled him and produced a condom. She guided him, her eyes disengaged from her smile, the motion of her body as fluid as a seal. It was over in seconds. Tom sat at the edge of the bed, sobered and unsure of what to do. He spied a small bin and reached for the tissues. He poured a glass of water that tasted of old pipes. Should he thank her? Ask about money? Did people tip? He collected his shirt, took out his wallet.

Your brother paid for forty minutes. You can stay.

He didn't turn to face her. *And what?*

Whatever you like.

He laid his body down beside her—resignation? obligation? Closed his eyes. The raw flesh of his tattooed shoulder throbbed needle hot beneath his weight. Tom felt desolate and brother-bound and on the verge of weeping. She took his hand, a curve of belly, a warmth of thigh.

★

The Light Keeper's Tree was so armoured with plaques that the trunk and larger branches appeared to sag with the weight of all that pressed tin and history. Most were small crimped sheets bent to hug the tree's curve, others were mounted onto wooden backings like baiting notices. Tom had been up here before but never stopped to read them properly. A pattern of pinholes through tin spelled out the name of each keeper, his wife and children, the record of their service inscribed with hammer and punch.

Stephanie searched for her grandparents. Tom looked through weatherworn inscriptions; you could determine the era by the thickness of rust. 'Here,' he called before he registered the graffiti scratched across the name.

John Cole. Mary Cole. Gretchen Cole
September 1969–May 1973

She knelt on the ground, used the sleeve of her shirt, and then her fingers, in a futile attempt to obliterate the words *ADULTERER BURN IN HELL* crudely gouged in tin against her grandfather's name. It was like something from his mother's bible.

Tom touched her shoulder. 'Some vandal. Doesn't mean anything.'

She shook her head. 'It's as old as the plaque. It meant something to someone.' Her voice was tight.

'I'm sorry.' Tom didn't know what else to say.

'The whole reason we've come here is to help Mum get over Callam.'

Callam? Tom waited for an explanation.

'My twin brother. He died. In Mum's mind everything about this place is perfect. This would send her over the edge.'

He wanted to ask about her brother but something told him not to. 'Perhaps she won't come up here.'

Steam rose from the forest floor as they hiked the final stretch of undergrowth to the summit of the island. They passed by a grove of tree fern. All around them was a waxy carpet of fronds. Through the foliage Tom pointed out Flat Witch and Big Witch Islands, the Hen and Chickens. Stephanie circled through the bush, peering out. Tom checked his clothing and his socks for leeches. In damp like this you only had to stay still for a moment. He spotted a pair of fine black threads advancing in waves across his boot. He saw a head lift, the sweep of a tail, double-ended sensory receptors that searched the air, guiding the leech until it found bare skin and suckered on. Tom flicked it free.

They started down the hill. 'Your brother. Was he sick or something?'

'An accident.'

'When?'

'Two years.'

'I'm sorry.'

She seemed to want to say something more but then she shrugged it off. 'You don't need to be sorry about everything.'

'It must affect you. All of you. Not only your mum.'

'My brother became … difficult.' Tom waited for more. 'Growing up we were like this.' She crossed her two fingers. 'It changed the year he died. He got weird. Drugs, maybe. Stealing. I don't know. No one does. What I do know is that at some point you have to let it go. You can't keep asking yourself why.' She walked on, her shirt catching on a branch and unknotting from her waist. She looked irritated when he passed back her shirt. 'What?' she said to him.

'I lost my father when I was three days old. He died of absestosis. I can't help myself thinking about him. What it would be like now. What he'd make of me.'

Her face softened. 'He would have loved you, Tom. How could he not?' He felt himself blush. 'I'm really sorry about your father. It isn't fair,' she said. 'It's not that I don't care about my brother. That I don't wish it was different. I want to live again, not be held down by it. That's what I'm saying.'

Tom found the path off the track that led to open slopes, an undulating sweep that looked as soft as pasture.

Stephanie laid her shirt down and parked herself beside him. He caught sight of her back. Five black leeches collared her midriff, bulbous as fingers, latched like mussels to a rock. Girls and leeches. Not a happy combination. 'How do you feel about leeches?' he enquired.

She gasped, shot to a stand. She twisted in an effort to inspect her back. 'Get them off. Please. Now.'

'They'll bleed.'

'I don't care.' She shook her hands but didn't squeal. 'Just get them off.'

He picked each one off and flicked it at the bush. Each wound streamed with blood from the anti-coagulant. 'Last one. Stay still.'

'Can I see it?'

He laid it on his hand.

'The size of it.' She poked at it. 'That's *my* blood.'

Tom chucked it away. He checked her back. 'You've performed a community service. That will keep a leech going for months.'

She beamed.

'What?'

'Mum will never come up here. She's petrified of leeches.'

Tom produced a Mars Bar from his pocket and held it up before her. She went to take it but he pulled it away.

'I've lost blood,' she cried. 'I'm anaemic.' She was trying to reach around him and he wanted to put his arm around her, hold her, but it occurred to him that she might not think of him that way, that she might just see him as a brother. He handed her the Mars Bar and she broke it in two.

If Tom blurred his eyes and searched the horizon he could make out the speck of Pedra Branca, the white rock a sanctuary for seabirds. Out there, the Continental Shelf formed a vast under-water terrain, deepwater troughs that enticed fishing trawlers and big-game fishermen. Reef breaks delivered glass waves as tall as a building and lured a new breed of hunter: big-wave surfers. They were all the talk around the boats. Surfers who forked out for a nine-hour boat ride, to take their chances against fifteen-metre death-pit waves. They were all beholden. Them. Him. Frank. The ocean ruled.

The coastline ran away to South East Cape. Around that corner a more genteel world awaited. 'We're headed up to town tomorrow. Tanks are nearly full.'

He felt thrilled to register her disappointment. 'You're coming back, aren't you?' she said.

'For sure. Later in the week. Or next week, depending on Frank. Depending on weather.'

'I've been listening to the boat talk on the radio. How much a kilo Asia's paying for live crays. What everyone's getting at the dock. Jules, Jake, Lee, Bluey, Rodgey Dodge. *Go the Jake*,' she put on a voice.

'That lot never shut up. Some choice conversations.'

'According to Dad it's rounding out my education. His, more likely. They all seem so *chummy*. Everyone looking out for one another in a blokey kind of way. I keep expecting to hear you, your brother's name.'

'We don't have many friends when it comes to fishing.'

'Why?'

Tom's gut tightened. But the words were out. 'It's just Frank's way. He can be difficult, like your brother.' He'd opened a wound he couldn't fully stem. She'd see it. Not now or tomorrow, but at some point she'd figure it out.

'Dad says after being here he'll never complain about the price of crayfish. The hours you put in. The conditions you work in. Dad says you and Frank earn every cent. *Honest, hard-working lads.*'

Tom ruffled her hair. 'Your dad's okay.' Flyaway strands caught the sun. He drew his arm around her shoulder. She laced her fingers through his hand. He pulled her close. Her hair smelled of almonds and apricot. Her head rested on his shoulder. Exhilaration pounded in his chest. He looked out at a groomed ocean, a depth of deceit.

11

The wind squealed like a terrified child. Steph braced herself, angled her body as she rounded the corner after leaving the weather office. She was ready for the onslaught. She made her way down the path to the house, mindful of her footing. The screen door of the laundry caught a squall and flew back on its hinges. Steph struggled to close it.

She peeled off her waterproofs and towel-dried her hair. She hung her clothes on the inside line to drip on the linoleum. The windows shook, translucent with salt, the Needles a blur of sea spray and mist. A squall raced across the ocean and laid down the waves. You could barely see halfway to the Cape.

Steph put the kettle on. She searched the kitchen cupboards. The smell of mould seemed worse when you first opened things. She tiptoed to the pantry to fetch more Milo.

'Is that you, Steph?' her father called from the bedroom. He was propped on his elbow, his hair mussed from sleep. 'Everything all right?' He cleared his throat.

'All good.'

'What's it blowing?'

Her mother stirred.

'Fifty-five, gusting sixty knots.'

He gave her a *didn't I tell you?* look. 'Have trouble getting up there, getting back?'

Her father had got out of bed at five-thirty, had offered to accompany her. 'I was glad of the handrails.'

'I bet you were. Looks filthy out there.'

Steph had been wishing Tom back—every day she'd been looking for the boat. Now she wanted to feel sure he was still in Hobart. 'Where do the boats go in this?'

Her father spoke too brightly. He knew she was worried. 'They'll be holed up behind one of the Witches. Some sheltered bay. Fishermen are used to this kind of thing.'

Her mother raised her head from the pillow. 'Everything okay, Stephie?'

'It's early. I'm going back to bed.'

'You're all wet. Dry your hair. I'll get up and make you a hot water bottle.'

'Go back to sleep. Both of you. Please.' Steph hated fuss.

She found her favourite mug and added extra Milo. She filled her hot water bottle with the remainder of the kettle.

Her father was sitting up in bed, staring out the window. It would all be a blur without his glasses. He looked plaintive. He probably thought no one had remembered. She went in and kissed him. 'Happy birthday, Jamesie.'

'So it is. Thank you, sweetheart.'

Mum patted his sleeve. 'Forty-five,' she muttered into her pillow. Her mother would cook him a special breakfast when she woke. Steph would save her present until then.

Steph climbed into her bed. She laid the hot water bottle against her stomach to ease the cramps. Other girls her age were on the pill. Their periods lasted three days. Her mother didn't see the point. *Not until you're . . .*

Sexually active?

Steph, you'd tell me, wouldn't you? If you were planning?

Hardly something you could plan for. Not here.

She studied the high ceiling, the rust stains circling the nails. Steph's eyebrow mirror and everything metal on her mantlepiece was already spotted with rust.

Steph kept a framed photo of Gran standing in front of the pink azalea outside her porch. She fussed over that plant like an old companion. Steph still made the annual Easter pilgrimage to stay with Gran in Canberra. It was their special time together. She studied the photograph with Lydia at Disneyland, two cousins screaming like lunatics, a tornado of hair reeling down Magic Mountain. Sammie and Tessa. The three of them piled on top of one another in the snow. Just the one small photo with Callam, her chasing him though the shallows when they were little kids. Everything was simple in the old days.

Steph tried to blank it out but the sombre image moved before her: a wooden coffin polished to glass, ornate brass handles like something from the pages of a gothic novel—the last thing Callam would have wanted. If they'd included Steph, asked her opinion, she could have told her parents what her brother would have chosen for himself. She and Callam had seen them on cable: happy boxes. Superheroes. Star ships. Motorbikes. Pandas. Balloons. Any picture you or your loved one wanted. When she and Callam were little kids, in the water wearing masks and flippers, they'd hold their breath and dive. They'd turn and twist and roll, make squeaks and underwater singing sounds. Callam used to wish he was a dolphin.

★

Her father sounded groggy. 'What time is it?'

'Nearly ten o'clock, sleepyhead. Steph and I thought you were going to sleep away your birthday.'

'Looking out there it's not such a bad idea.'

Steph stood beside her mother at the bedside, rain hammering the window. Mum held a tray decorated with sprigs of tea-tree, a bowl of homemade yoghurt and dried cranberries, toast and coffee. Steph's birthday gift rested on the napkin.

'You manage the nine o'clock weather?'

'She had me go with her,' her mother said. 'We were like two old drunkards, staggering arm in arm against the wind.'

'I can well imagine.' Her father sounded hurt. All the times he'd offered help and Steph chose her mother instead. 'What's this, then?' He shook the small gift. He wiggled his little finger into the lip of the envelope and drew out the miniature card. *For Dad*, Steph had written. *Now that you're the outdoors type.* Her neatest print. *Love, Steph xxx.*

Her father peeled back the tape to find the slim black-handled knife. The woman at the store had tried to push the kind Tom used, jammed with nail files and screwdrivers and *everything a bloke could want*. That woman didn't know her father. He'd have put it in a drawer with all the other things he didn't use.

Dad weighed the knife in the palm of his hand. 'Look at that. How light it is.'

'I bought it in Hobart.'

He opened the blade, pressed the tab and clicked it closed with ease. He turned it in his hand, rubbed his thumb against the textured handle. 'Just the ticket,' he said, reaching out to hug her.

'And this one's from me.' Mum opened the bedside drawer and presented a black leather box. A wristwatch with chunky chiselled edges.

'Italian.' Mum glowed.

'*Waterproof to fifty metres,*' her father read aloud. Her father had never gone deeper than a duck dive. 'Stopwatch. Dual times.' A face crammed with numbers, dates and circles he'd never figure out. 'Darling, it's perfect.' He kissed her. Mum looked full of herself.

'Breakfast in bed as well.' Dad rubbed his hands. 'Now that's a treat worth waking up for.' Her father took a noisy slurp of coffee, tore off a corner of toast. 'Coffee's good. I hardly notice the powdered milk any more.'

Mum sat beside him on the bed. 'What would you like to do today? It's awful outside. We could play Scrabble, do a jigsaw, listen to music. I'll make toasted sandwiches for lunch.'

He took another slurp. 'A day off is what I'd like. Maybe I'll stay in bed and get stuck into a novel. Nothing too cerebral.'

Her mother shrugged. 'If that's what you want.'

Mum got up to leave. Dad asked Steph, 'Any news from Tom?'

'Nothing.' Steph tried not to sound concerned.

'They'll be anchored over the other side. Watching videos and eating crumpets. The rigours of life at sea.'

★

Steph spread six crackers with butter and Vegemite. She sandwiched them together.

'Is that all you're having for lunch?' her mother said. 'You look pale, hon. You want some soup? A toasted sandwich?'

Her stomach cramped. She felt bloated and fat. 'Just this.' There were no bathroom scales in the house to even check her weight. Girls at school, far thinner than her, weighed themselves four, five times a day. They fasted the whole day if they gained half a kilogram. Steph had never had the willpower to get past lunchtime. Tessa's mother would laugh off the whole idea of dieting. *Girls your age haven't stopped growing. On the scale of things you're all still tiddlywinks.* Alison Tennant the hockey captain wasn't a tiddlywink. Or the goalkeeper Gemma Sinclair. If you believed the gossip, those two had been having sex for years.

An aroma of savoury and sweet wafted through the house. Mum was browning chicken on the stovetop. The birthday cake sat cooling on a rack.

Dad padded across the kitchen in his dressing gown and sheepskin boots.

'There you are, birthday boy.' Mum gave him a peck. Dad looked longingly at the chicken sizzling in the pan. 'For tonight,' her mother tutted. 'Your birthday dinner.'

'It smells good.' He kissed Mum's neck. 'You smell good.'

Steph returned to her dreary assignment; she failed to tune out her father's murmurs from the kitchen, her mother's titters. They hadn't been like this forever. Steph tucked a sleeping bag around her legs, pulled on her hat and scarf and crunched a cracker. Her textbooks consumed the dining table and spilled onto the floor. Some she hadn't opened for weeks. She tried to feel motivated, tried to discipline herself. Her heart wasn't in it. Dad paced through the lounge room. 'I don't know how you stand it.' He folded his arms. 'I'm going back to my electric blanket.' Fifteen minutes later her mother walked by. Steph heard the bedroom door close, her mother giggling. Steph shuddered. She didn't want to think about her parents in that way.

The second radio had picked up the police channel. Through the static Steph caught one-sided bits of conversation, a woman issuing directions. *Domestic disturbance*, Steph heard her say. Hobart seemed a world away.

Two fishermen were talking on the VHF. Steph cranked up the radio, hoping to hear something of Tom.

Won't chance pulling 'em today, Bluey. Leave 'em till the morning and hope to Christ it eases off.

I reckon we're here for the duration. Sit it out behind the Big Witch.

Who you got on deck with you?

New kid from up north. He's not bad value.

Decent deckie and you never have to leave the wheelhouse.

That's the general idea. Thought he was a goner yesterday. Big wave come over, next thing he was swimming down the back of the boat. Scared the daylights out of both of us.

Steph put her plate in the sink and checked through the window. The sea was pouring over Moderate and Heavy Rocks, the swell was pushing partway up the face of the outer Needle. The bay was streaked with foaming rollers that heaved in, one, another, another. They'd be pounding the cliffs below. The windows of the house, the lighthouse, the fence, the walls: every surface was crusted with salt.

Steph took up the microphone. She hesitated. If Tom was there, they'd all be listening in. She took a deep breath. 'Perlita Lee, Perlita Lee, this is Maatsuyker Island, Maatsuyker Island. Over.' She waited. Tried again.

A gruff voice broke through the crackle. 'Bluey MacIntyre here. If you're after Frank he's nowhere round here. I'm chasing him m'self. They could be up at town.'

Fishermen on the radio never said *Over*. They didn't repeat things the way she'd been taught. They spoke normally. 'Okay, thanks for that.'

'You one of the caretakers?'

'Me and my parents,' Steph said. 'I do the weather observations.'

'That's the way,' he said less gruffly. 'What are you like at reading the swell?'

He was testing her. 'About four point five this morning?'

'Be about right. She'd be running bigger now. Five, five and a half.'

'It looks big from up here.'

'You find a sheltered spot and stay the hell out of it as best you can.'

Steph waited. 'Okay,' she said. 'See you, then.'

'You mind yourself around Frank Forrest.'

'It's Tom I'm looking for. Frank's brother.'

'Mongrels, the pair of them. Frank's just the one that pulls the strings.'

She couldn't tell if he was serious.

'You see 'em,' he said, 'you tell 'em Bluey's onto them. You tell 'em Bluey's had a gutful.' He didn't sound like he was joking.

Steph returned to her books. She couldn't concentrate. A gutful of what? She took up her sketchbook and crayons, drew a curve of glass. She should be studying, not drawing. Raised voices from the bedroom. 'Callam,' she heard her mother say. 'As if I'm not coping if I even mention his name.' Steph held her breath. A door opened. 'That's not it at all,' her father said. Steph heard the shower run.

It was pouring outside. She ought to finish her assignment. She couldn't bear the thought of sitting wrapped against the cold in a sleeping bag. She pulled on waterproofs, stepped into gumboots. Anywhere but here.

Wind swept up the valley in shrill screams. It peeled back her hair. She passed beneath a tea-tree arbour encasing the road. Beneath the branches and foliage the air was suddenly still, entirely protected. She slowed. Small birds skittered across the grass road, searching for insects and worms. Beneath the arbour you'd never guess a tempest was raging beyond.

Water raced along the ditch beside the road. The stretch her father had cleared ran uninterrupted. But when Steph reached the crest, where the drain was crippled with debris and silt, storm-water spilled over the brim and flooded the width of the road. It ran through the grass in rivulets, filling the vehicle furrows with puddles and leaves. It occurred to Steph how much her father had done. The difference it made.

Rushing water. The downpour of rain. The day she'd missed the afternoon bus and walked home from school alone. Callam had been gone since morning, left her at the bus stop and wagged school with the older boy whose gang he'd started hanging around with. He'd made Steph promise not to tell. A look of pleading that could easily turn to anger was all it took to guarantee her silence. Rain had bounced off the footpath, had poured down the roads, the drains unable to cope with the deluge. She'd diverted down the grassy slope to a walkway that wound past the bay leading to their beach. She'd taken shelter at a picnic table beneath a grove of peppermints. Her school uniform, her backpack and school-books: everything drenched. The roar from the stormwater drain had drowned out the rain. It raged snarling and dogged like a monstrous living thing. Steph had watched the torrent gush from the mouth of concrete, watched it bloom into a bay whose surface was littered with grubby foam and swirls of scum, with leaves and sticks and manmade debris scooped along the way.

She'd stayed there for a time, watched sediment spread and overwhelm the slaty blue. She'd shivered in wet clothes—it made her shiver now. She'd made her way home, the rain a steady thrum, her feet squelching inside her leather school shoes. She'd heard her mother's wails before she reached the garage—the roller door left open, her father's car home early. Guttural moans and heaving breaths seeped from upstairs. It sounded like a distraught beast. It set Steph's skin prickling. Steph placed her hand on the bottom door, wanting to understand but too scared to go in. She'd put off the moment and dumped her backpack. She climbed the outside stairs. She looked in through a window at her mother in a foetal curl upon the floor. Her father on his knees beside her, rocking like a metronome, his hand limp against her mother's hair. Steph stepped through the sliding door. *Dad?* Her father turned. Part of Steph had known. *Where's Callam?* she said. Her father's eyes the murk of the bay.

Steph raced along Maatsuyker's road. She slowed at the place where the mutton-bird had burrowed its nest. The drain had turned tailrace, carrying away everything in its course. Surely the bird would abandon the nest, find some better place to go? Steph followed to where the drain met the culvert that ran beneath the road. Thick spears of grass matted the entry to the pipe. She laid belly-down at the edge of the road, ignoring the sodden mat of grass. She dug her hands down through the grass, giving no mind to the gush of water that ran inside her sleeves, up past her elbows. Her fingers touched a soft object. She drew back. She reached for it again: a small limp bundle tangled in a dam of sticks and leaves.

The bird lay lifeless in her hands, the feathers matted with silt. Wet seeped through Steph's clothes. Her throat thudded. Within those clouded eyes she saw things about her parents they couldn't recognise themselves. All of them eddying around the idea of Callam, with nowhere else to go. Her mother pined for a past that could never be returned. And while her father never spoke aloud of Callam, his voice had inextricably faltered, as if grief or guilt had silenced him. The hours her father spent clearing this drain: an act of making good that might release the stagnant dam that held them all.

Steph carried the small body back toward the arbour. She made her way into the bush, stepping onto tree roots, the fragile ground so undermined with burrows it would have caved beneath her weight. Beneath the ground the soft sound of bird trills, mutton-birds cooing. Steph found a place beneath a bush burgeoning with buds and the promise of yellow daisies. She scooped away handfuls of dirt. She placed the bird within the shallow pit and gently covered it with soil. A pair of robins, one vivid pink, the other pale, flitted and settled on a branch. She could bring Tom here. Steph wiped dirt from her hands, she leaned against the rough bark of the tree and listened to the distant pounding of the ocean. *Mongrels*, Bluey called them. Steph distanced herself from the awful, ceaseless rain.

The light had dimmed, the horizon shredded with red. She heard thunder, looked at storm clouds sweeping overhead. She'd missed doing the afternoon weather observations.

The outside light was on. Through the window Steph could see the table set, three wine glasses, her textbooks packed away.

Mum stood stiff-backed at the stove, the dinner overcooked and waiting to be served. 'You knew it was your father's birthday.'

'I didn't mean to be late.'

Dad was seated at the table, dressed in a good shirt. 'Where were you?' he said quietly. 'We were worried sick. I went down to the lighthouse. You've been gone for hours.'

'Walking,' she said. 'Just away.'

'Please tell us next time you're going to disappear like that.' His disappointment was worse than if he'd been angry. 'I did the weather.'

'Thanks.' She felt meek.

'And you missed your radio session with the tutor. I apologised on your behalf.'

Her mother set a casserole dish upon a mat and turned to go. She wrinkled her nose. 'Go and wash your hands please, change your clothes. You reek of mutton-bird.'

Dad looked defeated and old. Steph felt overwhelmed. She hugged her father. 'I'm sorry. I'm sorry, Dad.'

'Oh, Steph.' Her father studied her, his halting voice, his eyes slate grey. 'We're all sorry. More than you can know.'

12

The sou'-westerly doused the wheelhouse with spray. The engine farted and spluttered, ready to stall on them again. '*Slut*,' Frank snapped. As if fearful of his temper the motor surged into a roar. 'That's my darlin'.'

Dirty fuel, Frank had claimed last week. Now it was air in the fuel line, but bleeding the lines before they'd left the shelter of Rocky Bay hadn't fixed the problem. Too cheap to have the engine looked at in Hobart before they'd started out. Tom knew some of the short cuts Frank took at the end of a season, arrangements he made with certain mechanics and boat engineers. In kind, the preferred form of payment: a sack of undersize crays, fish from someone else's pots. Worst of all a catch of berried females, the platelets beneath their tails clustered with eggs. Why fork out ten grand to the boatyard when your papers could be signed for less?

Maatsuyker's light blinked. Tom saw the lights of the house. He'd never get the dinghy ashore to visit Stephanie. In the morning he'd call her on the radio. To the west, broken threads of scarlet had deepened into night. Sheet lightning scored the underbellies of thunderheads bullying their way across the sky, puffed up for fight. The caps of waves tore off into scraps streaked white across the water. The *Perlita Lee* struggled for control as she crabbed up a wave.

Frank gripped the wheel as she skittered down the other side and plunged into a trough. The swell was running five metres. 'It's not worth ten pots,' he said to Frank. *Gale eater*, Bluey MacIntyre once called Frank. *Your brother's got a death wish.* All week in Hobart Tom had wanted to get back down here. Now he wished they'd stayed in town. 'Let's come back for them when the engine's sorted.' Tom didn't care that he was pleading before his brother and Habib.

'Not at forty bucks a kilo.'

Frank swung the wheel hard to round the Needles. The water turned into a maelstrom of waves fit to knock each other out. The ocean felt wrong. Frank swore. The *Perlita Lee* charged over a crest and smacked hard onto the belly of a trough—the slam jolted Tom's spine. The boat came to a stop. A wave bucketed toward them, a surge that looked taller than the boat. Tom watched in a trance. The roll of water caught them on their hind, punched them sideways, the curl of the wave breaking over the gunnel and dumping a ton of water across the back deck. The vessel lurched, the stern shunted down beneath the extra weight of water. The back half of the boat looked like a swimming pool of bubble bath, the scuppers not equipped to drain such volume before a new wave pushed them under. The corner of the gunnel was flush with ocean. Too much water to even get to the tank boards to open the well. They were gone. They were dead. Tom looked at craypots and orange buoys, a tangle of ropes: everything afloat behind the wheelhouse.

He heard the engine splutter. He held his breath. Habib gripped the railing. Tom looked out at a swell that raced toward them. Part of him wanted it. All his imaginings that soured his dreams and left him drowning in the ocean, nightmares from which he struggled to wake. This was escape. The engine coughed and heaved. The world turned slow. He pictured bronze-skinned women in rolled bark canoes. Tom was amongst them, diving for shellfish, kicking down and down, lungs starved of breath and bursting for air and how could any human, no matter how good they were, ever make it back up to the surface? He saw his brother's forehead beaded in sweat. In Frank's blanched face, Tom imagined his father at the end, lungs choked of air. Frank caught his look. His brother swore and jammed his hand hard against the throttle. Habib stood owl-eyed. The engine chugged with life and the boat inched forward, dragging itself like a clubbed seal, the back half rendered useless. *Come on.* Tom's heart pounded. He gripped the handhold, willing the boat to move. Even laden with water the vessel lifted on the swell. Behind them two waves collided; water rained down on the wheelhouse roof. The *Perlita Lee* slid away, the water held in the stern cascading down toward the bow. A wall of water pushed against the wheelhouse door, ran in beneath, across Tom's feet and down the steps into the galley. The bulk of it poured by outside.

He watched it spew out through scuppers like a strainer. He watched their colander of boat purge itself of water. He felt her pull away.

Tom blinked to make sense of it. A second chance. The last wave should have sunk them.

'Jesus fuck.' Frank's relief sounded girlish.

Tom couldn't talk. He sat with his gut in spasm, his limbs trembling, his mind in vivid replay. Tom had welcomed death, a convoluted logic that meant he'd never have to work for Frank again. Tom was an idiot. He didn't want to die. Out there in the ocean he wouldn't stand a chance.

A deep guttural rumble—thunder right above them—put Tom's skin on edge. He pulled his eyes away from saturated carpet, his brother's sodden shoes. Beside him Habib stood in a kind of trance.

'Jesus wept.' Frank saw his Stormy Seas lifejacket worn by Habib. 'The going gets tough, the rats abandon ship. That the way it is, Hab? Ready to rob the skipper of his last means of survival?' Frank's voice cracked. He reminded Tom of a wallaby spooked by the headlights. His brother was afraid and he was angry with the world at being made to feel so. 'Might be the way things are where you come from, mate. You're in a civilised country now.' Frank was a beleaguered vessel in heavy seas, clawing up the back of a wave to regain control. It was attitude that got you through. 'Who's your employer, mate?' Frank poked his finger at Habib's chest. 'Who's your sponsor for your residency? Or maybe you don't give a shit if you and your knocked-up missus get shipped back home?' Frank gained vigour and strength in seeing Habib falter. He lunged ahead. 'Two more years you're on this boat, shithead.' Tom hated his brother. He was the personification of every bully Tom had known. Frank raised his voice above the din, the wheelhouse roof thrumming with rain, the windows a pattern of watery pins ricocheting off glass. 'Good thing you got your float coat zipped up, brother. The prick'd be eyeing that off as well.'

Habib spoke evenly to Frank. 'We passed beside life end.' He gestured to the heavens. 'We leave now. I ask you.' It came as a command. Hab held Frank's glower, he kept his head raised. Tom saw in Hab's defiance a quiet dignity, a glimmer of a former self that Habib Yılmaz had been forced—by circumstance, by striving for a different life—to set aside. Your real self, it might be buried for a time but it couldn't be completely quashed. Not even by Frank.

Habib gave Tom gumption. He stood head to head with Frank. He wasn't someone's little brother any more. He was as physically strong, as broad across the shoulders from all the lifting. 'You heard him, Frank. Give it away. We come back for 'em tomorrow.'

Frank's hands tightened on the wheel, pitbull terrier that he was. But then he swung the boat around. 'Cowards, the pair of you. Midnight. Take it or leave it.'

Hab held Tom's eye. Tom caught the silent thanks.

★

Barely hours enough to find shelter and anchor, change out of wet clothes, mop up the worst of the water, heat a tin of soup before upping anchor and back out in it. But the worst had passed, the wind had shifted. The pots were now protected. Tom and Habib worked side by side. Tom threw out the grappling iron to snag the line between the double buoys. He wound the line around the turnstile and started up the pot hauler. The first pot tipped against the gunnel; seawater cascaded from the woven basket.

The fishermen across Bass Strait and over in the west used plastic cages, throwaway things without a sense of history. Each of these pots had been crafted from tea-tree, most by Frank, the newer ones, the bark still on, by Tom himself. It was the single part of working on the boat that brought Tom peace—producing something tangible and good, holding its weight and strength within his hands. He could tell you which track he'd driven down, which tree among a stand of good trees he'd looked over and assessed. He knew now the effort in preparing and steaming the branches, the strength and skill it took to round them into shape. Once the bark peeled away, six months or so, the pots were seasoned, the better for catching crays.

With good care they'd get seven years from Tom's new pots. Frank looked after his gear, he'd give his brother that.

Tom slid the pot, heavy with crays, onto the steel platen beside the hauler. Even the storm had played its part, the swirl and current enticing crays from darkened crevices in through the neck of the pot toward the promise of a feed. They crawled in and out as they pleased. If Frank had left the pots till morning as Tom had wanted, the bait would be gone, with it a bumper catch. Tonight's haul was the reddest of red crays, the kind you only caught in shallow water: these fish were gold.

Habib used callipers to measure borderline fish from the horn along the carapace. He sorted crays by size and sex. You were only meant to take the males. Hab switched out the bait in the pot then waited on the cue from Frank. His brother manoeuvred the boat to within a length from the cliff. There wasn't a skipper behind the wheel, not even Bluey MacIntyre, as deft as Frank. He switched gears between idle and reverse, kept the revs up to nudge the boat in, drawing back to counteract the swell. Frank's eye didn't waver from the mark on the GPS yet he somehow tracked the depth sounder, positioning the boat precisely. Frank gave the signal and Habib released the baited pot. Their boat backed out before line and buoys had finished racing out.

The location marks were recorded in the book and saved in the GPS. Those marks were a measure of your time at sea. Frank could sketch a map of submarine ledges and bomboras as clearly as the rocks above the water. Frank, Bluey, any of the good skippers: they knew where a ridge began and where it dropped away. According to the Law of Frank, the ocean wasn't everyone's to use. Frank had come to think of certain patches as his and his alone.

Tom held the crayfish by its head and horns, careful not to bend or snap the feelers. A damaged fish paid a fraction of its worth. Grab the fish too far down the carapace and its tail would snap against your fingers until you dropped it on the deck. Take it by the legs and chances were one would snap right off—Tom had seen them drop at will.

A cray could shed its shell and regenerate another, legs and all. *It has to*, he'd explained when Hab first started on the boat. *It has to change its shell to grow.* He'd shown Hab the soft new shell—barely more than membrane—formed beneath the toughened carapace. Language with Hab had been a challenge then but Hab had understood when they'd caught a cray whose old shell slid away in his hands. Tom had plunged the cray into water and they'd watched it swell before their eyes, the exposed flesh absorbing water and expanding a fifth again in size. *The new shellers are too fragile for export*, he'd answered Hab's questions. *We sell them on the local market. They're our bread and butter.* Tom had held out the fish for Hab to touch the flimsy shell. *Two or three months and it'll toughen up.*

Every year, a new skin? Hab had asked.

Many times a year when they're small. Right through till they're mature. Those huge ones you'll sometimes see, the old men of the sea, they're dozens of years old. They reckon they moult every three, four years.

Tom opened the stern hatch and placed each legal cray down into the well where ocean water circulated. The fish would cling to the grates, fed and monitored until they reached Hobart's wharf. Some were flown in tanks to Asia, others packed in straw and chilled. They'd live three days like that, enough to reach some swanky restaurant in London or be set on display at a Tokyo sashimi bar.

Live export. *From pot to plate*, the slogan went. That's where the money was.

Tom stacked the females and undersized in a separate plastic bin, ready for Frank to deal with. The smallest he chucked back into the ocean. *Live another day.*

For ten pots it was a haul they'd talk about for weeks—premium crays, illegal extras that all up would fetch enough to make the month's repayment on the loan and keep Frank wife's Cheryl, who managed the books, entertained and clothed. Tom and Hab would get their percentage of the catch, no arguments with Frank over extra cash for keeping hush.

The vessel-to-vessel transfers happened in the dead of night, arranged by Frank or Cheryl back in town ahead of time. They'd choose some secluded cove away from other boats. Tom would creep up in the thick of night to drop the fenders and wait. He felt like a wary nocturnal animal crouched there on the deck. He hardly caught sight of a face or voice before the exchange took place and the boat retracted into night. *We're not plundering the ocean*, Frank said. *It doesn't make a shit of difference when it's just a few fish undersized.* Once Tom had believed his brother, chucking away Association newsletters, disputing falling numbers; *like climate change, scaremongering by the greenies and politicians to make life harder for the working man.*

A year ago Tom had thought himself too young, powerless to take a stand. This was Frank's domain, all of it his brother's call. But for every undersize fish Tom stacked in that bin, for every berried female whose harvest of eggs he scoured from her tail and hosed overboard, for every note of ill-gotten cash he shoved into his wallet or added to his savings in the bank, he felt burdened with unease. He slid the bin of undersized into the concealed compartment.

He was as culpable as Frank. They were pirates and thieves wreaking havoc on the future. They took and took and never gave back. *Perlita Lee*—even the boat was a desecration of their parents' good names.

Tom saw their escape from the storm as a warning. Every fisherman knelt to the sorcery of the ocean, the witch who kept watch and would bide her time for the moment to take back.

Come dawn they'd be out shooting pots again. This foreboding, his hatred of Frank, would dissipate like any passing storm. Yet something had been set in motion. Something visceral, winding like a clock key quarter turn by quarter turn, tightening Tom's ribs at the base of his chest. Tom had seen Frank scared. His tough-as-steel brother. Hab, whose life before Australia Tom had never much considered, had countered Frank's abuse with quiet resilience. Tom remembered what Hab had said about that first new sheller casting off its shell. *Brother, him.* Hab had prodded the soft new membrane then stepped back and put his hand to his heart in a way that endeared him to Tom. *New country. New big work. Habib New Shell Yılmaz.*

Nineteen wasn't old-old. There were other things Tom could do. It wasn't too late to cast off the old, start life anew. He'd tried explaining something to Habib but had given up, the point lost in language. He'd tried telling Hab it was the crayfish's *struggle* to free itself of its old shell, the energy required, that triggered the crayfish to take up water and expand to something new. Tom couldn't explain the physics of that weird osmotic process, but he knew it to be true. *Couple of months*, he'd said to Hab, *that new shell will harden up and fit you right.*

13

Steph was out of bed in a flash. She raced for the phone, ignoring the small voice that said it was way too early to be any of her friends. Steph grabbed the receiver and winced at the shrill fax tone.

She propped herself at the kitchen bench, yawning and barefoot in pyjamas. Pages stuttered from the fax machine, grinding through rollers impregnated with years' worth of compressed lint. At the top of the second page: *For Weather Girl*. Gran's new name for Steph. Gran. In motor drive before anyone was awake. A handwritten page for each of them. Steph switched on the kettle and found her mug.

How's life in the wilds, Weather Girl? What a treat to have a fax from you. We've had a week of late frosts here. More like July weather than November.

You sound fed up with your studies. It must be hard keeping up the motivation, especially when you're away from your friends. Try not to worry, love. I know you'll succeed in whatever you choose to do. (Gran's wise words.)

All well at this end. Yoga, Probus, Library morning. Busy, as always. On Friday Helen and I went to the Open Day at the ANU Glass Workshop. Helen brought her granddaughter, Lucy – did you meet her last time? Lovely girl, arty like you. I've popped

*the catalogue in your Christmas parcel, with a few bits and bobs
you might find of interest.*

*The whole world's in a panic over gearing up for the millennium
bug. I don't think anybody really knows what's going to happen.*

Love and hugs. Gran x

*PS: Casper's laid out by the heater commanding me to give him
his morning cuddle. 'Dogs have masters, cats have staff.'*

The sky was already bright when Steph began the weather observations. Dawn was earlier, the days growing longer. At home they'd
be preparing for exams, talking about the holidays, about Christmas,
about plans for next year. Normally Steph's friends were away on
her New Year's Eve birthday. This birthday she was being robbed of
the most important celebration of her life. Turning seventeen on the
eve of the new millennium. Her friends, everyone from school, all
of Sydney would be congregating in the city to watch the fireworks,
hear live music, dance and party through the night.

Beyond the Mewstone the morning sky looked petal pink.
Steph stood at the cliff top. The paddock was edged by a perimeter
of soil undermined by burrows. Steph always woke too late to see
the mutton-birds fly out to forage for the day.

A pair of unfamiliar motor launches chugged back and forth
below. Yellow, red, white and orange buoys dotted the water below
the cliffs. Steph drew in the scent of the bush, the smell of mutton-
bird, the sweetness of freshly cut grass. The mowing never stopped.
Endless lines back and forth, her father stopping only to wrestle with
the lawnmower. Give it a pep talk. *Come on, Buster. Nearly there, boy.*

Already the soft dawn colours were being bleached by the day,
the light turning crisp. The ocean barely drew a breath. Out there

was a shimmering lake that melted into sky. For every stretch of howling wind and rain, Maatsuyker delivered a day of perfect weather—two if they were lucky. A reward, Steph thought, that could lull you into thinking this place was special, something you might not easily forget. She wished her cousin Lydia could be here for a day. Not Tessa. Not Sammie. Those two would have made faces at one another to show that they were bored.

Today Steph refused to lock herself inside a perpetually cold house, wrapped in a blanket and hunched over dreary studies while an army of blowflies buzzed at the window or dropped dead along the sill.

The ocean sparkled. Down at the Needles, a small white launch motored in close. Steph's only contact with Tom, a week ago now, had been a brief, disjointed conversation. He was different on the radio, stilted, more conscious than she of others listening in. It left Steph disappointed. It made her unsure. Really, she hardly knew a thing about him. Or his brother Frank. It was weeks since she'd seen their boat working on the water.

Steph logged off the weather computer. A pair of green rosellas squawked and flew off from the outside railing. They'd be inside the weather office in a flash if she forgot to shut the door. She angled down the paddock. At the top of the lighthouse, a currawong surveyed its domain, perched on the prongs of the lightning rod.

Steph pulled back the lighthouse door to air the tower. She scaled the stairs and tied back the top door that opened to the balcony. The tower wasn't singing. It wasn't even humming. Among the palette of greens below was a dusting of white: the first tea-tree flowers. Steph raced back down the spiral staircase, giddy by the time she reached the bottom.

An overgrown path led her down toward the headland. She was wary of her footing where the path meandered near the edge. She was forbidden to come down here in the wind. She wound beneath branches, past the dainty violet flowers of dianella, past stalks of Christmas bells that rose toward the dappled light, the first red flowers as shiny as glass.

Steph felt a freedom in knowing that a rustle in the scrub belonged not to a snake but to a small bird or skink. The foliage opened out to waist-high shrub and the pungent scent of flowers. Flies droned around newly opened daisy flowers. Steph paced downhill through a carpet of pigface.

She stood on a platform of rock within reach of the ocean. Bull kelp rose and fell in tangles. Skirmishes and growls reverberated from the colony of fur seals sprawled across Seal Rock. The rock was painted white with excrement.

She heard the hum of a compressor from the motor launch anchored close in to the rocks. A Hookah line trailed across the water. A person worked on deck. Somewhere below would be an abalone diver. It was from these rocks that her mother would pick abalone when the weather was calm. Grandfather would throw in a crayfish ring. *He had to pull it up quick fast. Dad was very skilled.* One time, her mother said, she and her father had almost been washed off. Steph could see how. She had become so accustomed to looking down upon the ocean that standing here, staring out, it was as if the surface of the ocean was above her. *A big roller,* her mother said, *that kept coming up and up and up. Finally it slid away, combing back the kelp and taking Dad's cray rings with it.* Steph's eyes followed the flank of the island. This was how Maatsuyker looked from a boat: scoured rocks and cliff faces, a moat of kelp, jagged skerries as impenetrable as razor wire.

Steph climbed back onto the headland and chose a place to lie down among the pigface. She sunk into the spongy green, her fingers brushing fine pleated petals. The more time she spent at Maatsuyker, the more she got to see her mother idealise the past. Callam. Her mother's parents. Steph felt to be at the eye of a cyclone holding all the world's secrets. She hadn't spoken to Mum of the phone call from the woman. How to broach the subject of the name scratched across her grandfather's plaque? *Was something going on between Grandfather and someone else's wife?* Instead she'd asked her mother: *What made them leave here?*

They didn't have a say in it. You worked on the lights. You came and went as you were told. It killed my father, it literally did, being shipped back to town. He lived for the lights. Mum told her how the men took shifts in the tower: four hours on, eight hours off. *Fifteen minutes before dusk the light went on, and it burned through to dawn. Mornings they worked together painting, mowing, polishing, servicing all the equipment. I remember having to tiptoe around the house when Dad was sleeping.*

Steph tried to visualise her grandfather pumping kerosene bottles every half-hour to keep the light going, winding heavy weights each and every hour of his shift. The keepers kept logs for everything, a log for all the passing ships. Weather observations six times a day. *I'd hear Dad on the radio send a string of numbers back to Hobart. Then there'd be a crackly voice you could barely understand talking back at him. Dad had bread to bake, beer to brew. In summer the men kept fire watch along the mainland coast. Their work never ended.*

Steph pressed her mother. *Was there some kind of trouble between the families?*

Trouble? Why would you say that?

Steph backpedalled. *I just wondered why he had to leave when he didn't want to.* She'd seen her mother flinch. *Chill out, Mum. You're paranoid.*

Steph shielded her eyes from the glare. The flannel of her sleeve felt warm and stiff and smelled of sun-dried laundry—not aloe-scented from the dryer. Steph drifted in and out to the rhythmic drone of the Hookah compressor. The cry of gulls. Seals groaning and squabbling. Far away she heard her name. She felt Callam beside her, keeping pace, the two of them swimming out from the beach, turning and rolling like dolphins. Steph slowed—she didn't like the deep, the patches of weed below—but Callam kept swimming, out and out. Her brother turned and she thought he was coming back. *Stephanie*, he shouted. *Stephanie*, he beckoned. Callam never called her Stephanie. He shouted something else across the water, *Mongrels, the pair of them.* Steph woke to a whistle. She searched around. She heard her name. She looked to the lighthouse. Up on the balcony. Tom!

14

Tom yanked the outboard into life, reversed the dinghy in an arc and motored out from the Gulch. Stephanie sat perched at the bow, gripping the gunnel and looking back at the hill from where they'd come. 'It's like a big scar through the bush,' she called to him above the motor.

She meant the haulage way. He felt her watching him. Tom's stomach churned in equal proportions of zest and anxiety. *Yes!* she'd squealed when he'd told her the plan. She'd raced from the lighthouse, changed her clothes and was waiting with her backpack before he'd had a chance to properly chat with James, assure her father she'd be safe. *Have you packed a towel?* her mother called after them. *Did you get the bread, Steph?* Tom wanted today to be good. Let it be good.

The *Perlita Lee* bobbed at anchor, water shimmering, her red and white paintwork gleaming in the morning light. Frank was out on deck cleaning salt from the wheelhouse windows. Habib had moved all the pots to the bow. The day off was a bonus that Tom couldn't fathom—halfway through a fishing stint—he'd grabbed it just the same; he'd run with Frank's idea. *Invite her aboard, make a day of it, we'll run over the other side for a look-see. Any place you want to go.* Frank. Some weeks on top of the world, dealing out benevolence like a croupier with cards. *We deserve a day off,* Frank had said. That they did. Night and day, working the outside of South West Cape up to Port Davey, two, three shots a night. His brother ought to be stoked: four days and the tanks were three-quarters full with top-dollar fish.

Frank had changed from his track pants with the tear in the bum. He helped Stephanie aboard. 'Hi, Frank,' she said without waiting to be introduced. 'Hi, Habib.' Frank gave a nod of approval. Habib bowed and shook her hand and took her pack.

The wheel was Frank's throne, but once he moved the *Perlita Lee* away from the island, the GPS set for Louisa Bay, he motioned to Tom. 'You take her, mate. I'll sort a few things below.'

Stephanie was seated behind the wheelhouse talking to Hab. She turned to smile. The rumble of the engine vibrated through the metal floor, through Tom's legs and arms. Frank had dismantled half the engine before he'd found the fault. Since he'd put it back together it hadn't missed a beat. Trust the boat, Tom told himself. His mother would say, *Don't think badly of your brother. Look at everything he does for us.* Perhaps this time she was right.

Tom pushed the throttle hard and felt a surge of power, the same charge he remembered as a boy when Frank had first started on the boats. Back then Tom would blink awake to his Christmas sack hanging off his door. It made Tom squirm to think how quickly he could set his mother's gifts aside. Waiting in the lounge room was something she could never afford to buy.

His brother had a sixth sense, as if he knew before Tom exactly what a boy his age would want. His first bike a dragster with blue and black stripes. The next year a skateboard. Then the CD player for his bedroom. The mountain bike whose picture Tom had clipped from a catalogue and taped to his bedroom door months before, hoping Frank would find it. Frank's benevolence enveloped the house. A ham on the bone that filled a shelf of the fridge. Crayfish. Chocolates. A crate of Tom's favourite soft drink. A carton of fresh sweet cherries for their mother. One Christmas Frank staggered in from the garage with a new TV. He'd knocked his knuckles manoeuvring the box through the door. *Frankie*, Mum cried. *Oh, Frank*. She'd grown quiet, the way she sometimes did at Christmas. Perhaps the price tag of Frank's generosity and all that abundance amounted, in her eyes, to a hard-fisted reminder that her sons had been robbed of the singular gift every child deserves.

*

Louisa Bay. Even on a day as calm as this the waves rolled in; there was no bringing the dinghy straight up on the beach. Hab motored around the sheltered side of Louisa Island and Tom and Stephanie clambered over the gunnel into thigh-deep water. Tom shuddered at the cold. They waded, hand in hand, to the sand spit that linked the island to the beach. Hab gave a wave and angled back toward the big boat.

Stephanie meandered across the hard sand; he listened to her singing. Tom veered up the beach, past a flock of terns planted near the river mouth. A pair of oystercatchers tottered along the river's edge, halting to address their reflections skewed across the water. The edge of the river was patterned into rivulets of sand that seemed to shiver beneath the water's flow. The middle deep and dark, as steeped as a billy of strong tea.

'Tom!' Stephanie bounced past him, barefoot, she wore a bikini top, cut-off denim shorts. She threw down her backpack and towel, leapt upon the overhang of sand, squealed and slid down to a halt. Along the south-west coast, tannin from peat soil blackened waterways. By the time Louisa River reached the bay, its course ran parallel with the back of the beach like a thick leather belt.

Tom cupped cold water to his mouth. Stephanie looked dubious. 'It's fresh.' He wiped his chin. She knelt and drank. She was as slender as a waterbird, her body feather pale.

Tom could see aboriginal middens on the far bank of the river. There were caves if you knew where to look, stark reminders of a bygone time. Beyond the dunes a thick band of vegetation rose to the craggy slopes and bluffs of the Ironbound Ranges.

Frank had crossed the Ironbounds, had walked the length of the South Coast Track when he was fifteen. In record time, his brother liked to skite. Tom once suggested he and Frank walk it together. Frank shook his head. *You'd hate it, Tom-Tom. Mud, mountain ranges, wind and bloody sleet; your tent, sleeping bag, nothing gets a chance to dry.* As if Tom were soft, some kind of princess. Subject closed.

The *Perlita Lee* stood at anchor, a glare of brilliance, the aluminium dinghy tethered with a painter, bobbing at the back.

'Coming for a swim?' she said.

'The river? Have you felt it?'

Steph put her foot in. She gasped. 'A quick swim.'

An intake of breath as icy water rose to his groin, ballooned through his board shorts, girdled his waist. Stephanie shrieked with the cold. She was under, she surfaced with a ragged gasp, 'It's freezing!' She swam out a few metres, swam back and grabbed his arm. *No.* He whimpered. 'Yes. Yes.' He plunged through a shock of cold; the current easing him along. It was too cold to breathe properly. He retreated to the edge where he could stand waist deep, the water icy on his legs. He drew her close and she looped her arms around his neck, wrapped her legs around his. He felt her body shivering, her ragged breaths.

They laid their towels together on the beach. A bush bird trilled; the salt and kelp faded with the warmth. The scent and sound was this, skin and breath, the sun on his neck, an insect droning by. Tom closed his eyes to the softness of her lips. He stroked her arm with his fingers, studied her skin. He kissed her neck, her collarbone, the skin that curved toward her breast. She kissed his fingers. He contemplated going further but steeled himself against the thought. Something about the day felt as fragile as a shell.

They made their way along the length of the beach. Dotterels danced across the sand. 'Is that Maatsuyker?' She pointed out to sea.

'Yep. Flat Witch in front of it. Then the Big Witch.'

She stopped. 'You can see the sheds at the whim. I'd never thought about people being able to see us from the land. Out there it seems like you're completely alone, a speck on the ocean.'

Tom kissed her hair. 'Imagine how it feels in a boat.'

He helped Stephanie search for shells but none were to be found, just a scattering of flotsam: a plastic strap, a jam jar filled with tannin water.

A forested gully marked the far end of the beach, its rock face shiny with water that sprinkled a steady shower onto the sand. Waves washed around a small islet and whooshed through a channel in the rock. A pair of sulphur-crested cockatoos perched above them on a branch. Suddenly the air was filled with wings of white, cockatoos lifting from trees, their raucous shrieks rebounding.

A cluster of buoys marked a secluded campsite among the trees, protected from the weather by the cliffs. They followed the wall of cliffs through groves of fern, over fallen trunks wound in moss and lichen. The air felt cool. He saw Stephanie shiver. There was something primal about this place. 'There,' he said. Two small caves beneath an overhang of rock.

Stephanie took photos. 'Did the aboriginal people live in them? They look so meagre.'

'Not sure. I know they used them. For shelter, for cooking.'

'It feels a bit spooky,' she said, making her way back out to the beach.

They returned to their towels at the river's edge. He felt warm and lazy with the sun. She drew a pattern on his tattooed shoulder. 'Did it hurt?'

'I don't remember. A long story, involving alcohol.'

'My parents won't let me have one.'

'You don't want one.' He pulled at the ugly pair of anchors.

'I'd have dolphins.'

He kissed her unblemished shoulder. Tom rested his head on the crook of his arms. Stephanie propped against his back.

'What are you thinking?' she said.

'I'm not.'

'What *were* you thinking?'

'When?'

'The last time you were thinking.'

'Being here. With you. How it feels.'

'How does it feel?'

He hesitated. Her hair felt warm against his shoulder. 'It feels right.' The way that when the temperature is right you never really think about it.

'My brother,' she said. 'He would have liked you.'

'Yeah?'

'Yep.' She curled up, pulled the extra towel across her knees. 'Let's stay here. Let's live on the beach. Catch fresh fish. Bathe beneath the waterfall. Sleep beneath the Milky Way.'

'Give it another twelve hours. It'll be howling.'

'Do you think about next year? The new century?'

Tom raised his head. 'I won't be on a boat shooting pots.'

She tickled his side. 'What will Frank do without his Tom-Tom?'

'Frank's cool,' he lied. Not lied, exactly, he'd tell Frank he was leaving when the time was right. It sounded easy, saying it to Stephanie. He combed her hair with his fingers. 'You'll be at university, being smart.'

'Maybe,' she said. She crossed her arms and took a deep breath. 'Or I might do something radical.'

'Live on a beach?'

Tom heard the outboard. He wished time would halt. 'It's nearly half past two.'

She shook sand from her towel. 'You could come to Sydney. When you finish on the boat. If you want to.'

'I could do that.' Tom buttoned his shirt. There'd be plenty of work up there. He owned his car, had a stack of savings in the bank. There'd be choices. The beach crumbled into powder beneath his feet. He put his hand around Stephanie's shoulder, felt her arm around his waist. 'I'd like that.'

★

A large stainless steel shower was built behind the wheelhouse. 'Use the shower in my cabin,' Frank instructed her. 'You'll have a bit of privacy.'

There was no soap Steph could find, the moulded cubicle felt unused. Steph spread her things across Tom's bunk, changed into jeans. The cabin felt dim and airless with the curtains pulled, she caught a whiff of diesel fumes. Steph twisted the towel around her hair, stretched out on Tom's bed and rested her head on his pillow. Frank's double bed was at the very front of the boat, Tom and Habib's bunks within a hand's reach of one another, moulded to the curve of the hull. Steph listened to the rhythmic chink of anchor chain, the crackle of a radio transmission, muffled voices, ocean lapping by her head against the hull. The boat rocked. Steph hugged her arms. The way Tom looked at her, touched her skin. On the shelf above his bunk he kept his hairbrush, razor, a magazine on four-wheel drives, a book, *Van Diemens Land*, a photo of a man. She drew Tom's brush through her hair, imagined his hands touching her—all of her. She wanted it to happen. Her skin radiated heat from the sun. Her scalp tingled. She cloaked the sensation around her, wanting to carry the wrap of it home. Steph crammed her things into her pack. Tom and Stephanie. *Stephanie*, he called her. It sounded womanly; *Steph* sounded like a girl.

'Where in Sydney?' Frank tore the two thick pincers from the crayfish, his hands as tough and thorny as the shell.

'Forty Baskets Beach.' Lunch was a feast. Two crayfish, sliced meat and cheese, tomatoes, baked bread from her mother and three kinds of lettuce from the vegetable garden. Steph had expected a sandwich, sitting out on deck. Frank looked none the wiser. 'North Shore,' she explained. 'Near Manly.'

'On the water?'

'Behind the beach.' It felt odd sitting in a circle, the only girl, under scrutiny from Frank. 'It's not flash or anything. My parents bought before prices went up.' A sort of coveting that put Steph on edge.

'Tom tells us you're going to be a doctor.' Frank gave Tom a, *See, I do listen* look. 'Says you've all kinds of talents.'

Tom picked at his food.

'Doctor good job,' Habib said. 'At home, I study at the academy.'

'You?' Frank sounded incredulous.

'Not to finish.' Habib gave a gesture and a whistle. 'Come here, Australia.'

'I thought you'd been a chef,' Tom said.

'Study day. Cook nights at restaurant of my uncle.' Habib waved his hands. 'Now I chef every day, every night. Home from boat. I cook. I clean.' He turned to Steph and drew a bulging curve. 'Baby soon my wife. She most necessary rest. Be strong. Good health.'

'Sounds to me like you're under the thumb, mate,' Frank said. He turned to Steph. 'How do you like our little corner of the world? Bit of a change from home.'

'I sort of knew what to expect. Mum grew up on Maatsuyker. My grandfather was the light keeper, in the seventies.'

'So I believe. Back then the light would have been kerosene.'

'What was it like?'

'They'd switched to electric by the time I started. It still looked fucking awesome.' Frank stopped. 'Language,' he scolded himself. 'Better than the rubbish they've got up there now.'

'Mum calls it the Tupperware light.'

'Didn't matter where you were. Unless there was sea fog, in which case you couldn't see your hand in front of you, you could see the light from twenty-five, thirty miles away. You'd look up at it, flash, flash, every half a minute, and you knew exactly where you were. When I first started there weren't that many using GPS, all the fandangle we have now. You relied on the lights. You knew the keepers, you'd have a chinwag on the radio; if the weather was kind you might call in, give them a feed of crays and they'd make you a cup of tea. I wouldn't even know who's up there now. Except for you.'

'I never hear you on the radio.'

'Listen in, do you?'

'No.' Steph blushed. 'I mean, the radios are on in the house; we have to have them on for Tasmar Radio, or if someone's in distress.'

'Tom's the only one that talks, in recent times,' Frank cackled. 'I don't have any friends, do I, Tom-Tom?' Frank put on a sad face. 'Joking. Truth is, there are too many dropkicks out there. Eh, Tom?'

'There's a few.' Tom started clearing the table.

'We only ever have crayfish at Christmas. I suppose you have it all the time.'

'Hardly ever,' Tom said. 'We have whatever's lurking in the freezer. Or up there in the cupboard.'

'Slim pickings, some nights,' said Frank.

'Except for Hab's dinners,' Tom said. 'He can make a banquet out of anything.'

Frank collected a toothpick. 'As long as it involves rice, lentils or potatoes. With enough spice to blow the roof off your mouth.'

'Tom is good cook,' Hab told Steph. 'He this and this and this.' Habib took imaginary pinches of herbs and sprinkled them into a pot. 'Good taste.'

'Tom-Tom cooks a mean pizza in his special little oven at home.' Frank sounded mocking.

'Perhaps he'll cook for me.' Steph said it as a challenge.

Tom took her plate. 'Anytime. Anywhere.'

'You'll love our pizza oven at home—' She stopped.

Frank raised his eyebrows. 'Off to Sydney are we, Tom?' Frank looked to Steph. 'Is he?'

'Not until . . . when he finishes on the boat.'

'Ah.' Frank wiped his dirty hands on the tea towel. 'I see.'

★

The wind had sprung up, riffling the water. It blew away the smell of diesel. The change in weather matched the shift in mood aboard the boat. Great paw prints of cumulus galloped in from the west. Lenticular cloud looked motionless while alto cumulus billowed into gigantic jellyfish, climbing through the sky.

They detoured around the Needles so that Steph could take photos of the lighthouse. She zipped up her hoodie, stayed in the shelter of the wheelhouse canopy. She waited for the boat to ride up on a wave then quickly snapped a shot. The tower looked proud and stately perched at the edge of the cliff. Above it their house nestled among the tea-tree. It would have looked the same when her mother was a girl. It would have looked the same one hundred years ago. The paddock the same russet carpet of grass heads and tiny yellow flowers, and perhaps they did or didn't have the dande-lions back then.

When the paddock was long and unkempt, it brushed against Steph's calves in a way that made her want to lie down and roll through it. Dad likened mowing the pasture and lawns and road to painting the Sydney Harbour Bridge: you reached one end then started at the other. With the onset of spring, the grass grew almost overnight. Guano from the mutton-birds fertilised the grass and leached into soil. When Dad wasn't mowing he was clearing drains, *another thirty metres*, digging out the fetid slurry that with each new downpour unearthed topsoil and guano into milky rivulets.

From out here on this clean slate of ocean you couldn't imagine half the things Steph knew about the island. You wouldn't know that her father talked to the lawnmower as if it were a living thing. You wouldn't know all the times her mother spent being sad. You wouldn't know that every day when Steph tied back the door to air the lighthouse, she would stop to listen to it sing, she would stand with her arms outstretched and feel it breathe and hum through her chest. Every step, every footfall on those wrought-iron steps had become her daily ritual, the tower a refuge. All the times Steph would step inside the lens and put her face against the prisms of glass to look and look and look with the wish that the warped, contorted shapes beyond would sharpen into focus and form a human figure. That there through the glass would stand the world as it once was, that her brother—the boy he used to be—would press his hand to the glass and everything would be mended and whole.

The boat lifted on a wave. It was pointless wishing for the past. Pointless wishing she'd been strong enough to speak out, to tell her parents that Callam was sneaking out at night.

Steph looked past the weather office to the anemometer, to aerials and the automated light, to the great stretch of wild hill beyond. The air was so clear you could make out individual trees beneath a billowing of cumulus, the sky swirling to a bruise. Chaotic sky, the Bureau called it.

Weather girl, Gran called Steph. They kept a secret, she and Gran. Gran had been to a man who looked into the future and saw back through the past. And though that man knew nothing of Gran, he'd seen a pair of twins and told her of the boy caught within the light. *Caught?* Gran had quizzed him. *Held,* the man explained, *waiting to be allowed to leave.*

The boat motored past Moderate and Heavy Rocks, the land-marks Steph used to gauge the swell. From up there they were specks. From down here they were bigger than the boat. The *Perlita Lee* moved along the east side of the Needles, past towering slabs of rock, seabirds wheeling overhead.

They passed a blue cray boat, the greeting from its wheelhouse an angry jab of fingers.

'Pricks,' she heard Frank shout their way.

'What was that about?' she said to Tom.

The blue boat moved away. 'Don't worry about it.'

Tom pulled out the grappling iron, showed Steph how he'd throw it to snag the line between the buoys. He started up the pot hauler. 'The craypot rests here on an angle. You slide it down to here, take out your fish, put them in the tank. Buoys in this cage, lines in that one. Bob's your uncle.'

'You call them fish?'

'Fish, and rats,' Habib piped in.

'Rats are the small ones that eat all your bait. The ones you chuck back. There's a reef out there.' Tom pointed out past the Needles. 'Locally known as Rat Palace.'

One of the two cages was crammed with orange buoys, the painted letters chipped and worn. Steph felt the boat lurch, saw Frank yank on the wheel. He looked pissed off. 'What's he doing?' she asked Tom.

Tom walked to the side window of the wheelhouse. 'Frank,' he called in through the glass, the way you'd call your dog if it was about to roll in something putrid. 'We're not using it right now. Let it go.'

'Our patch, they know that well enough.'

Tom spoke quietly. 'Not now.'

'What?' Steph asked again.

'Nothing. Don't worry about it.' Tom moved into the wheel-house and rolled the door shut. He turned his back to her. Steph looked to Habib; he gave a shrug. She watched the brothers through the glass, saw the way Tom braced his body, the jerky movement of his hands. Frank shook his head.

'Let her decide.' Frank opened the door and called to Steph. 'I was saying Tom can pull one of the pots. Show you how it's done.'

Tom looked at her pleadingly.

'It's all right,' Steph said, confused. 'Don't worry.'

'Come on. A feed of crayfish to take home for Mum and Dad?'

She looked to Tom for guidance.

'Alrighty.' Frank took her silence as a yes, his eyes alive. 'Grab the hook, Tom-Tom. No point wasting time.'

A sheer wall of rock. Tufts of tussocks growing high up on the ledge. They were directly below the lighthouse. Frank pulled the boat alongside a pair of yellow buoys. Tom waited, a glazed expression on his face. Was he angry with her? He pulled on thick rubber gloves, took up the grappling iron. She couldn't gauge his face. He threw the iron as deftly as an athlete, hooked the line first go. She watched him drag it in, his actions honed. Tom looped the line around the wheel of the pot hauler, the ratchet of the motor a stuttering of discord.

Two yellow buoys and lengths of line were sprawled across the deck. Tom's jeans, his shoes, everything was wet. Steph looked over the side. She couldn't see the bottom. She held her breath and waited. A shape, a cauldron of bubbles turned the inky water turquoise blue. The craypot emerged like a living, raucous thing, a whoosh of water, snapping tails, the water streaming. She placed her hand against a curve of pot—wood wet and shiny, intricately twisted to a woven basket, a neck of fine cane. 'It's beautiful,' she said to Tom.

'Only the best.'

The pot sounded out a clatter of castanets; she looked in through a weave of wood to a shuffle of bodies and legs, antennae pushing through the open neck, dancing through the air.

Frank powered the boat away from the rocks. He turned and gave Steph a reassuring nod. She smiled back, a flutter moving through her chest. In that moment he looked exactly like Tom.

Tom reached into the pot and drew out a crayfish. He gripped it firmly by the back, turned it over, the feelers waving, the tail clacking at the air. 'Undersize.' He held it for her to see then threw it overboard. He pulled a larger crayfish. Another. Another. Habib held a wet sack and in they went.

'Hand Tom his knife, will you, Stephanie. Tom, finish her off, mate.'

Steph took the knife, held it by its orange sheath. The blade was inscribed with Tom's name. The way he resisted it. The hatred on his face when he turned his eyes to Frank.

Tom took the knife but then he dropped it on the deck. He grabbed the pot and heaved it out across the water as though it were a tainted thing. The line ran out in chase, whipping water across Steph's jeans. Tom scooped the yellow buoys, punched them like a ball out across the water.

Tom and Frank. No words exchanged, but within that loaded silence was an interchange of rage unlike any screaming match she'd had with Callam. Habib stood in silence, privy, Steph supposed, to a history of conflict that she could only feel. She saw Frank's look of defiance. She glanced at Tom, his back rigid, neck taut.

Frank punctured the silence. 'Where to?'

They all looked to her. 'I—I should probably get home. If that's okay.' She sounded little-girlish.

Frank nodded. 'Wind's getting up. The ocean's no place for a girl when it gets a temper.'

★

Steph clambered from the dinghy up onto the landing. Tom handed her the laden hessian sack. He didn't kiss her. He didn't say when he'd be coming back. She watched him motor out. She waited and she waited but he never once looked back.

She was on the track, hessian knocking at her legs, walking through a patch of waist-high yellow daisies. The island had turned spring. Somewhere ahead a cockatoo shrieked. She thought about the colour of the buoys.

Steph's face was wind burned, her arms and legs felt tight from sun, her hair was tangled from salt and wind. She felt worn down, dragged from the certainty of shore by a great rogue wave, left to flounder in the deep before being flung back onto land. Inside the sack crayfish clicked and clacked. It was heavy. She felt marooned, unable to hold her head above the truth of what she knew. It crept along the knuckles of her spine. It wound around her neck and squeezed her throat and turned her breath into a plaintive sigh. The cage of buoys on the boat had been a sea of orange. The yellow buoys from the pot they'd pulled had stood alone. Steph didn't need to compare the painted letters and numbers to know that Frank and Tom were stealing someone else's catch.

The angry thrust of fingers from the blue boat.

Frank handing her the knife to pass to Tom.

Steph stopped to rest, weighed down by tiredness, by a heavy sack of ill-gotten gains. Above in the branches a raven watched. From its elevated height that silken black bird could comprehend the length of track, the patterns of the bush, the cycle of seasons. Ravens were keen-eyed, they'd perch on the lightning prongs surveying their domain. A movement in the grass and they'd swoop from fifty metres to seize a worm. That bird would have seen long before Steph that a rope and its buoys were the lifeline to a craypot. Tom knew when he took the knife what he was being told to do. He knew because they'd done it all before.

Wind shrilled through the branches. Callam sniggered, *Mongrels, the lot of us.* He shimmied past, blowing hair across her face.

15

Rain. Relentless days of it. It came in waves like movements of a symphony, slowly, gently building to crescendos that pummelled the cement, burbled through downpipes, choked drains, spilled as waterfalls through every rusted gutter. Steph watched the sky empty, watched until it ebbed and eased into a steady drizzle.

She was on her own in the house, not that you would think it. The room was a crackle of static, a staccato of voices—both radios scanning frequencies—fishermen, Tasmar Radio, Hobart police.

. . . five dollars' difference between the brindles and reds. You start knockin' a couple a grand off a ton, that's . . . fifteen to twenty-five knots, increasing thirty to thirty-five knots in offshore waters between Rocky Cape and South West . . . log truck overturned on the northbound lane of Huon Highway, five kilometres north . . . the wives'll have to stop shavin' their legs because we won't be able to afford the disposable . . . white Subaru wagon, registration plate . . . if there's no other calls, Tasmar Radio going back to . . . either way you're fucked.

Steph put on her headphones and pumped up the music. It was stupid to listen for Tom. He could be in Hobart. He could be out stealing pots. The table was covered in scraps of recycled paper, a cutting mat and glue. She was working on her papier-mâché model of the lighthouse.

She turned at the movement. Her father stood at the table, saying something. The hair on his forearms was speckled with iron filings. He smelled of the garage. She hadn't heard him come in. He pushed the headphones back from her ears. 'Let's try again, shall we? I was asking about your study.'

'I'm having a break.'

'And what about the weeding in the vegetable garden that you promised your mother?'

Steph raised her eyebrows the way her father did to make a point, she motioned to the rain. His face tightened. He left the room. Then he was back. He took her CD player and yanked the cord out. His hands were trembling. He switched off both radios. 'I've had just about enough of you.'

'Huh?'

'Listen to yourself. You're sullen, moody, you're rude to your mother and me. You disappear off to your lighthouse for hours on end, last week we had to cover for you again with the weather, you sit here doing your art as if you're on holiday. As far as I can tell you haven't done a scrap of study. Your exams are a week away. One week, Stephanie. Are you intentionally trying to sabotage your chances?'

She shrugged. She didn't care. She didn't care about anything.

'We've put a lot of effort and expense into flying you to Hobart at resupply. Your mother's been on the phone to your school, the Education Department, getting everything set up.' He rapped the CD player. 'How do you expect to get into university if you don't try?'

She glowered. As if there wasn't enough pressure. 'I don't want to do medicine.' There, she'd said it. She'd never wanted to be a doctor. 'Mrs Burrows mentions it and next thing it's your and Mum's big dream. No one asked me, as usual.'

Dad shifted her books from the chair, sat down at the table. 'What *do* you want? I'm listening.'

Steph turned to the window. Rain fell in sheets. A currawong, bedraggled and forlorn, perched on the radio aerial. 'I don't know any more.' She couldn't think properly.

'Are you worried about disappointing your mother? Is it Tom? We can tell something's happened.'

'It was a dumb idea coming here. You didn't want to come. You just sat there at the interview agreeing with everything Mum said.'

Her father looked away. He took off his glasses. He laid them on the table. 'I wanted to support your mother. You know the reasons.'

Her mother had addressed the interview panel as softly as a song. *This is my chance to share a special place with the people I love, to give something back.* Mum had turned to Steph and squeezed her hand. Steph knew what was expected. *Mum's been telling me about Maat-suyker all my life. I feel as though it's part of me.* She was just as much a part of the performance. *Me,* Steph had said. *My life.* They all knew better than to mention Callam. It felt as though her mother's entire future, her road map back to happiness, rested on the outcome. The interviewers couldn't see the wreckage.

Her father rubbed the bridge of his nose. Rain filled Steph's vision, the noise swamped her head. 'After Callam, somewhere in all that mess, your mother disappeared.' He looked at Steph. '*You* disappeared.' His chin rested on the back of his hands. 'I thought I could cope. I'd push on, take care of you and Gretchen, get us back on track.' He shook his head. 'Gran held it together. For all those months.' He was looking through Steph, caught in a different time. He sat staring out the window. 'The rain. You remember?'

She was Callam's twin. How could she forget?

'The traffic was a crawl. I nearly didn't take the call. I couldn't hear properly for the rain. *Police*, I heard. And *your son*. I thought, *What's that damned kid got himself into?* I got to the other side of the bridge and waited until they rang me back.' Her father knocked his chest with his fist. 'I drove down to the water. Rain on the roof, the bonnet, pouring down the street, you couldn't see the harbour. I had the motor running, the heater on high—I couldn't get warm. I curled across the front seats like a little kid. Watching the floor lights dim.' He turned to Steph. 'You know what I was thinking?' Her father's voice was silk, his words unbroken. *'You can't beat German design.* Isn't that an odd thing?'

'You were home when I got there.'

'Steph. It must have been awful for you.' He rubbed at his face. He looked grey. Her father took out his handkerchief, ironed perfectly into three. Dad wiped his eyes and nose. His voice halted. 'Poor old Cal.'

Steph placed her hand on his forearm. 'It'll be all right,' she told her father. But she felt as empty as a sky drained of rain. Rain always made Steph think of weeping. For a long time now she'd trained herself not to cry—their house at home had been ready to subside with the volume of her mother's tears. What held her to Callam was a confusion of feelings and an inability to express grief as any normal person would. It was a stricture as mysterious and fickle as her father's strangled voice. 'When you were talking,' she said to Dad. 'Did you notice? There was hardly a break.'

'Go figure,' he said as if he'd pondered that himself. 'A dodgy link in the neurological chain. People think I put it on.'

'Will you go back to work?'

He shook his head. 'I doubt it. Not on air.'

'Mum says you should have the injections. Then you'd manage.'

'They're not a cure, Steph. A few months at best.'

'Then you have another one. You'd be fine.'

'I doubt the producers will look at it that way.' He patted her hand. 'We'll see about it all when we get home.' He inspected her model lighthouse. 'You're so creative. Do you know that?'

'Does it hurt to speak?'

'It's exhausting. The physical effort of forcing out the words. Of having to find words that aren't as hard to say. It's easier to say nothing.'

'Is that why you don't talk to us any more?'

He looked taken aback. 'It's not ... I don't ... I have no *position*.'

'Position?'

'Voice is who I am. Who we all are. Being able to express what we think and feel.' His hand collared his throat. 'This won't let me be me. Perhaps, looking on, it doesn't seem that big a deal—I'm not even sure your mother understands. I feel as if my whole identity's been stripped away. At work, at home. Every turn.' Steph didn't know how to answer. Her father looked embarrassed by his admission. He took a breath. He checked his watch. 'Almost time for the weather.'

Steph collected her socks from the laundry basket. 'Dad.'

'Yes?'

'I know it's big. I do. But you're still you. Underneath. I think you need to figure out how best to manage it. Be open to the options.'

He gave a flicker of a smile. 'Are you all right, love? Not just this,' he motioned to her schoolbooks. 'Being here. Without your friends. Everything a bit off kilter. It can't be easy.'

She couldn't remember anyone but Gran asking that. 'Mostly it's okay.'

'You don't talk to Mum or me about your brother. I worry for you.'

'You don't talk about him either. It makes me feel like I shouldn't. Like we're all treading on eggshells in case Mum has another break-down. We're not allowed a single happy memory. Or to say it like it really was.' Steph paused. 'Everybody compensated for Callam. All the time. He wasn't perfect, Dad.'

'I know he wasn't.'

'Does Mum?'

'In her own way, I think she does. Steph, I wish we could have done better. It wasn't fair on you.' Her father's face looked thinner, he'd lost some weight. 'I know you and your brother were close, but you were so different from one another. Right from the start.'

'Different, how?'

Dad thought for a moment. 'Cal thought himself invincible. He thrived on risk, on stretching the rules. Ever the showman, sad to say.' What did that make Steph? Conservative? Dull? As if tuning in to her thoughts, Dad met her gaze. 'You were the one we never had to worry about. Accepting of people, their differences. The little girl with a big curiosity for the world. You could never get enough of learning.' Steph couldn't even conjure an image of that person. Dad tapped her schoolbooks. 'Now look at the pickle we're in.'

Steph released a huff of tension. The mood between them lifted. 'Gloom Central around here.'

Her father gave a smile. 'I'll leave you to talk to Mum about medicine.'

★

The rain gauge had overflowed into the outer cylinder. Steph measured the plastic beaker, emptied it, filled it with the excess and added up the total. Thirty-two millimetres since nine o'clock. Rain trickled off her hood, polished her waterproofs. She wiped a drip from her nose and checked the thermometers. Twelve point five degrees. She recorded the figures and closed the screen door, dropped in the nail to secure it. All second nature now.

She surveyed the thinning stratus, the outline of a weakened sun trying to shine through. Far across the water the clouds had opened to glimpses of blue sky that felt like a reminder of a larger world in motion. Rays of light glossed the tip of South West Cape and turned the ocean pewter.

Inside the weather office she took up binoculars and measured the sea state. She could estimate visibility without checking the map. She knew how far off each mountain stood, the distance to each bluff and bay.

She keyed the data into the laptop, then recorded it by hand in the old-fashioned log, the way her grandfather and all the other keepers at Maatsuyker had done. The final column was where the observer wrote a general note about the day. Some were formal, others conversational. She leafed back to Lindsay and Brian's pages: *Wild and woolly; Cleared by afternoon; The Southern Ocean going off; Blue skies—a cracker-jack day.*

Wildlight, Steph wrote. *A shiny, wet Maatsuyker day,* thinking as she did that that's how Gran would look upon this day. Gran, who found the good no matter how bad, who, after Callam, had driven up from Canberra and stayed with them for months. She was still there in February when Steph came home late and dishevelled, knees scraped, her new school uniform stained with dirt and gravel dust. Steph ignored Gran's pent-up worry, she couldn't tell Gran where she'd been. Somehow Gran knew not to ask. *Throw your uniform in the laundry, love; I'll rinse it out tonight*, she said, then went back to cooking dinner.

The place that all their lives she and Callam had been banned from going. She'd walked there after school, the streets, cars, shimmering with summer heat. She'd climbed through the gap in the fence as her brother had done, crouched at the edge of the stormwater drain. Heat pulsed from the cement. He was always up for a dare. She'd never have had the guts to leap across a chasm of slippery drain. Steph forced herself to look, to see her brother teeter, water coursing at his feet. If he hadn't turned to face his friends, if he hadn't been distracted by their awe.

Steph crawled in through the tunnel of the drain. Gravel pierced her knees. She gave no care to her school skirt or new leather shoes. The air in the shadows felt cool. Steph was beneath the road, encircled by concrete, engulfed by a fresco of graffiti. She shivered in concert with the tremors from cars passing above. She moved toward the beam of daylight, tracing her brother's last moments of life. The torrent of silty water that would have carried and jostled. A ride that tore at skin and battered limbs. Steph breathed his struggle for air.

She reached the crisscross of light, the two of them together now, escape blocked by a grate bolted and padlocked. She was no longer in or of herself, separate from fear, from grief, a sister looking down at the build-up of dust and filth, cans and syringes, a rag of underwear. And there, within her reach, a desiccated bird, the wing bent back, its head and neck jammed through the lattice of steel.

16

'Watch it,' a voice cautioned. Steph pulled back from the kerb as cars swished by. The lunch hour glared with traffic and fumes and sharp grating sounds. She had woken at dawn at Maatsuyker. Now, standing in a crowd at traffic lights, Hobart felt alien.

Everyone around her maintained a certain space but still Steph felt squeezed and jostled by the proximity of *people*. City workers waited with intent, their eyes set ahead. She watched a guy on a bike, a faded backpack slung over his suit, one hand on the handle-bars, checking back for traffic as he snaked across the lanes. The Walk sign *rat-tat-tatted*. Steph joined in the line of shuffling feet and tight sombre faces. She melded into the congregation of students that moved to a silent dirge along the footpath to the steps of the exam hall.

Steph clung to the thought, as she walked the aisle of the hall and took her place among the screech of chairs, that by lunchtime her first exam would be over and then there was nothing anyone could do to change the outcome.

She used every minute of the allocated time and still she didn't finish all the questions.

Afterwards, Michelle, the ranger from the Parks office, drove Steph through the city, pointing out bus stops and landmarks on the way to Mum's old boarding school. Steph would board there for the week of the exams.

She spent the afternoon at the school library with other boarders, everybody cramming. Her brain physically ached. She drifted, reading the same passage of text without digesting the meanings. She felt displaced, disembodied, on the verge of nausea. She took an audible breath, took a walk outside. Back on Maatsuyker, they'd have finished the resupply. There'd be mail waiting, gifts for Christmas, fresh fruit and groceries ordered from the supermarket. There'd be treats, her mother had promised. She'd stood at the helipad teary-eyed and clasping Steph like she was leaving for a year, not five days, saying how it wasn't right that she, her mother, couldn't go as well. *We can't leave one person alone on the island*, Michelle said kindly. Dad squeezed Mum's shoulder. *Steph's a big girl. She'll be okay.*

Too big for her boots, thinking she could manage Year 11 and 12 studies in the same year, and nail her Higher School Certificate. Earth and Environmental Science—she hadn't read the last two chapters of the book.

The boarders' dining room felt warm and airy, not the spartan hall her mother recalled for her. Boys and girls her age filled the tables near the window, younger groups congregated according to their age. Steph sat with a small girl at the only empty table. 'Are you new?' the younger girl asked.

'I'm just here this week. Exams.'

The girl nodded knowingly. 'Everyone's going home at the weekend. The little kids have left already.'

She looked so small herself. 'When do you go home?'

She counted with her fingers. 'Tuesday, Wednesday, Thursday, Friday. Mum's driving down to pick me up.' Her name was Marcie, a chatterer, and though she was small she ate a mountain of mashed potato. Marcie slowed at the other vegetables, nailing one at a time with her fork, peas inadvertently pinging off her plate. 'Are you the girl that lives in the lighthouse?'

'Beside the lighthouse. It's just me and my parents on the island.'

'I've seen a lighthouse but I've never actually been inside a light-house. Does it shake in the wind?'

'Not at all. It hums when the wind blows. Sometimes it sings.'

Marcie blinked. She picked at the remaining peas with her fingers.

Steph stood in line to rinse her dishes and stack them in the dishwasher. A duty team of students wiped tables clean, put the food away.

Silent study time began at seven. The dining and common rooms transformed into workstations for Year 7s, 8s and 9s. Marcie waved to Steph from the far table and put on a tortured face. The residence supervisor, mug of tea in hand, moved between the two study rooms. Year 11s and 12s, he explained to Steph, had the option of studying in their rooms.

Steph moved past student rooms, moons of light spilling beneath the line of doors. She passed through the deserted foyer and felt looked upon by decades of bygone boarders whose framed photographs covered every wall. She trailed back through photos and years until she found her mother's era. Steph had to trawl through printed names to recognise her. She looked as small and sweet as Marcie, swamped by a uniform large enough to see her through.

Steph moved out into the courtyard and sat at a bench in the shadow of the light. The air around her feet felt cold. She checked her mobile, brightening at the promise of a message. Telstra: a reminder that her phone plan had expired.

Steph had been allocated a bedroom in the Nan Chauncy wing. Heated air pumped through the vent. She clicked on the bedside lamp, threw off her jumper. The room was cheerful enough, a bright doona cover and curtains, a desk and work chair. But the window was permanently sealed—there was no escape from manufactured air. A boarding school did its best, Steph supposed, but here you were watched over, wound in a swaddling of sign-in sign-out safety and parent-endorsed care that, for all its good intentions, offered a hollow imitation of home. She thought of Marcie, counting down the days until home—Steph's mother would have been no different, she had lived for the promise of Maatsuyker, school holidays scudding by like a storm front of clouds.

Steph unpacked her bag. Between the layers of clothes she found a sprig of tea-tree Mum had wrapped in kitchen paper. It smelled of Maatsuyker. It smelled of fresh salt air. Steph laid it on the bedside table. She changed into a T-shirt for sleeping. The sheets felt stiff, stamped at the edge with the name of the school. *All the hopes my mother had by sending me off to school,* Steph's mother once told her. *And all the time I couldn't wait to finish. Then after Dad died, I didn't care about a career, what work I did. All I could think of was leaving home, going somewhere new.* At seventeen Gretchen had moved from her home in Melbourne to Sydney, hardly older than Steph was now. Her mother hadn't known anyone. She'd worked as a receptionist then met and married Steph's dad. Her mother was beautiful. She was brave.

Steph's eyes felt gritty. She fought to finish the chapters from her textbook. Twenty past ten. Perhaps it was enough to get her through.

It wasn't. She propped the pillows, blinked herself awake and leafed through her notes, through doodled arches and whorls running down the margins that brought to mind the lighthouse glass. Steph still hadn't confessed to her mother that she wasn't going to do medicine. If she didn't pass at all, what would she be qualified to do?

She thought of Tom, loyal to his brother as she had been to Callam, trapped in a job he didn't like. Steph wished she hadn't jeopardised her chances. They weren't so different, she and Tom: their futures teetered on the knife edge of other people's expectations.

She opened the curtains, she set her phone alarm early, to study, knowing she would wake an hour before, conditioned as she was to get up for the early morning weather.

She tried to block out the strident noises of the street, cover them with wind squealing up the hill and buffeting the house, with mutton-birds calling and cooing, settling down into their burrows for the night. She masked her eyes from the headlights of passing cars and searched for a single beam of light sweeping past the window. The room smelled of disinfectant. Steph pushed back all but the sheet, kicked it loose around her feet. She turned her back on the heated room, flushed by the weight of three more exams, her head pounding with facts and numbers and the lifeless cloying air.

*

A group of girls squealed and hugged. Two boys perched at the hall steps like groomsmen at a wedding, high-fiving each student as they emerged from the final exam. A stranger patted Steph's back. 'Well done.' She felt vacant and stunned from concentration, but she turned and smiled, the thrill and relief and all these happy faces contagious as she made her way to the street. It was over! The kerb had turned into a taxi rank of parents' cars, eyes searching expectantly, an arm beckoning, a mother clasping her daughter, a father ruffling his tall boy's hair. A shimmer of goodwill radiated from the crowded square. The prospect of summer holidays rose like a weather balloon.

Students peeled away. You could sense the buoyancy in the way people walked and talked and how riffles of laughter split the air. Even those leaving on their own punched trills of numbers into mobile phones, backpacks bobbing down the street.

Steph made her way down to the water. She was off to Salamanca to eat lunch, to window shop, to celebrate. She'd find a public phone and call her parents. She had some money to phone her friends at home.

A refrigerator truck pulsed a warning as it inched back toward the edge of the wharf. Below, men from a cray boat hauled up heavy crates. Steph recognised two blue boats tethered side by side. Here, at the fringe of this small city, the rainbow of coloured hulls clashed with the image of vessels pitching and tossing through cascades of spray. Pockets of conversation from tourists glanced through the air, some in different languages. Passers-by slowed to inspect the flotilla of working boats, to photograph handmade craypots and cages crammed with fishing nets and buoys—mementoes from an ocean that in this tranquil setting gave no clue of hard-bitten lives. Steph's focus sharpened on the curve of red, the white of the wheelhouse: the *Perlita Lee* was tied up to a second wharf beyond.

Tom wore white rubber boots, an old T-shirt and jeans. Steph waited on the wharf as he finished hosing down the deck.

He clambered up. He still hadn't seen her. He stood at the tap gazing up toward the mountain. She covered his eyes. 'Guess who?'

Tom turned. He shook his head in disbelief. 'I was thinking about you. Right then. I didn't think I'd see you again.'

'Had enough of me?'

'I meant after last time. I meant—what are you doing in town? How long are you here?'

'I've just finished exams. I'm hitching a helicopter ride back with the Tasmar Radio guys. Tomorrow.'

'When tomorrow?'

'Early, if the weather holds.'

'Are your parents here?'

'Just me. I'm staying at Mum's old school.'

'We just got in last night,' Tom said. He looked dazed to see her. 'Lots of crayfish?'

He gave a wry smile. 'Never enough, according to Frank.'

Steph looked about. 'It feels a bit strange.'

'What?'

'Being here instead of there. With you.'

'Can you wait?' he said. 'While I finish up?'

'I'm totally free.'

'No hot dates?'

'Never know your chances in the big city.'

He beamed at her. 'Would you still let me cook for you?'

Steph affected casual disinterest. 'Depends what's on offer.'

'Wood-fired pizza? Tom's Garden Restaurant.'

'I'd need to phone my parents. The school won't let me out without a leave pass.'

Tom helped her down onto the boat. 'Mum's in Melbourne for the week.'

No need to tell her parents that.

17

Tom watched Stephanie fold her arms around a small freckled girl with red plaits, huddled on the front step of the boarders' house. 'You sure you'll be okay, Marcie?' she said gently. The girl nodded. She'd been crying.

Stephanie got into his car. As they drove away she turned back and waved. 'Is she all right?' Tom said. 'Does she need a lift?'

'She was meant to go home today. There's some trouble with her parents and now Marcie doesn't know when they're coming to get her.'

He'd driven Stephanie home from town two hours before, then dashed home to shower and change and shop for dinner. In those two hours she'd changed into someone older. Her legs looked longer in tight jeans. She wore makeup and earrings, she looked different with her hair tied up—she looked much like her mother.

Perhaps it was the change in pitch from afternoon to evening—colour speared across the sky—that made Tom feel alive with promise. They'd spent the afternoon along the waterfront walking, talking; he'd blinked himself back into being when she'd pointed to yachts sailing on the water, a dog wading in the shallows, barking at the seagulls. Tom had been locked in a bubble of disbelief that she was there beside him, talking and laughing, her fingers snagged in the belt loop of his jeans as if nothing, nothing at all, had shifted in the way she felt toward him. They'd danced around talk of the boat; he hadn't mentioned Frank and she hadn't asked. Now, here in the car, the night sky charged with indigo, Tom felt renewed, a second chance that glistened like a cliff face after rain. 'How long do you have?'

'My leave pass expires at midnight.'

'Cinderella,' he said. The sky was clear, the forecast good. Tom spoke to make conversation. 'How's it looking for the morning?' He'd already checked the weather. He already knew the answer.

'They rang just now. Seven-thirty at the heli place.'

'Ships in the night, you and me.'

She kissed his hand. 'There'll be a next time.'

'Can I drive you out there?'

'Really? You want to get up that early?'

'I'm awake at four. Once a fisherman—' He stopped. Every word counted. Everything felt breakable. Beneath his skin Tom felt bruised and weatherworn. It was more than the physical aftermath of heaving across an ocean, growing wet and cold then thawing out with a deck shower whose water never grew hot enough. Putting on the least rank of your work clothes. Tom was tired of crap tinned soup, he was tired of baiting and stripping and shooting pots. Baiting them again. A kind of fatigue that went beyond flesh and bone: it came from tight-lipped days and restless nights of trying to withstand the final stretch with Frank.

It had all gone belly up the day Stephanie came aboard the boat, when she let slip Tom's plan to leave. He could have expected an earful from Frank but his brother was too cunning for that. His punishment had taken the form of a public exhibition of the man

Tom Forrest had become. The degradation of stealing pots made all the more tawdry before the girl Tom wanted to impress.

The fishing went on, but Frank sensed a shift in Tom—Hab felt it too. Tom and Frank were a continent buckling, a tectonic rift, one half wrenching itself apart, whatever the collateral damage. Perhaps Frank had cause to be pissed off with Tom, but he'd played it wrong. He'd forfeited the fucked-up obligation Tom served for a lifetime of big-brother benevolence. Frank had given Tom his exit plan. As soon as Hab's wife had the baby. When Hab came back to work. Tom wouldn't leave Frank short-handed. He owed his brother that.

'Are you all right?' Stephanie said.

He squeezed her hand.

Tom parked the car on the road; he led Stephanie down the side of the house.

'Wow.' She slowed at the sight of the garden. 'Is all this your mum? Or you?'

'Some of both.' He'd forgotten how this garden might look to someone else. Even around the perimeter of vegetable beds, spring onions vied for space between rosebushes and azaleas; garlic filled the gaps between the lavender and ranunculus; across the back trellis snow peas curled around the dried remains of his mother's sweet peas. Tom walked Stephanie past the fruit trees to the glasshouse. He showed her the seedlings and herbs, grumbled about the valuable bench space taken up by his mother's orchids and African violets she rotated from indoors to the glasshouse to guarantee perpetual blooms. 'The place needs weeding,' he said as an apology.

Stephanie fingered through the old shoeboxes—seeds stored and dated in recycled packets Tom saved from the kitchen. In a dishevelled kind of way the place held an order. He could put his hands on anything.

'All this.' She looked at him in a way that lifted Tom. 'This is you. This is how I think of you.'

He took a deep breath. The air trapped by the panes of glass felt warm and dank on his skin. He pinched off herbs, cupped the aromatic rub to his nose. 'What?' he said to her smile.

She rubbed her fingers. 'That thing you do. Sniffing leaves. I love it.'

The promise of a giant moon glowed beyond the old iron rooftops of the street. Pizza dough proved in the warmth of the kitchen; it swelled above the rim of the bowl. Stephanie stretched out on the lounge room rug, searching through CDs. 'Tom?' She held up Mariah Carey, acting out a look of *death by hopelessness*.

'It's Mum's. I'm more your Whitney Houston kind of guy.'

'Tell me you're joking.'

Stephanie watched him as he floured the bench and rolled and stretched the dough. He spooned homemade sauce across the base, giving it the flourish of a painter. He'd never cooked for anyone but his mother. Or on the boat, for Frank and Hab, but that was fuel that filled your belly and didn't count for anything. Beastie Boys pumped from the CD player. The big speakers were last year's Christmas gift from Frank. The only other females Tom could remember in this house were Aunt Fina from Melbourne, and Frank's wife Cheryl when she and Frank first started going out. In the years they'd been married Cheryl had never visited; Frank always showed up on his own.

Beyond the patio, the adobe oven pulsed with heat. Tom raked the coals to the back. A rush of sparks flared up into the night through the open chimney. He used a metal paddle to position the granite tile and slide the pizza in on top. *Built yourself an igloo,* Frank had mocked Tom's home-built oven. He'd never seen their mother turn on Frank to give him such a dressing-down. Tom knew she fretted. Nights, she'd look up from the television, rest her knitting in her lap. *Is everything all right with you and Frank?*

What could he say? She was mother to them both. Tom watched mozzarella melt and spread. His gut twisted at the echo of his brother's latest declaration—*Forrest Brothers*—Frank had hyped up on the boat trip home after another top catch. Tom had stayed silent, hadn't flickered at Frank's bait that snagged like a dirty hook. Thank Christ for Cheryl, who would look at the books and tear down Frank's grandiose talk of a second boat with the fierceness of a Tassie devil. The last thing Tom wanted was to skipper his own vessel. He'd served his time. He was sticking to his exit plan.

The air beyond the fire grew damp. Stephanie shivered. Tom brought his Gore-Tex jacket from the chair. 'It will be too big.'

'It's toasty.' She turned up the padded sleeves.

She set the tiny patio table with a cloth and serviettes, found cushions for the wrought-iron chairs. 'Shall I light this?' She held up his mother's votive candle.

'Go for it.'

She held the match to the wick. 'Make a wish,' Tom said, unable to stem ingrained habits. Stephanie closed her eyes in concentration.

Her hair smelled of wood smoke, his hands of fresh herbs. They stood together at the open oven, his girl blanketed in his jacket, the night air aromatic.

★

Steph followed Tom through the kitchen. She'd stacked the plates from dinner on the sink, left her scarf and backpack on the table. She felt her heart pulsing in her chest. She hoped she wasn't trembling.

Beyond the brightness of the kitchen and lounge the house changed mood. This narrow hallway, these dark wooden doors. She felt a heaviness distinct from the night and put it down to first-time nervousness.

Tom opened the door to his room. A night-light at the floor cast a reassuring glow. Steph paused. His bed. She took a breath.

'Are you sure?' Tom said softly.

She couldn't trust herself to speak. She squeezed his hand. As sure as a girl could be before leaping off a cliff.

★

'Back in a minute.' Tom grabbed his keys and went out to the car. He searched the glove box, looked behind the seat. Where? He'd gone into the chemist before picking Stephanie up—a lady with a baby had watched him knowingly from the other side of the shelves. Lubricated, Ribbed, Form Fit, Ultra Thin, illustrated packs of twelves and twenty-fours bearing a form of intimacy that spoke of late-night American TV, not him, not this tonight. Tom had prickled with uncertainty—he'd grappled with his own presumption at how the night might go. He thought to slink out of the pharmacy and leave it all to chance. But wasn't the onus on *him*?— *safe sex*, they harped on in his final year at school. If he hadn't been prepared, if things had gone this way—which obviously they had,

149

or would, if he could only find them—then what? He'd picked the plainest pack, blue and white, *Chekmate*, trying to find meaning in the misspelled name. He'd waited till the girl had finished serving at the counter. No, he didn't need a receipt, thanks. No, he didn't want a bag. He'd put them—

Stephanie looked at him enquiringly. She was curled against the pillows where he'd left her, still wearing his jacket. She reached into the pocket. 'Looking for these?' she said shyly. He gave a feeble simper. Chekmate.

★

Steph lay across his radiating chest, the race of his heart beating in her ear. 'Okay?' he said. Steph nodded. Tom pulled the bedcovers over her shoulders. Should she feel more special? Womanly? She felt unlinked from her body, a little dreamy, the way she felt on New Year's Eve after guzzling champagne. Tom had read her inexperience from the start. He hadn't laughed at her awkwardness. He'd whispered she was beautiful. He'd touched her skin, he hadn't hurried her. Everything was caring.

His breathing had eased, his chest rose and fell in a sleeper's rhythm. Steph felt wholly alert. She turned her ear to the sounds of the house: a creak of timber, a branch scraping the gutter outside the window. Around her—in the smell of the air, the set of old drawers, the flattened pile of the old-fashioned carpet—was the contrast of Tom's growing up to her own. His room was neat, unadorned—personality withheld. Tom's selfhood was the greenhouse, the garden—an outdoor oven he'd built himself. Steph looked around the walls. The bedroom had no posters, no art on any wall she had seen.

A statue of Jesus stood on the phone stand, another of Mary on the mantlepiece; you could hardly call *them* home furnishings. Only photos—the story of his family in flowery ornate frames, set out along the mantlepiece. His mother's wedding portrait reminded Steph of Gran and Pop's. Then Frank the baby, Frank the toddler, Frank in school uniform, Frank with his father showing off a catch of fish. Tom's father, older, hooked to a tube and seated in the recliner beside which the photo now stood. It touched Steph to see Frank back then, his head resting on his father's arm. The first photo of Tom, his father hollow and grey against hospital sheets, a tiny naked newborn propped against his chest. *Thomas Lee*, weight and birth date labelled in the corner. Photos of Frank cradling little Tom, ushering Tom as he took his first steps; Frank earnest and proud with Tom riding on his shoulders the way a boy would with his father. Frank and Tom seated on the bonnet of Tom's car. Frank and Tom together on a slipway, the *Perlita Lee* dressed up with bunting.

Tom stirred, he turned to reach his bedside clock.

'It's early still,' Steph said. 'Just eleven.'

He stroked Steph's leg, the dip of her waist. 'I wish you'd stay, Cinderella.' He touched her breast and kissed a curve of skin.

A thread loosened. She pressed herself against him. She could go back to the school first thing, before anyone woke, knock on Marcie's window. She drew her body close to his.

'Wait,' he fumbled with the packet. Steph lifted her body over his. Tom put his hands around her hips. She kissed him. She didn't feel anxious or unsure. 'You're beautiful,' he whispered.

Her body moved to a murmur, she closed her eyes and let it lift and carry her out upon a wave. In the corner of her senses a branch scraped at the gutter, murmurings that might have been her own.

'Stop,' she heard Tom whisper. She felt his body halt. He gripped her arms. A fridge door rattled, a voice, the sharp scrape of a chair.

'Your mother?'

Tom scrambled for his clothes. 'It's Frank. He'll be drunk.'

She listened to Tom's steps along the hall. The floorboards creaked. 'Well,' she heard Frank in the kitchen. 'While the cat's away, eh, Tom-Tom?'

'What are you doing here?'

Frank's words were slurred. 'Thought you might want company. Mum away, all on your lonesome. But I see you're managing just fine.' Frank let out a belch.

Steph dressed with trembling hands; she fumbled with the laces of her boots, combed her hair with her fingers as she moved along the hall toward the light.

Frank was seated at the kitchen table, her scarf wound stupidly around his head.

Steph waited at the kitchen door, the armour of Tom's jacket wrapped around her. Frank blinked. 'Stethenie.' Too drunk to say her name. 'Wasn't expecting you, sweet pea. Correction,' he held up his hand. 'Tom-Tom's sweet pea. But I'm his big brother so that makes you everybody's sweet pea.' He pulled the scarf from his head, swept his arm across the kitchen table, bowling his stubby of beer across it.

Tom picked up his car keys. 'I'm taking Stephanie home.'

Frank cackled. 'Helluva drive to Maatsuyker Island.'

'Get a taxi, Frank. Go home.'

'Home? Cheryl's a bitch. Cheryl says she hates my fuckin guts. Not very ladylike, is it darlin'? Not very Forty Buckets Beach.'

Tom summoned her. He held the door.

'Tom-Tom tell you our big news?'

'You're pissed, Frank.'

Steph couldn't help herself. 'What news?'

'Top Fuckin Secret,' Frank ranted. 'Everybody has to sign a con, a conf—one a those. But we'll tell you.' Frank turned to Tom with a theatrical wave of his arm. 'Is it a bird? Is it a plane? It's Captain Tom-Tom, skipper, I said *skipper*, of his own Forrest Brothers' cray boat. How good is that, girlie!'

'Don't listen. He's full of shit. Come on, Stephanie.'

Steph followed. The wall of cold snapped her back into time, the moon distended, its icy light glancing off the roofs and road.

Tom drove. He gripped her hand. Steph sat in a daze, caught between her body and the clutter in her head. Her voice trembled. 'You said you told Frank you were leaving.'

'I am leaving.' He sounded strange. He sounded on the verge of tears. He pulled up at the gate of the school. 'I'll be here in the morning. I'll pick you up at six-thirty. I'll explain then.'

'Explain now, Tom.'

He took a deep breath. 'Frank knows I'm leaving. I haven't said when, but he knows. He's saying all this stuff as a way to make me stay.'

'Why doesn't he just ask you to stay?' *Like any normal person would,* Steph felt like saying.

Tom rapped his fingers on the steering wheel. 'It's his way. Frank doesn't say sorry. He'd never come right out and beg. He thinks if he spouts big plans and I don't say anything to the contrary, that it will all blow over and I'll have changed my mind.'

'Have you changed your mind?'

'I told you. I'm leaving.' Tom's voice sounded tight. 'I have to wait until Habib gets back. Till his wife has the baby. A couple of weeks. I can't leave Frank without a deckhand.'

'Why not?' Steph said. She waited for an answer but Tom just shook his head and stared up at the moon. It threw her back in time to Callam. Steph had turned a blind eye to her brother's fur-tiveness, his sneaking out, rumours at his school of someone selling drugs. She'd denied it from herself, the way she had with Tom. Steph might have drifted along in a bubble of illusion had she not found the roll of notes hidden in her brother's bookcase. The feel of other people's money soiled her hands. Every fulcrum has a tipping point. Statues of Jesus and stealing people's pots. 'I know what happens on the boat,' she said to Tom. 'I know what you and Frank do.' Steph couldn't be a part of that.

18

Out and around the Needles, a steep bank as the helicopter rounded course and turned to face the island. Steph couldn't claim to be at ease, but gone was the terror of her first flight. From the back seat she loosened her grip on the seat and looked down to a pair of yachts beating westward. The ocean sparked and glittered in the breeze, the lighthouse tall above the vegetation, the canopy of tea-trees laden with white flower. Maatsuyker had turned to icing on a Christmas cake. They flew over the weather station and house, across newly mown lawns and road. Every tree, every bush in flower. Steph saw the blue truck, her parents standing either side, reaching up to wave.

The helicopter rocked on the pad. Steph let herself catch up while she waited for the shutdown—it felt like peeling back the skin of town. It felt like coming back as someone new. The pilot did his paperwork, the rotors warbled to a stop. He opened his door. 'Special delivery,' he called to Mum and Dad. 'Two for the price of one.'

Beside Steph, the radio technician fumbled with his seat buckle. He remembered his headphones then heaved himself out. Steph was next. Her parents enveloped her, squeezing her, firing questions one over the other. *How were exams? How was the school? Which room did they put you in? Gosh, we missed you. How was your dinner with Tom? It's been like this all week. Your mother even sunbaked on the lawn. Wait until you see the mail.*

Steph took a deep breath. 'Mum. Dad.' Steph beckoned to her friend. 'This is Marcie, from the school. I invited her to spend the day. A rescue mission,' she said to Mum.

Her mother gaped. Dad blinked. 'Does the school know Marcie's here?'

'Not entirely.'

Marcie blurted, 'Steph said you wouldn't mind and there was a seat in the helicopter because a person couldn't come and I really wanted to see the lighthouse and the island and where you live and everything. I hope it's okay.'

'It is okay. Isn't it?' Steph said to Mum and Dad.

A second radio technician carried the gear to the truck. 'Be there in a minute,' Dad called to them. 'Excuse us, Marcie.' Her parents walked Steph to the front of the helicopter. 'What were you thinking?' Dad said. 'You can't go abducting someone else's child. What if something were to happen to her?'

'Like what?'

'She could fall down a cliff. The helicopter could crash. If the wind got up she could blow away—how old is she? Ten?'

'She's twelve, Dad.'

'She's no bigger than an ant.'

Mum clucked. 'So it's fine for our daughter to be in the helicopter when it crashes?'

'That wasn't—'

'What about the school?' Mum said to Steph.

'We left a note.'

'Stating what?' Dad said.

'That she'll be back tonight. Weather permitting.'

'Good golly.' Her father was working himself into a tizz. 'Her parents will have called the police, rounded up a search party. They'll be beside themselves.'

'That's just the point,' Steph said. She should have guessed this was a bad idea. 'Her parents are in the middle of a break-up and her mother's gone AWOL for the weekend. Her father says he's too busy with the farm to come down for her until next week.' Steph appealed to her mother. 'She would have been at the boarding school completely on her own. I felt sorry for her.' Her mother's eyes flicked in Marcie's direction. 'Tom's going to pick her up tonight.' Tom had offered to get Marcie back to school. Steph hadn't thought that far. 'He'll make sure she's okay.'

'Stellar job!' Dad exploded. 'Imagine what they're going to make of that: in a car with a nineteen-year-old boy.'

'I'll phone Marcie's father,' Mum said. 'I'll speak to the school.'

Dad shook his head. 'I can't believe you would do something so impetuous. It's the sort of thing your brother would do. No regard for consequences.'

'James,' her mother said, pulling him aside.

Steph slumped. She hadn't slept. She'd lain awake through the night, replaying what had happened with Tom, what she'd said, trying to convince herself of what Tom was and wondering how a single conversation could turn something intimate and tender to a ragged, ugly screech.

They hadn't talked on the way out to the airport, not with Marcie in the car. She'd felt Tom's upset—his hurt at Marcie being there, a wedge between them that insured nothing could be said.

Perhaps that was why she'd asked the smaller girl. No. Steph had wanted to protect her, had wanted to do something decent and nice and kind. She'd tried to give Tom's jacket back; he'd insisted that she keep it. *But it's yours,* she'd said. He'd pleaded. *I want you to wear it.* She'd kissed him the way you would to be polite, to thank someone for their help. Marcie had taken to Tom, hugged him like a favourite brother. Now Marcie waited by the helicopter, looking anxious. 'She thinks you're mad at her,' Steph said to her parents. 'She thinks you'll send her home.'

'It's okay, darling,' Mum called. She drew Steph and Dad together. 'For better or for worse, Marcie's here now. She's in our care and by tonight she'll be back in town, safe and sound.'

Dad shrugged in abdication. 'I have to help the men.' He strode away to the truck.

Mum turned into protective dove, her wing folded around Marcie's shoulder. 'How about we take you down to the house and get you settled in? Then you and Stephanie can go exploring while I rustle up some morning tea. You like Anzac biscuits?'

Steph changed into her favourite old shirt and jeans. The smell of Omo, sea air. Wood smoke lingered about Tom's jacket. Steph resisted the urge to look through the box of mail.

She did her best to be cheerful and sociable when all she wanted was to curl up in the lighthouse and be alone. She showed Marcie the weather station, checked through the week's entries made in her absence. Steph pointed out the Mewstone, the Needles. 'Big pointy stepping stones across the sea,' said Marcie. Marcie followed along the path, running and leaping, too short to reach the branches of the arbour. Encircling them, embracing them, a living garland wound with tea-tree white and coastal daisy, the bush bejewelled with bells and berries. The air felt cool, alive with birdsong, the drone of insects muddled on nectar.

Marcie gazed upon the lighthouse. She broke into a squeal. 'This is just about the best lighthouse ever.'

Steph opened the lower doors. 'How many have you been to?'

'Just this one.'

Steph showed Marcie the canisters. 'From the light-keeping days. Only one of them still has a signal flag inside. Want to guess?'

Marcie studied them. She shook the M, the S, the A. She reached for Z. 'This one.' She prised open the lid and pulled out the flag.

'Z for Zulu,' Steph explained.

They climbed the steps; Marcie stopped at each floor to stand on her toes and peer through the narrow clouded windows. She ran her fingers along lintels gritty with loose mortar. She wiggled her nose. 'It smells a bit funny.'

'Mould. You get used to it.'

She stopped at the old kerosene lanterns. 'We have some like these in the shed.'

'They used them in the old days, in case the light broke down. My grandfather was the light keeper back then.'

'I don't have a grandfather any more.'

'Nor me. Just Gran. My dad's mother.'

Steph gripped Marcie's hand as they circled the balcony. If Marcie blew away Steph would never hear the end of it. Wind parted the line of tussocks along the cliff edge, laid them flat like crowns of hair, russet and blonde, silky as a pelt. How the island had changed in the space of a week.

'Look. Way out there.' Marcie pointed.

Far out past the Needles a bulk carrier ploughed westward. It was only the second big ship Steph had seen. 'They must have passed by all the time in the old days.'

'Do you think they can see us?'

'With binoculars. If they're looking this way. At night-time, in the lighthouse days, the ships could see the light all the way from the horizon.'

'Could they see the light from Hobart?'

'Maatsuyker's too far around the corner.'

'I'm going to be a lighthouse keeper.'

Mum arrived laden with a basket, a thermos, the old grey blanket. They sat on the lawn shielded from the wind. 'I spoke to your father, Marcie.'

'Is everything all right?'

'He was a bit shocked at the thought of you flying off in a helicopter to a remote island. We had a good talk. He's going to call the school and let them know you're here. He's driving down tomorrow to pick you up.'

'Tomorrow?' Marcie said. 'Am I in trouble?'

'No, pet. He just wants to make sure you're safe. That you're okay.'

'See?' Steph said. 'I knew it wouldn't be an issue.' Her mother gave a *don't push your luck* look. 'What's Dad doing?'

'They're working on the VHF. Installing a bigger aerial.' Her mother laid out mugs and a container of milk, a tin of homemade biscuits. 'It isn't until we have visitors,' Mum said, 'that I see how rundown the place looks. We had a Heritage woman over at resupply recording the cracks in the walls, photographing the plaster. *Decrepitude* was the word of the day. I couldn't help feeling a little insulted, as if I hadn't cared for the place properly.'

'What do they expect?' Steph said. 'A house as old as ours is bound to have a few scars and wrinkles. It's still a great house.'

Mum blinked. She shook her head at Steph. 'Who *are* you? And what have you done with my daughter?'

'I love old houses,' Marcie said. 'They have a certain atmosphere.'

'It's not as if I don't keep it clean,' Mum appealed.

'Is there any sugar?' Marcie asked.

'Steph, can you run up for me?'

'I can get it,' Marcie offered.

Steph laid out on the blanket, closed her eyes. 'Is everything okay?' her mother asked.

'Yeah.' She nodded.

'You seem . . . distant.'

'I'm all right.'

'Did you enjoy Hobart?'

'It was okay.'

'How's Tom?'

Steph sighed. 'Can we talk about something else?'

'All right,' her mother said. 'How were exams?'

'Mum.'

'Then *you* tell me what I can talk about.'

'How was it here this week?'

'The big flurry of resupply day; after that it seemed extra quiet, just Dad and I rattling around.'

'Who did the weather?'

'We started out doing it together but we could never agree on the clouds, the heights. Dad, bless him, did the early morning shifts and I did the afternoons.'

'I can do the weather now. I want to get back into it.'

'Time's moving fast,' Mum said. 'December, January, then it's all over.'

Steph had spent the first month counting off the days. 'Do you think about Callam?'

'Every day,' Mum said. She was quiet for a while. 'You spend your whole time on an island looking out to sea. It's a kind of meditation. Perhaps what you're really facing is yourself. I always want to remember, but I want to feel good. I want to feel . . . alive again.'

She hadn't said that before. Her mother sat up, stretched her arms; she took a deep breath. 'I started yoga this week.'

'You haven't done anything since . . . Callam.'

'It's a long time since Callam.'

'Mum?'

'Yes?'

'I won't get into medicine.'

'You can't know that. You always do well. It will be another month before you get your results.'

As good a time as any. 'Even if I did get in, which I won't, I don't want to do medicine.'

'Since when?'

'I said I would to make you happy. It was your dream. Not mine.'

Her mother pulled at bits of grass. 'This isn't about me. It's not my life. I'd be unhappy if you did something you didn't want to do just to please me.'

Marcie bounded around the bend, clasping an eggcup. She skidded on the blanket in a scattering of sugar crystals. 'Never mind,' Mum said to Marcie. 'Isn't it meant to be good luck, spilled sugar? Or maybe it's salt. We'll salvage what we can; the wind will scoop up the rest.'

There was something timeless about sitting in the shelter of the lighthouse on an old army blanket, dunking Anzacs in a mug of tea. Mum and Marcie chatted, seals bleated, the underlying rumble of an ocean that pushed and pulled and dumped itself against the rocks below. 'Did your mum say why?' Mum asked Marcie. Steph tuned in.

'She says it's lonely and boring and all Dad does is work. She wants to move to the mainland but Dad doesn't want to sell the farm. I love the farm. What will happen to me if Mum leaves?'

'Well,' Mum said, searching for an answer.

'What if neither of them want me?'

Mum shook her head. 'My guess is your parents need some time to work things out between them. But I can assure you, they'll both still want you. You're their little girl. How they feel about you won't ever change, no matter what.'

'Listen,' Steph said. She closed her eyes. She heard the lighthouse breathe.

'It's humming,' Marcie said. 'It's humming like you said.'

'It takes me back to Dad up on the catwalk,' said Mum, 'polishing the glass.'

'Was it brilliant? The lighthouse and your own island and everything?'

'It was special. The hardest thing was going back to school.' Her mother turned to Steph. 'Your grandmother wanted me to have a proper school education. So I'd have choices. Not that I ever made proper use of them.' Her mother collected up the mugs. 'Then it all came crashing to an end. I didn't even know my parents were leaving until I came down to the island for Easter. They weren't told until a few days before.'

'Why?' Steph asked. 'Why was it so sudden?'

Her mother sighed. 'It was complicated.' She put the mugs on the tray. 'It broke my heart for Dad. It was more than a job, it was his whole identity. It was that way for all the men—they worshipped the lights. And now it's gone. Everything automated.' Mum turned her gaze out across the sea.

'Only the ocean stays the same,' Steph said. Her mother looked at her enquiringly.

Mum took the basket. Marcie followed up the path with the empty thermos. Steph gripped the corners of the blanket. It caught the breeze; it tugged and yanked against her hold. Part of her wanted to carry it up the lighthouse stairs and free it from the balcony. Callam and Grandfather would be All Aboard, wheeling off at breakneck speed toward the Mewstone. Steph reined in the corners of the blanket and turned toward the house.

*

She stepped into a warm sea of fruity bubbles, wedged her feet against the foot of the bath. The helicopter would be back in Hobart. Right now Tom should be driving Marcie home. Steph reached for the pages on the floor and reread Tessa and Sammie's letters delivered with the resupply. She tried to concentrate on events and parties and names, a score of make-ups and break-ups. She'd forgotten how intense Tessa could be. *The most horrendous evening of my entire life. And now he wants to go out with me again!!!!* Sammie had a boyfriend. Daniel Satterley. Six months ago Sammie loathed Daniel. *I don't know how you bear it down there,* Tessa wrote. *Poor Stephie,* Sammie drew a sad face. The edges of the paper were tissue limp from steam and water. Steph let them drop to the floor. The window looked out across ocean to South West Cape, a taper of hills that marked the corner of Tasmania. Mutton-birds rafted on the ocean in steely evening light. Fishing boats were on the move, their pinpoints of light like lantern fish across a watery expanse.

Steph studied the curves and angles of her body, her legs and feet, her faded tan, templates of milky skin that never saw the sun. Her body was changed, inscribed with adult meaning. It could never go back to being what it was before last night. In something found, a part of her was lost.

The water, thick and warm, enveloped her breasts and shoulders, coated her arms in warmth. She closed her eyes and sunk into Tom, to the feel of his skin against hers. She let the water envelop her head, felt a swirl of hair across her face. She listened to the drumming in her ears that pulsed like the heartbeat of an ocean.

She had moved through the day separate from herself. Not until the final minutes, at the helipad, Mum hugging Marcie goodbye, Dad shaking the pilot's hand, *All the best for Christmas and New Year,* had Steph been jolted into action. A scrap of yellow graph paper from the glove box of the truck. A chewed tradesmen's pencil. *Come for New Year's—it's my birthday.* Righteous stands were no match for the forces of your heart.

The message looked last minute, throwaway. *For Tom,* she'd scratched in pencil and folded it around a sprig of tea-tree. A line thrown out. She placed it in the pocket of Tom's jacket. Closed the zip. Passed the jacket to Marcie. 'Can you give this back to Tom? Tell him to check his pockets.'

Marcie hugged Steph. 'I wish I could stay. I wish I lived here.'

'I wish you could stay.' Marcie climbed into the back seat. Steph helped her with her seatbelt. She bundled Tom's jacket at her feet. 'You'll tell Tom what I said?'

'Cross my heart.'

19

Halfway through December, supposedly summer, yet fog blanketed the island, the pall unrelenting. Her father had gone to bed early. It was Steph and Mum in the living room assembling a jigsaw from a box held together with yellowed sticky tape, bits of draft horse and windmill mixed in from other ancient puzzles.

A thud from a mutton-bird hitting the porch roof. In the fog, the landmarks that guided the way to their burrows now stood as unforgiving obstacles.

'There must be something we can do,' Steph said.

'What?' Her mother shrugged. 'Birds, people, boats—we all bow to the weather. It's the light and dark of being at this place. You plant yourself on the edge of an ocean and you see how startling nature is, that it's fierce and beautiful—totally indiscriminate.'

'Was it nature that got Callam?'

Mum closed her eyes. Her breath came out like wind fluttering a sail. 'It was Callam being Callam. A precious silly boy who'd lost his way. Who made a terrible mistake.' Mum wiped her nose with her sleeve. 'I loved him,' she said. 'God knows he drove me round the twist.'

'Callam?'

Mum kissed Steph's forehead. 'I know I don't always get it right. But I thank the stars for you. Truly.' Steph couldn't speak. She pushed back tears. Her mother cleared the coffee cups. 'I'm off to bed. You'll switch off the Christmas lights?'

'Mum.' Steph wanted her to stay. To talk some more. 'A woman phoned.'

'When?'

'Ages ago.'

'Who?'

'Cathy someone. She knew you from Maatsuyker, when you were growing up.'

'Cathy Smithies?'

'She said something. About Grandfather.'

Her mother looked wary. 'What did she say?'

'That it was a shame what happened to him. That none of the light keepers were angels.'

Her mother shook her head. 'I don't know what she was on about.' She looked upset. 'Cathy Smithies hardly knew us. What was she thinking speaking to you like that?'

'I wish you'd tell me the truth. I'm not a child that needs protecting.'

Her mother set down the cups. She looked at Steph. 'What do you want to know?'

'Why they had to leave. What he did.'

'I was only fifteen,' her mother said. 'I don't know all the ins and outs of it. There was tension between the families, the keepers. You could feel it. Mum and the other mothers used to take turns visiting one another's quarters for afternoon tea. All of a sudden it stopped. Mum wouldn't talk about it. She'd say she was too busy for cups of tea.'

Steph waited, to see what else she knew.

'I came down on the supply boat that Easter and there was a new man aboard. We chatted on the way down, he asked about the island, what Dad did. I was so naive. He was Dad's replacement. Dad and Mum were waiting at the landing ramp with all our boxes packed.'

'Did you find out why?'

'I can guess why,' her mother said sadly. 'Dad had a drinking problem.' Steph was thrown. The bottles of rum her mother had found in the roof. 'He'd missed one of his shifts. One shift and they claimed he wasn't doing his job properly. They gave him three days' notice. For a lifetime of service.'

Drinking? Steph thought about the plaque. *Adulterer*, scratched across his name. 'Was there more to it? The dismissal?'

Mum blinked, confused by the question. 'Not to my knowledge. Isn't that enough?'

Steph went to speak. She stopped. Her mother didn't know. But this wasn't Callam, where speaking out might help, might change the course of things. Who would it serve? Whatever had happened was long ago, her mother still a girl, privy to her father's drinking; protected, perhaps, from other adult things. Steph backtracked. 'You always said you had the perfect growing up.'

'I did.' Mum sounded defensive. 'I adored my father. He always seemed larger than life, boisterous and happy, always playing pranks and showing off.' The man Callam would have become. Her mother's gaze shifted to somewhere in the past. 'Dad would infuriate my mother. Not me. I'd get a stitch from laughing.' She gave Steph a sad smile. 'When you're a child, so long as you're safe and loved, the details don't matter. I wouldn't have swapped my father, or my time on Maat, for all the riches in the world.' The cups clanged when she picked them up. She stopped at the kitchen door. 'I never liked that Cathy Smithies. My father did his job as well as anyone. Better.'

Her mother came back from the kitchen.

'Mum?'

'Yes?'

'It makes him seem more real.'

'In what way?'

'Nobody's perfect.'

Her mother kissed her. 'No, they're not. Far from it. Goodnight, my love. Don't forget the Christmas lights.'

The tea-tree branch, propped in a bucket of dirt, consumed the meagre room. The foliage sparkled with scraps of balding tinsel and flaking baubles, cheered by a set of wonky lights whose working bulbs shuddered more than blinked. You wouldn't call it a glamorous Christmas tree but it was earthy and real.

Steph wound up the volume on the new VHF. Mutton-birds and boats were out there in the fog, as hidden from one another as they were from the island. Even in Steph's world, nothing was instantly apparent. She'd believed her mother's love was all for Callam. But Mum thanked the stars for her—*her*. A small string of words so pure and unexpected that Steph summoned the echo of them again and again, their meaning washing through her like a cleansing. Only now could she admit to the resentment she'd felt toward her brother.

She tuned in to the chatter on the VHF amongst the fishermen.

M'pots have been out since yesterday morning. The air's so thick it's like a fuckin Sherlock Holmes movie.

It's no Teddy Bear's Picnic over this way.

Got any company?

Jasper's next door. Not that we can see him.

Steph collected the packet of booklets and papers Gran had sent with the mail. Australian National University glass workshop. They'd been sitting unread for weeks. She tucked the blanket around her feet. She flicked through photos of the glassworks in the catalogue. Sculptures and vessels, abstract shapes and forms, curves and prisms, sweeps of colours, swirls and patterns locked within an outer seal of glass—how did they even do that? These pieces were the real thing. It wasn't some dinky student exhibition put on for the paying parents of Steph's school who gushed over their child's efforts at art. Steph had seen girls at her school shrink in the presence of their parents, their false accolades an immediate recognition of lack. It was something Steph loved about her parents, especially her father, who would walk around the hall of artworks giving each a respectful airing and finding something, the one original thing—the use of colour, a technique, the choice of composition—that could be remarked upon genuinely, positively. *Clever*, her father might say quietly in a way that others would look again to see what they had missed. Now, without a voice, her father just looked and blinked as if in conversation with himself, before moving on.

Steph looked through the catalogue's pages of artists with their work—students no older than herself. In all the pieces the light seemed to pour like liquid through the glass. Was there any greater contradiction than glass? The ink bottle her grandfather had found had endured for hundreds of years. Had withstood being thrown up on rocks. Had shattered in a second.

Undergraduate students are introduced to the workshop and develop a sound understanding of glass, its processes and techniques . . . students develop their own artistic identity.

Steph leafed through panoramas of the workshops, girls and guys, oven mitts and leather aprons, bandanas and Blundstone boots. A cohort of artisans wielding blacksmith tools and shining with sweat, a forgery with molten baubles being turned and teased and shaped with human breath. New voices on the VHF:

Twenty feet the other way and we'd have deplanked her.

The only time you're really vulnerable is when you're sleeping. The wind moves around and straight away you're on edge.

I used to sleep like a baby when I come out with the old man.

Steph focused on the catalogue. *The workshop includes a fully equipped hot shop with tank furnace, colour pot furnace, annealing kilns . . . individual work spaces.*

She flipped through the pages. Visiting artists, field trips. She could stay with Gran.

It's not me, but the wife's at home doing the books and she starts fretting when the money isn't coming in.

Selection Criteria, Steph read. *A portfolio of drawings and sketchbooks, examples that demonstrate an aptitude for three-dimensional work, motivation and commitment, ability to articulate ideas in a visual form.* If she tried, if she was motivated, she could put a tick against every one of those requirements. Her body felt gripped. A heavy door had come ajar, a current of light charging through her.

How about the sea lice? Soon as it's dark the bastards're everywhere.

You wouldn't want to be in the pot; there'd be nothing left of you.

She checked the clock. It was too late to phone Gran. But her grandmother would be up at dawn when Steph was awake to do the early weather. She turned the page: *Academic Requirement: Higher School Certificate.*

20

New Year's Eve. Steph's seventeenth birthday. Dad set aside time for her driving practice. Her friends at home would all have their licence, by now some would have their own car. Her father sat beside Steph in the passenger seat, gripping the handhold at each downhill run. *Bend up ahead*, he'd sing out at any moment. He put Steph on edge. What would he be like when they got back to Sydney, cars swerving across multiple lanes? The little blue truck trundled along like a creaking funicular, wheels locked in the road furrows and not enough speed to even move past second gear. 'Bend up ahead.'

'I see it, James.'

Finally the road flattened out and they reached the old helipad at the northern end of the island. Steph brought the truck to a halt, turned off the ignition. 'Been through your checklist?' he said in his instructor tone.

She'd packed the tent, the ground sheet, her pillow, the sleeping bag—'Oh,' she realised what he meant and pulled on the hand-brake. Mum hardly ever used the handbrake but it was wise to keep your parents' contradictions to yourself.

Steph unloaded the camping gear from the truck; her father helped set up her tent on the old grassed helicopter pad. 'Not the middle, Dad, I'll be trampled by the mutton-birds.'

'It's an awful night for camping. Nothing's had a chance to dry.' Her father suddenly looked as wounded as her mother that she was choosing to spend the occasion without them.

It's the new millennium. It's not as if we'll get the chance again. Mum had stood at the twin tub pulling work clothes from grey water and dropping them into the spinner. But Dad had emerged from the kitchen to rescue Steph as he slurped on his mug of tea. *There'll be other birthdays, Gretchen, other New Years' Eves.*

The twin tub had shuddered on its feet, the spinner squealing. The shadow of Callam reared up; Steph nearly changed her mind. She wanted to wake before dawn, she explained, be up to watch the birds take off, be somewhere special that she'd always remember. That was the truth. At least it was most of it. Dad tightened the guy ropes of the tent. 'You're all set up for tonight.'

Steph drove the truck back along the road toward the house. Dad had an uncanny knack of tapping into her thoughts. 'Are you and Tom still an item? Or shouldn't I go there?'

'I don't know what we are. I invited him for New Year's. I never heard anything.' Steph told herself it didn't matter. *No looking back*, her New Year's resolution.

'We're leaving in a few weeks. Don't go breaking his heart.' Dad sat with his knuckles taut on the handhold as they jerked along, the truck shuddering with each change of gear. 'So,' he said. 'Mum tells me maybe Canberra next year for you. Off to glass school.'

'Only if they take me.'

'And if they don't?' A reference to her mediocre exam results. At least she had passed.

'If they don't then we'll both be figuring out what else to do, Jamesie.'

'Touché.' Dad instructed her to slow down.

'Dad?'

'Steph.'

'Is it actually legal to maintain a speed of less than ten ks per hour? Doesn't it violate some international driving rule? People walk faster than we're travelling.'

A smile played at her father's mouth. 'You'd do well to keep your eyes on the road, young lady.'

Steph stayed at the house for dinner, she opened her presents, blew out the candles on her cake, she made a wish. It was close to dusk when she left. She pulled on her beanie, zipped her jacket and backpack. The day hadn't risen above fourteen degrees. The air felt yanked and jostled. Steph made her way along the road. The sky was vast and wild and commanded that you pause and breathe it in. The sound of ocean and wind played out in her dreams and was imprinted on her senses. Steph believed that if she lived to be one hundred she would still be able to conjure its immensity and summon how it made her feel. This sky, this island and ocean would forever be a part of turning seventeen.

Seventeen. It was the start of something, a new beginning urging her on as she walked through arbours enfolding the road, the champagne in her pack cold against her back. The stress of high school, exams, deciding on her future was behind her. Gran had phoned through her results after Christmas. Steph had scraped over the line in Maths, but had mostly done okay in other subjects. When she saw her friends from school she wouldn't get caught up in the I-could-have-done-better-if-I'd-tried routine, because it sounded like a cop-out.

Between Mrs Burrows at school and Gran in Canberra, they'd cobbled together her portfolio to send to Canberra. She'd had the phone interview on Christmas Eve and the man had asked so much about Maatsuyker and hardly anything about art that when he said, *Talk to me about your interest in glass,* the image that glanced before Steph was the lighthouse. She explained about the prisms, the tonnage of glass and how the light danced through the Fresnel lens to turn the Needles upside down—a ragged-edged mural as broad as the sky. She heard herself babbling when she'd promised herself she wouldn't; that at first the glass looked clear but when you really looked it was the most delicate sea green imaginable, each curve infused with hundred-year-old bubbles. The lighthouse glass was sunlight punching through the back of a wave and that's how she saw it, the swirl and twist and how the ocean's energy seemed locked inside the glass. Light set it in motion. The third week of January, the man said, one way or the other, she'd be informed.

An ocean chopped with breeze. Not a boat in sight. The only evidence of fishing boats were necklaces of coloured buoys strung around the raspy throats of rock.

Steph paced from her tent set up on the old helicopter pad to the repeater antenna. She walked back down. The light was dimming fast. She climbed inside the tent and checked the air bed. She unpacked her backpack: mosquito repellent, pyjamas, water bottle; she inventoried her snacks: corn chips, dried apricots, birthday cake for two, champagne, glasses. She climbed back out. The *Perlita Lee* could still be up in Hobart. Or Tom might walk straight past the tent and miss her altogether. She checked her torch was working.

The other boats might have headed back to town. This night was made for celebration. In ten years people would remember where they were when the countdown sang off the old millennium and shouted in the new. A new year so big that every wild dream was possible. She felt a lurch, a voice. Callam had been silent for weeks. Steph resisted his hold. Two years of being torn ragged with the hurt of him; she and her parents clinging to grief. Steph had somehow followed the lifeline of bubbles and made it to the surface. She was a fledgling bird, the readiness of flight upon her as surely as the sky's creep of darkness, as surely as the first mutton-birds swooping in from sea and returning to their burrows. Steph opened the corn chips. She watched the sky. She waited.

*

Tom's jacket hung on the bulkhead of his bunk. He'd wanted Stephanie to keep it but she'd sent it back with Marcie as if it were a tainted thing. He'd shoved it in the boot of his car, chucked in with boat gear and a stack of hessian sacks that soon enough would stink of stolen crays and grimy payouts. Give anything on this boat enough time and see it turn bad.

New Year's Eve and they were off the back of Maat, swinging on the anchor. Below deck Frank was napping. Tom wrapped his hands around a mug of sweetened coffee squeezed from a tube and propped himself on lookout behind the wheelhouse. Maatsuyker's light had been on for thirty minutes. Further down the hill the grand old light tower stood as solid as a sentinel. Even decommissioned it would outshine all their lives.

Tom took too big a gulp and felt the coffee scald. He thumped his chest. Back in Hobart he had hinted to his mother about leaving the boat. Not straight out. *A few ideas I'm working on*, dropped into the conversation. Give his mother time to grow used to the idea.

She'd spent nights sewing signal flags, not quizzing him initially, but when he said, *They're a present for a friend*, he caught her expression of concern. *Don't go getting serious, love. Frank says you have a big, bright future on the boat.* Tom guessed Frank had already been in his mother's ear. He could hear it: *She's filled Tom's head with so much rubbish he's no damn use to anyone. She'll rack off back to Sydney and Tom won't hear from her again.* He wouldn't give Frank the satisfaction of telling his mother it was over, that Frank was probably right. Tom was leaving the boat. He'd made up his own mind, regardless of Stephanie.

When he'd collected Marcie from the helicopter and returned her to the boarding school, she hadn't drawn breath for talking about her big day at Maatsuyker, the lighthouse, her ride home in the helicopter. He'd caught her looking across at him; she'd blushed when he caught her gaze, like a kid with a crush. *One day I'm going to be a lighthouse keeper,* she declared to Tom.

It made him smile. That she was a generation too late for a role that no longer existed didn't factor into the equation. *Stephanie happy to get back on the island?* he casually asked.

She was in heaven, Marcie said. *She got loads of presents and letters from everyone at home.* Tom asked about the jacket. *She said she doesn't need it. She has her own jacket.*

Over one hundred pieces cut out and hemmed. They'd been pinned together, ready for stitching, laid out in his mother's sewing room the night Stephanie had come to the house. Tom had hurried her past the door, afraid she might walk in and discover his surprise, his grand scheme to slip the new flags inside the old lighthouse canisters, leave a Christmas card beside the lanterns with clues on where to look.

There was no Stephanie now. No flags. He'd driven to a building site, ready to dump them in a skip bin. He couldn't bring himself to do it—all the hours his mother had spent, the metres of material she'd bought. Waste on top of waste. Tom toyed with the idea of donating them to the new caretakers, but he would be long gone by the time they arrived. In desperation he'd swung by the boarding school, found the front door locked, asked the woman at the library to hold them. *Marcie who?* she asked. Tom didn't know. She was just some sweet little kid with big-arse dreams to be a light keeper. He saw wariness written on the woman's face. *Our students don't return until the new term. Can I have your name?*

Let the woman think what she wanted. *Just tell her they're from Tom.*

Frank was stirring down below. It would be the two of them working through the night, fuelled on Rice A Riso, mugs of tea and a charge of adrenalin pumped by recklessness and risk. They should have done the decent thing and motored up to Little Deadman's Bay, celebrate New Year's Eve with others from the fleet. Insurance, Tom's first thought when Bluey MacIntyre radioed to include them in the New Year invitation. Tom had looked to Frank, already gauging his resistance, Frank a hardened junkie for the clandestine rush of robbing pots and offloading illegal cargo in the thick of night—the sweeter knowing every other boat would be away. Tom wished Habib were here to fill the void. Hab was still back in Hobart waiting for the baby, his smiling wife as enormous as a try-pot. They'd induce her this week if nothing happened on its own.

Next round Hab would be back. Two weeks. Tom could stomach anything till then.

★

The night sky had cleared, the wind petered out. The Milky Way a spangled sweep of graffiti. Orion. Pleiades. The Southern Cross low down in the sky, her pointers not yet showing. If Tom could name one thing he'd miss when he was gone it would be a starry sky at sea. Their running lights were off, the air thick as pitch, the waning crescent moon a no-show for at least another hour. Frank's timing was honed to perfection. Only one hitch: the transfer boat hadn't shown.

Frank took up the radio and transmitted another run of clicks. 'They should have been here half an hour ago.' They waited fifteen, twenty minutes, the only light Maatsuyker's beam cutting through the night.

'There she is.' Tom pointed, a running light rounding the Needles a kilometre away, a pinpoint of promise twinkling through the night.

Frank moved inside to blink the running lights that echoed as a chequerboard before Tom's eyes. The transfer boat responded.

'Get them ready, quick smart.'

Tom hauled the first sack across the deck, twenty-five kilograms of stolen crays, snapping tails, feelers poking through the open weave of hessian and snagging on his shirt. Frank dropped the fenders along the starboard side. The transfer boat was bearing down, the throaty rumble of its engine rollicking across the water. Frank and Tom heaved the sacks into position. His brother halted, his ear cocked, intuiting his surrounds in a way that brought to mind a creature on the prowl.

Frank's grunt exploded. 'Not our boat. Not our boat. Christ. Chuck 'em over.'

'What?'

'Police boat. Get 'em overboard. Now!'

Tom took the neck of the first bag. Frank grabbed the tails of hessian and together they hauled the sack up and over the gunnel, contents smashing on steel in a carnage of legs and shell. *Shplosh* into the ocean. Frank grabbed the second bag by the neck, Tom the tails, thousands of dollars' worth of live crayfish scuttled to the deep. Four, five, six bags—four more to go as the police boat bore down like a steam train, engines racing in a whine. A minute more and its spotlight would ensnare them in the act. Tom saw it in a wounded flash: Bluey MacIntyre had tipped the police. Seven bags, eight. Wet hessian snagged on something steel and tore. Tom pulled it free, hauled it up and got it to his chest, his shirt soaked through. Bluey making out that he and Frank were welcome to join the celebration when all the while it was an orchestrated plan to do them in. Counting on the fact they wouldn't come. Nine. That they'd use this night to do what they were best at. Pirating. Bluey, who'd be first on the radio to help out in a jam, had excised the Forrest brothers like a tumour. Tom burned with the sting of betrayal. With shame. Ten.

He checked the empty deck. He leaned over the side and stared down at blackness—God help them if one of those sacks chose to float. A fist of light punched his back. Tom shielded his eyes, willed the bags down and pictured them thudding to the bottom, hitting reef and seabed in an upwelling of sand. Some of the bags would break on impact, the walking wounded given a reprieve. For most there'd be no second chance, crays too tightly packed, the bags too well lashed for the fish to work their way out in time. Hunters and the hunted. First would be a swarm of sea lice, burrowing in through open weave and bodily orifices, bedding down beneath the membranes of shell to feast on living flesh. Octopus next, suctioning on and drilling carapace with their jackhammer beaks.

Tom faced an assault of light. He caught the silhouette of Frank crouched down out of sight, slinking back around the corner of the wheelhouse. Tom tried to slow his chest from panting. He was hot, cold, his crotch and underarms chilled with ocean water and clammy with panic. He stood caught in a blinding spear. Fox, feral cat, take your pick of vermin—he and Frank so ignoble a beast there'd be no qualm in finishing them off.

The police boat bumped against their fenders. Someone threw a line to Tom to secure, a second spotlight scouring the surface of the water. They knew. Everyone knew. The game, claimed Frank, was in not getting caught in the act.

The police would come aboard—Tom had seen it once before—they'd check Frank's papers, storm the two of them with questions, inspect the tanks and measure every borderline fish until they found one undersized to hang a fine on. The slap on Frank's hand would be sharp enough to sting but way too paltry to warrant the effort and expense of such a stake-out. Pissed-off cops. No payout for Frank. Smashed crayfish. Who knew the fate of the transfer boat? A night where nobody had won.

Frank emerged from the bunkhouse in his tracksuit and sheepskin boots, scratching his bum and squinting at the light. Turn it into a pantomime, Frank, rub it in their faces.

Frank put on his best indignant. 'You pricks got nothing better to do than hassle me and my deckie?'

The fisheries officer stepped aboard. 'Happy New Year to you, too, Mr Forrest.'

★

Her foot found a rung. The wind moaned like a ghost. Another step. She heard a ripping sound, felt the ladder part. She reeled, everything slow motion, she couldn't free her arms, her body on the brink of plunging. She woke to her whimpering, to a throng of plaintive cries. She was twisted in her sleeping bag, the tent fly flapping in the wind. The dream state faded. It wasn't night, wasn't day. Three fifty-five.

Mutton-birds coursed down the pathway in a stampede of fretful cries and scuffles of dust. They skittled like dragsters round the bend and burst across the helipad. The view from the tent was charcoal wings and spindly legs, ungainly webs of feet that ran across the grass. Clots of birds—twenty, thirty, forty at a time—jostled for space, urged on by the need for speed. Birds scooted past Steph's tent. An endless cluster, a rocking gait of waddle and scramble. Steph lay in her sleeping bag, close enough to smell the birds' musky odour, to watch their wings unfold, heads craned to the sky as if sheer will would send them airborne. She grimaced as the birds careened toward the fortress of bush. They were running out of launching pad. But these birds knew better, the breeze scooping them up at the last moment in a mad beating of wings, their feet grazing the bracken in riddance to earthly stricture.

All around her the sky was crowded with weightless acrobats, veering out to sea to forage for the day. The procession eased, the sky lightened to a new year. A new millennium. In dawn's prewash the crescent moon looked tissue thin. Rain clouds marched toward the east.

The air felt thick and damp with misty rain. A black thread of leech advanced across the ground sheet. Steph flicked it away. She was chilled to her core. She didn't want to walk back to the house. It was hours too early for the weather. She dressed and laced her boots, made her way down the track toward the Gulch, past branches of trees and thickets of bushes trilling with birdsong.

The track opened out to where she could see the old wooden sleepers of the haulage way. She looked down to the honeycombed foundations of a cement landing where fur seals stretched out. Gulls stood as a flock in a flutter of breeze, their beaks tucked beneath their wings. Beyond the protection of the Gulch the ocean was empty of boats. No Tom; Steph knew that now. Just ocean and white caps and a girl at the brink of an uncertain beginning, shivering against the whistling rise of wind.

21

They retrieved the pots they could get to, but the last, set amongst bull kelp at the base of the cliffs, even Frank wouldn't take the risk in weather as foul as this.

The heave of ocean spewed water and spray metres in the air. They motored through mounting seas around the headland to New Harbour. The engine smelled hot. Frank tucked the *Perlita Lee* in as far as he dared to ride out the storm without being washed up on rocks should her anchor chain snap. Only another fisherman would credit the worst storm of the season waiting for mid-summer. Even here, in relative shelter, the wind shrilled through the rigging and caught so hard against the wheelhouse that Tom expected the windows to stave in with each new squall.

By midnight the whine altered pitch—squalls upping seventy knots. Tom and Frank switched between standing at the galley bench, both fighting seasickness, to keeping watch through the wheelhouse windows, the spotlight angled on the anchor. They both wore full gear. They needed to be ready.

By two in the morning the anemometer stopped working and the squealing began. Frank estimated the wind had risen over eighty knots. Squalls funnelled around the headland and laid down the *Perlita Lee*. They had out a full length of chain, the motor idling, each watching the GPS, their eyes shifting to the bow. Each was waiting for the anchor to drag or the chain to part, for the untethered vessel to be wrecked against the shore.

With each new gust the pots tied down behind the wheelhouse lifted with the loosening ropes and hovered weightless above the deck. They crashed back down like a percussion of cymbals. Already, some would be smashed. Tom zipped his red float coat and clipped on a harness. He felt his gut retch—seasickness laced with fear. He swallowed it down.

He left the wheelhouse to be knocked from his feet by a slam of air. He stayed down on his knees and crawled toward the stern. There was something mildly comforting about staying low, hidden from view of the ocean. The boat jolted; Tom felt himself thrown against the boat's steel rib. Rain fell as a sheet, poured out of the scuppers, the noise of the storm tremendous. Tom wedged himself against the side, wiped water from his eyes. He forced himself to focus. Rivulets ran inside his collar and down his spine. He braced himself against the lurching of the boat. He managed to grab the end of rope, looped it through and yanked it hard. By the time he'd tied it fast, his fingers were wooden from cold. Tom swallowed ocean salt, tried to stem the rise of bile. He gagged and spat a mouthful, let the wind wipe it away. The boat lurched, yanking on its chain.

Frank waited until he got inside and slid the door shut. 'Good job, Tom. Well done.' His brother cranked the engine into forward and manoeuvred their position to push the *Perlita* up into the wind to ease pressure on the chain. They had nowhere else to go. Even if there were a better place, you'd smash a hole through the boat upping the anchor. Or risk your engine letting you down.

Tom and Frank worked together in the wheelhouse—there wasn't need for talk—Frank used all his skills to keep the boat from parting from its chain. The power of the storm made Tom and Frank equals, dependent on the boat, on luck, on how long such a force of nature could endure. Through those hours, Tom loved his brother. It felt like he and Frank were one. Tom lost track of time. It wasn't until the squalls and rain subsided that he looked out to see New Harbour edged by a silhouette of light. Come daylight they'd see that beach strewn with torn-off buoys and tea-tree ribs from shattered craypots. Tom could make out lines of surf. He pictured them flinging ashore their night-time offerings of sand-crusted weed, bowel-like loops of tangled line.

★

Tom spooned extra sugar in his morning tea to keep himself awake. Frank was having the first hour of shut-eye. Tom turned up the VHF at the sound of fishing talk: a swell of ten metres, two squalls peaking ninety knots.

Bluey MacIntyre: his voice sounded thin. Old. *She was a long night over this way. Eight pots lost. Below deck looks like a bomb's gone off. How'd you get on?*

Just. We're all fucking rooted. May as well pack up and go home for good, way I feel at the moment.

It wasn't the usual banter. Tom felt the same fragility, the aftermath of shock—the hollowness in knowing how close they'd all come. He listened in to Bluey. *You have to wonder how many chances you get before you run out of lives. I'm sixty-six next month. Must of used up my share.*

Few more left in you yet, Bluey.

You start thinking about what you're doing, what it's all for, the wife at home worried if you're all right every time she hears the forecast, the grand-kids you're missing out on seeing because you're always bloody working. It's not about the money any more. The money's not worth your life.

How about Julesie? He over your way?

★

You got on with it. Except for those who'd lost too many pots or damaged their boats, everyone went back to fishing. You had no choice. The same routine of baiting pots, shooting pots, pulling pots. Dawn, dusk, night.

Tom watched the rope curl around the turnstile. The pot banged against the boat with a shake-out of water. He dragged the pot across, pulled out two good sized crays. The third fish caught on the pot wire and when Tom yanked at it he felt its gristle tear. *Careless fuck*, Frank would say when he saw the leg hang limp. Tom placed it in the holding tank and walked the empty pot to the stack across the bow. Frank swung the boat alongside the next set of buoys. Tom threw the grappling hook, snagged the line. He hauled it in, wound the rope around the turnstile. His mind-numbing lot. Tom couldn't still his mind. It was like sea lice crawling inside his skull; his flesh jittery, innards peristaltic, ready to gag or shit or spew out a turmoil of contents. Maybe this was how it went, not depression but an unbearable soup of ferment that drove you to consider the unthinkable. Nah, he wasn't up for any of that. He stopped the winch and pulled out a cray: a storm survivor three legs short.

Late afternoon and the light felt off. It smelled off; an ammonia stink from strands of kelp torn loose in the storm and left to rot on the surface. The ocean had withdrawn, stretches of eerie calm interrupted by sets of long slow rollers that rose out of nowhere and lifted the boat. Fog drifted in and out and the damp air and physical effort made Tom rub at his face with his sleeve.

Beyond the diesel fumes and burring of the engine, the other-worldliness of the surrounds came from a yawning silence. It would forever be this cycle of storm and wind and calm, long after he and Frank were gone. Tom fancied the ocean murmuring: *Get out while you can, mate.* Out before your boat gets heaved on rocks, out before a rogue wave catches you unawares and flips you overboard. The standard joke amongst the fleet: always the deckie, never the skipper, that takes the wave.

Frank was back to harping about being one hand short, all the time Hab was having off when Frank hadn't had a decent break in years. 'His missus picks the busiest part of the season to squeeze out her sprog.' Frank with a mouthful of foulness you couldn't switch off. Tom emptied the final pot and stacked it at the front.

They were moving across the ocean, through patches of semi-clear then back into fog, veering off course to Bluey MacIntyre's pots. 'No.' Tom shook his head at Frank. He'd had enough of stealing.

I'm in charge Frank's face said. *On deck and get yourself ready.*

Frank pulled up the boat at Bluey's buoys. Tom threw out the grappling hook and missed. Frank cursed at him and brought the boat around again. Tom looked at the thing in his hands and couldn't recall its name. Grail ... Cradle. To do with struggle. Gravelling ... Grappling.

He felt it slip, he let it drop, the hook tumbling and bouncing against the lip of gunnel. It wasn't only his brain refusing to work, he was unable to physically move. Tom wondered if it was conceivable at nineteen to suffer a stroke—his limbs felt leaden. And there came Frank marching from the wheelhouse and shoving Tom off balance and hurling the hook and scooping up the buoy and cutting the pot free without even taking Bluey's catch. Just to make a point. Show Tom who was boss. The whole thing. He and Frank. Worthless pieces of waste.

'You're a girl.' Frank turned back inside.

They used the GPS to navigate through fog, back to New Harbour—the promise of another evening meal of defrosted chops and instant potato, peas from a tin, a nothingless night.

The days were long—dusk didn't fall until late. At times the fog lifted enough for Tom to sense that somewhere up there out of reach beckoned clear air and blue sky. Then it closed in and you couldn't see beyond the bow. Frank rolled out the anchor chain himself; he couldn't trust his halfwit brother to get it right.

The occasional set rolled in, then the ocean lay as lifeless and flat as a drowned man's lungs.

Both sat silent through dinner, just the gabble on the VHF sucking air from the galley, the sound of Frank chewing. Tom pushed his plate away, his food uneaten. Frank wiped his mouth on the tea towel and killed the VHF. 'What's this about?'

Tom shook his head. It was about every dead-end moment of his life. 'This,' he finally said.

'This, what?'

Tom stemmed the urge to shout at Frank. 'What we do. This.'

'Bluey?'

'Everything. Fishing, the boat, the crap—wrecking gear.' *You*, he almost added. 'I've had a gutful.'

'A gutful.' Frank scratched at his head. 'What are you now, Tom, getting on twenty? How much money you got stashed away since the boat?'

'It's about having a purpose. Something that counts.'

'You know what I was doing at nineteen? What my purpose was?'

Tom made a weary face. Frank reached across the table and grabbed the neck of his shirt. 'Don't gimme that attitude, you little prick.' Tom pulled free. 'Working my guts out, that's what I was doing. Two jobs, payments on Mum's house so the bank wouldn't take it; school uniforms and sports shoes and schoolbooks and Christmas and all your fucking birthdays. You think Mum did all that on her own?'

It always came to this. Tom stared at the chop bones chewed clean beside Frank's fist.

'She been putting ideas in your head?'

'Mum?'

He nodded out to sea. 'Her on Maatsuyker with the silver spoon up her bum. You think she'll hang around waiting for you when she gets back to Sydney? You're not even in her league.'

'This isn't about Stephanie.'

Frank laughed. 'She's just a root, Tom. Take what you can and move on.'

'This isn't who I want to be.'

Frank chucked the tea towel at the sink. 'Who are you, then? What could you do without someone to bail you out? Go back to uni? You didn't even last a semester. You're unskilled. You don't have a trade. You don't have anything. We've been through all this crap.'

'You're right,' he said to Frank. 'I'm unskilled. Maybe I don't know what I'm going to do. I know this much: when we get back to Hobart I'm getting off the boat. The day Hab comes back.'

Frank's eyes flickered. He looked pitiful.

'I won't leave you short,' Tom said.

'You serious?'

Tom felt sick, heroic, exalted. Alone. It was cutting your own lifeline before you knew if you could float.

'I've slaved my guts for you. Christ.' Frank's voice high and strange. 'You can go now.' He rose from the table. 'Get your shit together.'

'What?'

'I'm taking you in.'

'What are you on about?' Tom's own voice sounded odd.

But Frank was gone, at the dinghy hooking up the hoist with that same fixed expression Tom remembered from years ago when all he'd wanted was for Frank to stop the car at a roadhouse—Tom had had his own money, he'd just wanted something to eat. Back then Frank had thumped the steering wheel and shouted *For Christ sake*, and pulled the car over in the middle of the night to yank Tom from the seat and swing him out on the road like a bag of bait. *I've had a gutful of your whining.*

Tom gathered up socks, beanie, his Blundstones, he pulled his Gore-Tex jacket off the bulkhead and punched it in on top. He grabbed a box of matches, crammed the pockets of his backpack with chocolate bars and instant pastas from the cupboard. He picked up his toothbrush and put it back down. He wasn't good at thinking on the run. He grabbed his wallet and pocketknife from the hatch above his bunk.

The dinghy rose on the shoulders of a wave, another and another before the set rolled by. They crept through fog, the throttle of the outboard held back, Frank's eyes fixed ahead. His brother was giving Tom time to change his mind. For all their differences, they were enough the same that a conversation could be exchanged without a spoken word:

You can't do this, Frank. You can't just dump me. You know it isn't right.

Watch me.

The rocks of New Harbour bay materialised, a skirt of kelp, then slipped from view. Frank slowed the engine.

Give the word and we go back to the boat. We get on with the day and put this all behind us.

They were close. Tom still couldn't see the beach for fog but he heard water sucking back on sand. Frank swung the boat parallel to the shore and headed left, not this side but the far side of New River that split the beach in two.

You're a bastard to the finish, Frank.

'You won't be taking that.' Frank motioned to Tom's red float coat. 'Property of the boat.'

Tom wouldn't lower himself to object. He yanked at the dodgy zip to get it loose and placed the jacket on the seat. Through his flannel shirt the air felt sharp. The fishing knife, a gift inscribed to Tom from Frank, hung from Tom's belt inside its orange sheath. Stuff it. 'Take your knife back as well,' he said to Frank. 'Scratch out my name and cut your own miserable ropes.'

Mist opened to a stretch of sand, the bush behind the beach lustred with wet. Frank pushed the outboard into neutral and coasted in. They were fifteen, twenty metres from shore, the ocean side of the drop-off, the water still deep.

Tom hoisted his pack high on his shoulders, tightened the straps. He watched the water change colour, shallowing to frills.

Frank caught his eye. *You get out, Tom, you're no longer my brother.*
You watch me, Frank.

Tom kicked off his gumboots and stuffed his socks inside; he
wedged the boots beneath his arm. He hoicked his legs over the
side, felt the boat keel. He slid free, the shock of cold ripping
through denim to skin, water tipping his waist.

Tom gripped the gunnel of the boat to steady himself. He
wanted to say something big, but Frank had the outboard in reverse
and was turned the other way, backing over the drop-off to circle
out. Tom balanced his pack on his head, the wash from the dinghy
lapping cold against his chest.

He waded in toward the beach, moving slowly so as not to falter.
Tom stopped and turned seaward to look but the outline of the
dinghy had dissolved into fog. The atmosphere dampened the outboard's drone.

Tom rolled off sodden jeans and carried them up the beach to
where the sand felt fine and squeaky underfoot. Fog had swallowed
all but the beach line of ocean. He felt wet, shivery with cold, but he
sat on the sand in his underwear and shirt. He waited and looked out
at the fog. The call of gulls, dotterels running across the sand, a pair
of oystercatchers pecked amongst tossed weed. From somewhere
behind him the cawing of a currawong. No whirring of an outboard
engine returning to collect him. Soon it would be nightfall.

Tom rubbed his legs to keep his breathing steady but a sound
escaped his lungs. He couldn't hold it in. He was back on the side
of the road, a worthless nuisance kid, a set of tail-lights blurring in
the distance, tears spilling, a hank of snot hanging from his nose.
Tom huddled at the edge of nowhere, a long way from home.

22

A duet of oystercatchers tottered along the water's edge. Sunshine. Waterbirds. From the beach of New Harbour, Maatsuyker shimmered as a mirage, the island hovering above the ocean, the lighthouse distorted and magnified, each of the cottages a spangling fortress in early morning sun. Nothing seemed fixed to Tom. Even the rocks at the entrance to the harbour looked to float. He couldn't see around the corner to know if the *Perlita Lee* was still at anchor. Had Frank taken off before first light? Was he waiting until after breakfast? The tannin water of the river carved the beach in two and streamed out into ocean: Coca-Cola wavelets stretched along the shallows, capped with creaming foam. The bay looked like an ice-cream spider.

Tom had spent a cold fitful night, had downed a Mars Bar for his breakfast. Now in the sun he felt overcome with drowsiness. He lay down on his jacket on the beach, rested his arms across his eyes. He couldn't still his mind. *Don't waste more time,* the waves seemed to heckle upon the sand. *No one's coming back to get you.*

★

Tom left the beach and scrambled up the steep track, over logs sopping with moss, the morning brightness dimmed by a canopy of leaves that dripped continually. The rainforest smelled lemony, a soggy crush of humus underfoot. Over the brow of the hill, banksias opened out to scrubland, the track eased to undulations, marked by rusting star pickets staked into the high points. Tom could no longer hear the ocean, only whispers of breeze and the rabble of braided streams—golden syrup water across porcelain gravel plates.

Tom stopped to drink. The thrumming of the stream and the babble in his head was Frank; he tried to block it out. The stretches of bog weren't anywhere as bad as his brother claimed. The greater the distance Tom put between himself and the ocean the better he would feel.

He propelled himself on, marched through water and mud. With things set in motion he felt stronger and steady—even in gumboots he paced at a clip. He stopped to inspect a small burrowing crayfish resting in a puddle in the middle of the track—a creature miles from the ocean. It reared its claws when Tom knelt down to touch it.

Along the track he passed wombat droppings but no animals to be seen. There was hardly a bird—the only calls came from small knolls of trees. Away in the distance Tom saw where the skin of the bush had been scraped back to flesh: Melaleuca's airstrip. At the next hill he could make out the windsock, pieces of machinery.

Tom halted at the junction. To his left an easy walk to Melaleuca: sit it out in the hiker's hut and wait for a plane. To his right a track that wound for kilometres along the coast, through plains of button grass and over mountain ranges.

He knew what to do but still his feet refused, his boots defiant. Two hours to Melaleuca. By tonight he'd be home, showered, fed, asleep in a comfortable bed. Had he known it would come to this?

He'd been trying to silence Frank's abuse since leaving New Harbour. *Too much of a chicken shit; you'd never manage on your own.* Seven days, Frank had walked the South Coast Track. Maybe it was six. Tom couldn't remember how much food he had stuffed into his pack. He had no fuel. No stove. He hadn't proper footwear, only gumboots and his Blundstones. He had no tent or sleeping bag. Everything was stacked against him, but still he couldn't will himself to move.

Something deep spoke back. *You have a box of matches, spare socks, you've got your Gore-Tex jacket.* Tom could find a length of fishing line, limpets from the rocks for bait, sleep beside a roaring fire.

Tom-Tom, listen to yourself. Without the proper gear? Go left, you dickhead. Admit defeat.

He was every bit as strong as Frank. He was good at making do. Tom's heart drummed inside his chest. The South Coast Track: the tough way home. His feet took charge and strode out on a mission. He'd show his brother. He'd show them bloody all.

23

Steph rounded the corner of the house. Her mother was on the ladder, reaching up to clean the outside window. Dad was at the bottom. He looked upset. The phenomenal wind gusts from Monday's storm had smashed across the island: branches down, bits of gutter swinging loose, windows opaque with a new crust of salt. None of that mattered. Steph was bursting to share her news.

'Pass me up the other cloth, James.'

Dad's voice cracked. 'Months of loyal service when all he needs is some TLC. It isn't right.'

'Who needs TLC?' Steph said. Mum gave her a beseeching *don't go there* look.

Dad motioned to his lawn mower parked on the paddock. 'They're shipping Buster back to Hobart when we go. To use as parts. Sending a new one across.'

'Poor old Buster.' It was no good reminding her father that even a lawnmower with a name was an inanimate object. Wasn't a new mower a good thing? Buster was always having some kind of hissy fit, though her father believed they shared a mutual understanding. *I decide where we mow, Buster decides how.*

'I have an announcement,' Steph said.

Mum clasped the cloth. 'You're in.'

'They just phoned. ANU. The glass school. They offered me a place.' Steph's legs turned to jelly. She felt giddy. She rested against the wall of the house.

'I knew they would,' her mother said. 'This is your time, sweet-heart.'

'Well done, Steph,' Dad said wearily.

'Dad. It's good. Be happy for me.'

'It's tremendous news. Really. It's going to be a different world. Isn't it, Gretchen?'

'I was saving the last bottle of champagne,' her mother said. 'We'll have a toast tonight at dinner.' She inspected the window. 'At least you can see through it again.'

'Until the next onslaught,' her father grumbled, heading off to Buster with a jerry can of fuel. Since the storm there was nothing anyone could do or say to console him. After months of work Dad had finally finished clearing the drain: two and a half kilometres, all by hand. He'd walked Steph and Mum the length of the road to show it off. *Restored to its original tiptop condition.* The drain ran twice as deep. Water burbled clear along its course. Nothing to hinder the flow. *The whole way through. Right back to bedrock.* He'd looked eager for Mum's praise and she'd linked her arm through his in a way that seemed to Steph motherly and tender. Mum knew. *For Callam,* her mother said gently.

Dad patted her hand. *That's it.* He grew teary. *Our boy. We did a couple things right.*

We did a lot of things right.

If her brother was looking down, if he did have a say in what happened that night, it seemed all the more vicious. The storm uprooted trees, felled them across the road, stripped buds and new leaves from the island's two apple trees planted decades ago by the old light keepers. In a single night the sky dumped one hundred millimetres of rain across Maatsuyker Island. Steph understood now what it meant when people claimed they couldn't hear themselves think. The squeal of moving air, the roof alive with rain, and what sounded like ball bearings continuously fired at the windows—the storm had overwhelmed all conscious thought.

In the daylight her mother's crop of lettuces was splayed open, torn apart and splodged with dirt like war-field poppies. Tomato branches hung broken-boned and tattered; the stalks of spring onions and parsnips bowed down across a breadth of ruined garden bed, transformed into woven mats. Vines bearing snow peas were chewed into remnants and spat across the grass.

Every dip in the road dammed a reservoir of milky sludge. The immense run-off had unearthed soil, gushed down Maatsuyker's slopes as unstoppable as the rain that fed it, stormwater amassing mud and guano, leaves and twigs, mutton-bird eggs, carcasses of birds, old bottles and tins, an amputee doll, a baby's shoe, a vinyl tablecloth, a bicycle wheel—a delta of silt and debris that filled and clogged the drain. Dad had returned from surveying the carnage stooped and defeated.

The lighthouse still hadn't dried from the deluge that had found its way in through leaking windows and the perished seals of doors, each floor cascading like a fountain. Steph had quite enjoyed being head of a human chain gang: she and her parents emptying buckets and sloshing in gumboots through calf-deep water.

The clean-up from the storm melded into final preparations for next week's departure. Mum and Steph bleached and scrubbed walls free of mould; the weather office was ready with the next few months ruled up in the logbook, a graveyard of blowflies vacuumed to make way for a new generation. Mum re-cleaned windows. Dad mowed and brush cut. The big paddock was all that remained. Buster's last stand.

★

The lemony needles of paperbark had paled and desiccated, falling about Steph's hair and catching in her clothes as she ran from the end of the road back toward the lighthouse. She missed Tom. It made her sad, wishing for a second chance, wishing they could talk. He could have found a way to come for New Year's Eve. Or called her on the radio. He'd made it clear that it was finished. Over and out.

The tea-tree flowers were blown, daisies past their best. Maatsuyker was reverting to a camouflage of green. *This is your time*, Mum had said. All that rain and still the fronds of bracken had shrivelled and browned, their once slender stalks now thick and woody with age. Christmas bells had lost their puff and shine, slowly deflating, the petals bruised and tattered from the storm. Steph stopped at the creek that ran through a culvert beneath the road. She stopped here each time she passed, searching for a pair of robins that hadn't shown themselves for weeks. Had the storm claimed them too? A small plane droned low in the sky, following a triangle along the coast to South West Cape, across to Maatsuyker Island, back in toward the mainland. It wasn't the usual back and forth to Melaleuca, setting down hikers, flying back to Hobart. Three times Steph looked up and saw the plane cross overhead.

She climbed the lighthouse. She knew every footfall, the number of steps between floors; with eyes closed she could trace the filigree pattern of iron. She felt the chalky cold, the different textured surfaces—crumbling brick to her left, iron railing to the right. She tied the top door open. Above on the hill, Dad and Buster ploughed across the final strip of paddock, stemming the wild. By the time the new caretakers arrived they would be greeted to the illusion of civilised order, not the wild swathe of unkempt grass that Steph loved, swollen with seed heads, buttered with dandelions, liquid in the breeze.

Steph sat on the balcony, her back against the wall. She would have settled in this spot a hundred times, scanning the curvature of ocean, soaking up the shrieks of birds and bleating from the seals. A wash of umber edged the Mewstone; soon the evening sun would turn as coppery as flame.

She caught a distant ruffle on the water. A whale? She tracked the movement as the mass sharpened and expanded, galloping out toward the Mewstone. Steph called to her father but her voice was lost against Buster's; Dad looked hypnotised beneath his headphones. Steph took up binoculars, set her focus on the ocean. A great cavorting fleet of tails and fins carving through the silk. Dolphins. Adults and calves. Two hundred or more. Dad stopped and looked up to the lighthouse. Steph waved, she pointed. Something inside of her wanted to cry, *Callam's going past!* But Dad wasn't seeing. He wiped his brow with his handkerchief and resumed his procession with the lawnmower.

The mass moved away, a blur dissolving into ocean until the surface resettled to its evening sheen. Steph turned to Dad and Buster, their final march. Her father's arms were taut, keeping Buster true to course. Steph watched her father slow and pull back on the gear lever before the final downhill slope. The motor whirred, impatient to devour the last unkempt stretch. Dad stood still, searching out toward the Mewstone, at the sliding sun, his face bronzed by precious-metal light. He turned to look back over his shoulder. He pushed back his headphones, gave the lawnmower a nudge, released his grip. Buster inched forward alone, grazing on a final feed of grass. He gathered speed. Steph waited for her father to walk after him, haul him in like an unruly child. But Buster gained momentum, trundling down the hill. Steph tried to call but her breath caught in her chest. Buster continued on, closing the distance to the cliff, bouncing harder and heavier through a track of green like a runaway cart. He met the edge, his motor stuttering; he careened out over nothingness, free-wheeling and momentarily weightless. He dropped like a stone.

Steph listened for the crash, the moment of impact when Buster smacked into rock face or ocean, when he burst apart, dismantling himself into a catalogue of useful mower parts.

★

Mum popped the champagne. 'Congratulations.' A chink of glasses. Dad downed his in a mouthful. Between bursts of static, Tasmar Radio issued a special land forecast. *Expected overnight . . . to five degrees along the coastal region . . . and Melaleuca. Intermittent showers in the . . . increasing . . .* 'We can do without that noise for one night.' Mum turned off the radios. 'Finish the mowing?' She sat down at the table.

'All finished.' Her father shook the cask of red wine. 'Rotgut,' he said, and poured himself a giant glass.

Mum took the lid from the casserole dish. 'If we do get delayed by weather I can tell you now I'm not cleaning the windows a third time. And you shouldn't have to do any more mowing.'

'He won't have to worry about that,' Steph said knowingly, but Dad refused to meet her eye. Chickpea and tinned corn curry. Again. All that was left in the pantry was a seemingly bottomless bucket of pulses, uninspiring tins, rolled oats, salt, a last bag of flour.

'So,' Dad said. 'Canberra in February.'

'I'll be home for Easter. For holidays. I'll have my driver's licence.' Plans were darting through Steph's head. 'Do you think Gran will let me use her car? She might. It depends. She's funny about her car.' She couldn't stop talking. She was giddy on champagne. In a year she'd be eighteen. In ten more days they'd be back in Sydney. Her mind halted. 'What about you, Dad?'

'Dad's been talking to some of his colleagues,' her mother said. 'There's an opening coming up.'

'Your own show?' It had always been her father's dream.

'In a manner of speaking.' Her father sounded wry. 'Producer for one of the Western Australian regional channels.'

The other side of the continent. Steph sat up. 'Why not New South Wales?'

'It's a case of what's available.'

Mum went to gather up the plates. 'You don't want more, Steph?'

'What about us? What about home?'

'That's all weeks away,' Mum said airily.

'Have they offered you the job?' Steph said to Dad.

'Pretty much. Steph . . .'

Mum shot him a look.

'She's an adult, Gretchen.' His teeth were stained claret red. He sounded tipsy. Mum took the plates away. Steph could see she was annoyed. 'When we get back, I'll shift over to the west, Mum will follow—we'll put the house on the market.'

Her mother came back with a tea towel in her hand. 'James, this isn't how we planned. Not tonight.'

Steph looked from one to the other. 'Why? Why now?'

Mum sat down. 'We wanted to make sure you'd be settled before we made any final decisions.'

Steph felt stunned. 'Do I get a say?'

Her father looked to her mother. 'None of us do,' he said. 'It comes down to financial necessity. Simple as that.'

'And you'll be in Canberra, staying at Gran's,' Mum said. 'You'll just be coming home to somewhere new.'

'The other side of the country?'

The phone rang in the kitchen. Dad looked at the time. 'Perhaps it's Gran.' He closed the door behind him.

Steph slumped in her chair.

Her mother said firmly, 'It's a new beginning for all of us, Steph. Not just you.'

Steph pulled back tears. 'Callam and I grew up in that house.'

Mum looked past Steph. Mutton-birds streamed past the glass. 'Will it change how we feel? Will we remember him any less?' She sounded like she was trying to convince them both.

'Why can't Dad have his old job back?'

'You know why.' Mum looked sad, exasperated. 'He can't go back on air.'

'He can have the injections. You'll see. I'll talk to him.'

'Coming to terms with his voice has been harder on Dad than either of us can imagine. It's his decision to start a new job. I want to support him, Steph. I want you to support him.'

The kitchen door opened. Dad returned to the table.

'Who was it?' Mum said.

'The police.' Her father's voice was a whisper. He looked ashen. He sat at the table, took Steph's hands in his. He was frightening her. 'A fisherman found a dinghy overturned. From Tom's brother's boat.'

Steph pulled free. She couldn't make sense of what he was saying. 'Where's their big boat?'

'Anchored near New Harbour. There was no one on it. They found the dinghy over by some cliffs, a kilometre away.'

Steph prickled. 'Where's Tom?'

Her father shook his head. 'The police are looking. The fishermen. Everyone's searching.'

Mum stood up. 'What do they want us to do?'

'Keep the radios on in case we hear anything. They want us to carry the handheld when we're away from the house. They've had a plane looking, a land crew are over there searching the coast. If the weather holds they're sending down a helicopter first thing in the morning.'

The water would be freezing. 'What about Frank?'

Dad rubbed at his face. 'They don't know if one or both of them were in the dinghy. The prop of the outboard was fouled with rope.' He spoke slowly. 'They found Tom's knife caught up in it. They think someone had been trying to cut it loose.'

'That poor woman,' Mum said.

Dad looked bewildered. 'Who?'

'Tom's mother.'

Dad's voice was sharp. 'I'm sure Tom's father is just as distressed. About both of his sons.'

Stephanie slumped at their exchange, at the echoes of Callam. A girl's pain: what did it count? 'Tom doesn't have a father,' she told them. 'He died when Tom was born.' Steph switched on the radios, filled the room with static.

24

Tom's first failing: the box of waterproof matches he'd grabbed from the boat without checking the contents. A sorry collection of spent discards and unused matches that refused to strike no matter how carefully he tried. Waterproof? Fireproof.

The first part of the South Coast Track meandered through coastal scrub and along sandy beaches. Tom found a discarded spaghetti tin purged by the ocean, its razor-edged lid prised back. He could use it as a tinderbox. He peeled the slimy label to dry inside his pocket.

At dusk Tom stopped at a clearing within earshot of hikers' laughter and the crackle of their campfire. He huddled in his jacket until the night was quiet.

When he circled their campsite he saw in himself a scavenger whose need for warmth and nourishment had no room for shame or indecisiveness. He shovelled dying coals from their fire into the spaghetti tin, imagining what he might say if they woke and caught him in the act. He could put on an indignant face the way Frank would have done to tell them that fires were prohibited along the South Coast Track. He sneaked around the tents like an opportunistic quoll, surveyed a rubbish bag pegged to a line, whose contents amounted to three used tea bags, plastic wrap, a tampon wrapped in a wadding of toilet paper that Tom tore off for later use.

Tom would no sooner seek help than admit to anyone his gnawing hunger. He shuddered at the prospect of being the object of people's pity, or kindness, or one pushed inside the sleeve of the other. He returned to his scratching. To sleep. To manage alone.

*

Beyond the prospect of warmth from the embers he carried in the tinderbox, Tom's world grew sodden and reduced. Even as he walked he shivered. His padded jacket, the only thing that kept his body warm and dry, dripped rain onto his jeans until the denim dragged and chafed. The elastic of his underwear drew bands around his legs.

The track veered inland from the coast. He trudged through depressions turned to waterholes, across submerged boardwalks. Where the boards ended the track turned into wading pools of mud. Tom sank to his thighs. Twice he fished through the slurry to retrieve his gumboot. His clothes smelled fetid. His toes rubbed against the rubber of the boots. His soles and the pads of his toes grew loose and puckered from being perpetually wet. Hikers took on this walk with the same optimism as those bygone Diggers who'd signed up for war on the promise of adventure. Bog-ridden battlefields. Mud and filth. Trench foot. Facing death day after day. If they could manage all that, he could do this.

The track was clear of hikers and Tom was grateful not to raise attention. People would think he was an idiot in jeans and gumboots, nothing but a ratty daypack. No proper shelter in which to retreat and wait for the rain to stop. Nowhere was completely dry. Tom's only barrier was a torn sheet of plastic he'd foraged from a shoreline that reeked of rotted kelp.

He carried the tinderbox, fed the coals with tiny twigs he hus-banded along the way. Tonight he'd make a roaring fire, cook himself a good hot meal.

Rain dripped from his cap. He passed through threads of mist. He couldn't see three hundred metres along the track. Tom grew to resent this sodden walk in the same way he resented his brother as the cause of all his hardship.

★

The track crossed Louisa River. The course of water that flowed to Louisa Bay where he and Stephanie had spent a day. This leg of the river was a long way inland. A sign warned against crossing when the water was high and fast-flowing. A safety rope was strapped from a tree trunk on Tom's side of the river over to the other side. The water rushed, dark and deep. He would camp on this side, wait until morning to cross. He laid out the plastic sheet. What if the river was still rising? By morning it could be too high to cross. He remembered a saying: rivers that rise fast fall fast. But Tom didn't have the luxury of waiting for the water to reach its peak and then subside. He hadn't enough food to last.

He wrung out his socks, folded his gumboots, stuffed all his worldly goods inside his pack. The tinderbox he packed in a sock and wedged at the top.

The skin of Tom's feet looked sallow through the liquid brown. The iciness of water stole his breath. He gripped the rope and pulled himself across. His arms felt on fire with the effort. He couldn't touch the bottom.

The night was still and cold. Mist hung in branches. Mosquitoes were fierce. Tom camped on the edge of Louisa River beneath a grove of towering trees. He scoured the ground and scrambled beneath bushes for anything flammable and dry. He trembled with the cold. The spaghetti label still felt slimy and damp. Tom fished inside the other pockets of his jacket and felt a boyish thrill to find a piece of yellow paper—graph paper—folded around a dried sprig of tea-tree. Necessity was all he saw. He shook out the small cluster of coals—the tin felt barely warm and he fretted that he'd left the coals too long. He tore the yellow paper into strips and latticed them on top. He hunched over the coals to shield them from rain. He used his breath—not so hard as to dislodge the paper—halting at the first spindle of smoke. Tom watched the paper curl and singe and the instant it flared he was ready with the sprig of tea-tree that ignited in an instant—an ember glow that quickly died away. It reminded him of sprinkling dried herbs into sauce, but this was a pinching of tea-tree litter from the lining of his pocket. His eyes smarted with smoke. He waited. It caught. He laid upon the top a single leaf and listened to it spit against the moisture and then catch light. Another leaf. Another. Tom felt a tiny halo of warmth. He added a handful of twigs and felt his chest tighten when the wet bark doused the flame. He stopped his mind imagining a night as cold as this, a person wet and hungry without shelter and warmth.

He closed his eyes to the spindly trail of smoke. Tom conjured an image of heat. He created a cloudless blue sky and a day thick with sunshine. When this was over he'd go some place warm, escape this state as his father had once done. But Tom wouldn't come back.

He pictured his father at his age in a rundown jeep, in baggy shorts and rolled-up sleeves, roaming Australia's north-west, working town to town. The flame took. Tom snapped a branch into smaller pieces, fed it bit by bit. Lee Forrest, a good week's work—labourer, cattle hand, a two-month stint of mining, cash in hand. His farewell gift from Wittenoom a shard of blue asbestos embedded in his lung that wouldn't show itself for twenty years.

Tom corralled the small fire with a wooden border of larger pieces that he didn't dare add before they'd dried. His stomach gurgled with hunger. Steam rose from the knees of his jeans. The rain had stopped. Tom warmed his hands. He laid out the contents of his backpack on the plastic sheet: four cup-a-soups, two meals of pasta with creamy bacon sauce (*8 minutes to cook*), the smashed remains of a packet of Iced VoVo biscuits, a half-tube of sweetened condensed milk. His second big mistake: the two Mars Bars he'd scoffed down before he'd understood the need to ration. He pulled out the three misshapen tea bags he'd stolen from the hikers' rubbish bag. With the tannin colour of the water, Tom couldn't tell if they had any actual tea left in them. It was more the ritual. A keeping-up of domesticity.

Tom rinsed the tinderbox in the river—it nearly slipped from his hand in the rush of freezing water. He used his pocketknife to pry the lid enough that it would fully bend back without snapping off. He half-filled the tin with water, careful not to let it topple when he set it down among the bed of coals. He added wood to the fire, fashioned a branch into a stirrer.

His father's decline was a slow-cooker measure. Even through his final year, his mother spoke about him bouncing Frank, scarlet-faced and breathless, Frank too old to settle on his father's knee, too young to understand he should. The start of spring, the fruit trees outside his parents' bedroom swelling with new buds—*Lee's favourite time of year; he really loved his garden*. Tom saw his father look through the bedroom window at a world burgeoning with life as his own wound down. Tom arriving in the world three days before his father left it. *Miracle baby*, Frank called his conception in a way that made his mother blush. *The old man still had it in him.* Tom was special to his mother. No one acknowledged it out loud but Tom knew and Frank felt it too. The naming of the boat, all the things his brother paid for. If Frank couldn't be first in their mother's affections he'd be first in both their debt.

Tom extracted every chip of dried pasta from the sachet to add to boiling water. He licked the foil lining. His stomach cramped with emptiness.

What Mum earned barely made the payments on the house. His mother and Frank had excavated the entire back lawn and turned it into growing beds. *Weekends I'd be digging chook poo into the compost while Mum delivered eggs.* What she hadn't fed the three of them she'd bartered at the shops or sold to help with bills. *You were too young to remember, Tom-Tom. She worked all the time. It was killing her. It wasn't fair on you.*

Tom remembered scraps of it. Frank arguing with Mum, his brother hellbent on leaving school early to assume their father's role. Frank talked to a man who talked to a man who gave him a tryout as deckhand on his cray boat. Then Frank was gone for weeks and the house turned still and dank, as if Frank had yanked away its energy and scattered it across the ocean in foaming streaks of white. Inside, the house smelled of stale lavender and a feeling that only now, sitting alone by a campfire beneath these trees, Tom identified as loneliness. On their mother's bedside table sat a cut-crystal bowl, her rosary beads as polished as river stones; above on the wall a miniature Jesus with womanly hands nailed to the cross. Growing up, those trickles of painted blood had made Tom dig his thumb into his palm and hold his breath until he launched outside and filled his lungs with citrus air. The garden an ocean of blossom, rainbows of poppy and freesia, the air tangy with lemon and the sleepy drone of bees.

He used the stirrer as a scoop and made himself eat slowly. He savoured every noodle, every lip-smacking mouthful of cheesy bacon sauce. He'd normally scoff at packet mix—Frank called him a food snob—Tom usually hated creamy sauces and would turn up his nose at dehydrated chips of bacon that were probably synthetic. But this, Tom relished the salty aftertaste, the coating of fat on his lips—this was superior to any gourmet dish he could name. Pasta with creamy bacon sauce was possibly the finest meal Tom Forrest had eaten in his life or would ever eat again. He felt a giddy rush. He used his finger to gather the last smears of sauce from the sides and bottom of the tin. He licked his fingers with squelching noises that could have been Frank chewing bones. He felt ravenous. Tom contemplated cooking up the second packet—he needed all the energy he could muster to cross the Ironbound Ranges. He went to tear open the second packet. Reason kicked in. He was days from finishing the track at Cockle Creek. He barely had food for two. He squeezed condensed milk onto his finger—a five-cent's worth to cut the longing for savoury and line his mouth with decadence. He turned his back to the fire to dry the seat of his jeans. The contrast of air felt chill and damp. The night sky was moonless. The river rushed by. Small glints in the dark reflected from the fire—eyes watching through the night. Tom was cut off from the ocean.

His brother would be out there now, scouring it of life while others in the fleet did the decent thing. Tom couldn't dwell on Frank. He had to push his focus on tomorrow. He had to be up and on the track first thing. He had to make it up and over the Ironbound Ranges in daylight.

★

Tom woke to pain. His hip and shoulder ached, his right arm and leg had numbed to pins and needles, impressed too long upon mortuary cold ground. His neck cricked. He stretched his limbs. Grey sky. Rain. His face and hands itched with bites. Tom slapped at a mosquito hovering about his hair. He'd overslept.

He picked at the remaining coals: not a skerrick of warmth. His hands and fingernails looked as grimy as charcoal. With a surge of resentment he pictured Stephanie, her model family, her friends, her clean-cut life. He needed to walk, take his mind off food, off pain, off feeling miserable and cold and sorry for himself. A mosquito whined around his ear. 'Fuck you.' He smacked his head and left Louisa River Camp.

The boarded walk through bushland gave way to open muddy slopes, the wind bitter and strengthening along the rising trail. Tom buttoned the collar of his shirt, drew his jacket hood tight. The low clouds that rolled in belonged to a different season's sky, laden and silvered with hail or snow. The high steps that cut into the moun-tainside made his muscles burn. Tom was out of shape for climbing, too long confined to the deck of a boat. He lost concentration and tripped over his gumboots, fell hard on his elbow and arm. He picked himself up. He was high enough now that he could look out to the ocean, down to Louisa Bay that appeared as a gleaming crescent. It glittered like shiny bullion, then dulled to tired metal beneath a new front of cloud. Out to sea a blur of islands: Maat-suyker and the Witches.

Tom stopped to catch his breath at the first bluff, felt sweat chill on his skin. The rock was marbled white and earthy pink, jagged formations with overhangs and shallow caves. He looked to the ascent before him, looked back down from where he'd come. In different circumstances he'd have savoured the view, sat with his lunch to take in the coastline. He'd been on the track for hours. He felt winded and weak. By his calculations he should by now have reached the top if he was going to make it down the other side before nightfall. He pulled down his beanie to cover his ears, found his spare socks and pulled them on as gloves. He trudged to the next bluff, stopped to catch his breath, made himself push on. He reached a saddle that was level with the cloud; to his left, wind whooshed up the wall of rock, bellows of air that Tom reached out to touch. He crossed an open plain and made his way over lengths of bleached boardwalk, rough-hewn planks so old they'd paled and split. Was this the top? The vegetation had turned alpine, cushion plants, pandani trees, highland heath stunted from a mean wind that shunted Tom forward. It pummelled his back and slapped his sides and punched him off the track into the scrub. He got himself up, trudged on. The second his focus wavered he stumbled, dizzy and light-headed when he righted himself. The rock, the vegetation: everything worn down by weather. The wind was determined to do the same to him. He felt conspicuous, an alien being, as out of place as that burrowing crayfish he'd seen in the middle of a track. He couldn't remember back to where that was. His teeth chattered. Even with his jacket zipped and his hood drawn tight, he couldn't stop the shaking. The afternoon light slumped in a portent of rain. Clouds split open but it was sleet that the wind gathered and hurled like lead shot against his back. Tom scrambled for shelter; he could see nothing higher than his knees. He left the track for a narrow trail that led uphill to a knoll—was that the top?—he found a meagre overhang and squeezed his body beneath. He wrapped the plastic sheet around his legs and hunkered down, his head on the crook of his arm. The sky turned jackhammer, the noise deafening. Bullets of hail pummelled the rock and ricocheted from the ground.

The hail finally eased enough for Tom to start again, the atmosphere replaced by scurries of snow that melted on contact with his clothes. Tom could no longer see the ocean. The air felt frigid, visibility reduced. Five-forty in the afternoon. It had taken him since morning to reach this point. Three hours of decent light remaining. The eastern side of the mountains should have afforded some protection but Tom crossed another open plain where the wind screamed more fiercely than before. He braced himself and waited for a lull. He took a run of steps then braced himself against the next blast, his plastic tarp flapping from his pack like shredded bits of sail.

He reached the shelter of taller foliage and felt the angle of the track descend. Tom paused at a clearing of marsupial grass set amongst the trees, saw a planked bridge above a creek. A campground?

Scrub thickened to rainforest; the light grew dim. Tom tried to set a faster pace but run-off cascaded down the track, every handhold and foothold wet and slippery, the mud the worst so far. The track was criss-crossed with slimy tree roots ready to catch his leg or trip him up and catapult him forward. Long deep steps jarred Tom's body—steps that would be hard in good weather, in decent light. His pace slowed. His limbs felt weak and shaky. His feet slipped from under him and he landed hard and slid. He gathered himself together, surveyed the torn pocket of his jacket. Thirty metres on he fell again, his foot catching on a tree root and twisting back his leg. If he sprained or broke something, what use would he be? Rain fell constantly. Tom was too tired to think. He remembered a clearing. His head felt foggy. A campsite, a planked bridge above a creek. Was that today? He had to go back up, he had to shelter for the night. He'd cook something hot, warm himself by the fire. *No coals, Tom-Tom.* He couldn't right his brain, the bush around him skewed and crooked.

★

Tom sat upright, the plastic sheet wrapped around him. For some reason his trembling had eased. He didn't feel warm. He didn't feel cold. The night sky had cleared to pockets of cloud that raced across the moon. There was an urgency about this evening. He should be some place else but Tom couldn't think where. He felt the urge to laugh out loud. Everything but Tom was in a hurry. He thought he heard a woman laugh but when he listened there was nothing but trills of wind singing through the branches. He gathered up a leaf, held it by its stem. The shape looked identical to the feather of a bird. Why, when leaves don't fly? Tom couldn't fathom it and then the thought slipped away. The full moon flooded the slopes below, the sand of some faraway beach glittered like a necklace of shells. The moon blackened the valleys and made the ridges stand in bas-relief. Tom felt himself rocking. Was he aboard the boat? Was he in his bunk? Where was he? Grass, the sound of rushing water: a small rough campsite. His left side felt bruised and inflamed from where he'd fallen on the track. His shoulder felt as painful as a tattooist's needle. He ought to heat a stick in fire and sear the skin, eliminate his brother from his life. Would it blister? Would it hurt? The conversation in his head made no sense at all.

Far away a beam of light blinked. He was staring across the water; he was looking at Maatsuyker. Tom cast about. He stared down at his feet. He was standing on an edge of rock. Below him, nothing. He felt wind against his face but had no sense of cold. His gumboots were gone, only filthy socks with a hole in each big toe. His mother would darn those, if she were here. He should bathe, rinse his socks, renew himself. He could hear a creek. *Come back*, it beckoned. He looked around, searching for the sound. The small light blinked in an oceanic rhythm. He felt a little seasick. 'Frank.' Tom heard himself say the word aloud.

Tom sat. He took off his jacket, unbuttoned his shirt, extracted his arm and pushed up the sleeve of his T-shirt. Frankie anchored on his shoulder. An ugly tainted layer. Tom opened his pocketknife and scraped the blade across his shoulder. Blood beaded like dew drops on a leaf. *Stop*, the same voice called. *Tom, don't*. A small figure walked barefoot from the bush: a girl, a shaven head. She knelt beside him, rocking on her haunches and looking out across the slopes. She sounded out the rhythm of the lighthouse. Her breath whistled with the wind. She was sequined with scraps of twig and broken leaves. Tom brushed her with his fingers and she leaned her head against his hand. Her eyes were amber, forlorn as a seal pup's. She motioned that he pack away his knife. Then she helped ease his arm inside his sleeve. She was small. Her skin was the tannin of the darkest creek, glaucous as if she'd smeared herself with ointment. He studied her fingernails and toenails, thick and nacreous as seashells, chromed as the moon. She crouched behind him, knees either side. She levered her arms beneath his, grunting as she strained to pull his body up to standing. He didn't have the energy to help. Really, he didn't want to move. 'Just leave it.' He listened to her small pitiful grunts that sounded out her struggle. He felt annoyed. 'What does it matter?' The small girl put her hand in his and drew him back along the ridge.

25

Steph's last days on Maatsuyker Island drifted without will or direction, her mind and body dislocated. After each weather observation she returned and sat beside the VHF, her tea growing cold as she listened for news of the *Perlita Lee* and scrawled in her art pad. When Steph thought about time, how it could thrust you forward or drag you back, these months on the island had been a continual push and pull. Now time ebbed. The clock on the wall seemed never to change, every minute a drag through the waiting, the ticks clicking through the air and grabbing at her skin, leaving her clammy and jittery and unable to settle. Her stomach felt empty but she had no appetite for food. She was unable to think beyond the room or concentrate on packing, on anything connected with the future. There was no future: no more Maatsuyker, their home in Sydney to be sold off and with it everything of Steph and Callam. Her parents would begin a new life without her, far away. Everything precious was being taken from her. Tom. She couldn't think of him without weeping. She couldn't not think of him. Her whole body, the inside of her skull, seemed bruised and tender to the touch. She was held in limbo, waiting for news. For something to happen. Anything. She kept a vigil by the radio.

Rain fell in a monotonous cycle: angled sheets easing off to drizzle, escalating to a downpour. Each morning and afternoon a currawong appeared on the aerial, forlorn beneath its water-beaded coat. Her world and everything within it became a mindless pattern. Even Tasmar Radio's unanswered calls came in a futile cycle. *Crew members from the Perlita Lee. Crew members from the Perlita Lee. Crew members from the Perlita Lee. Do you receive?* Each call made her pen bleed into paper.

'It's midnight. Try and get some sleep,' her mother said as she did each night. Her parents looked haggard with worry, as much for her wellbeing as for Tom and Frank's. Steph dreaded sleep, she had no control over fitful dreams of being stranded on the lighthouse roof, about to fall, her voiceless call for help, *Tom, it's Steph. It's Stephanie. Do you receive?*

From the house the search helicopter appeared as an indiscriminate dot trapped in the interstice between an angry ocean and a glowering press of cloud. It stayed low because the weather was so bad. The land party confined their search to South West Cape, the taper of coast so rough it was rarely visited by recreational hikers. Steph pictured the party wet and clambering through scratchy bush, scouring every lonely cove and beach. At night she heard their weary voices on the radio. Fishing boats set aside their work to look—Bluey MacIntyre, others in the fleet. At the end of the week the sea search was scaled back, the hope of anyone surviving in cold water extinguished, though no one said those words aloud. Gradually fishing boats resumed their work. Hikers turned for home. Everything but the inside of this house seemed reset to normal.

Steph woke in the morning to static and the sharpness of a voice: *All Ships. All Ships. All Ships. Calling for any boats in the vicinity of Telopea Point who can assist the police to monitor an item.* Item? They'd found the dinghy a week ago.

A gruff reply. *This is* Sea Echo *again. We're still waiting for someone to show up at Telopea. How long before the police boat gets here?* Steph sensed the man's distress. She'd missed hearing something vital.

ETA midday. Tasmar Radio spoke evenly: *Sir, are you in a position to remain and assist?*

Steph felt the weight of the fisherman's reluctance. A spear of indignation moved through her. What would it cost him to help?

All right, he finally said. You could tell he didn't want to.

Sir, can you give me the coordinates?

Mate, it's a body, not a craypot. What's left of it.

Steph rose. She knocked her tin of pastels from the table; coloured sticks rolled across the carpet, beneath the chairs. Her limbs turned wooden. She studied the map on the wall. She couldn't focus properly. Telopea: halfway between the tip of South West Cape and New Harbour Point where the dinghy had been found. The ocean had dragged a body all that way. Steph halted. She tuned back in. *Red float coat*, the fisherman said. *It's got the kid's name on it.*

Tom.

★

By evening the room was filled with radio talk, a medley of fishermen's voices.

You couldn't tell from looking at it, Dave said. *Something had a meal. Crayfish finally got their own back.*

Steph grimaced. She thought she might throw up.

Poor bastard.

Poor Dave.

Someone else broke in. *Do they know which one?*

Younger brother, they think. Had a tatt on his shoulder. They picked up his jacket nearby.

He had no shirt on?

Dunno the full story. Might have got knocked about against the rocks. Police have taken him back up to Hobart for identification. Dave's on his way up. Coroner's problem now.

Fuckin 'ell, who'd study dead people for a living?

Have they told the mother?

You think they'll find Frank?

I hope to Christ he doesn't turn up in one of my pots.

Someone scoffed. Steph winced before the words were out. *Free bait.*

Ease up. Bluey MacIntyre. *Frank gave me enough grief to send me to my grave. But no one deserves what those two got. Especially young Tom.*

There but for the grace of God . . . said someone in a pious tone.

God, fate, call it what you like, Bluey said. *Perhaps just being at the wrong place at the wrong bloody time. Jeannie'll visit the mother this afternoon. See what can be done.*

I'll get Ange to call a few of the girls, check on Frank's missus.

She'd know there isn't a hope in hell. Still, until they find something.

Bluey, what's the story with the boat?

Everything in order. Sitting on its anchor. Police took it up to Hobart.

Any idea what happened?

Dunno. Retrieving a pot. Checking something. We'll never know.

You think his missus'll put the boat on the market?

Give her till the day after the funeral, that one.

Wouldn't be a bad buy, right price.

You're a callous prick, Wattsie.

I'm just saying . . .

★

Steph walked the road to the garage, found two offcuts of tin. She used a punch to form the names. *James & Gretchen West, Stephanie West, Sept 1999–Jan 2000*. She started on the second. *Tom Forrest*. Every hole a puncturing of sorrow. No dates; she wanted something timeless. Not *Fisherman*. Tom was of the land. Tom was being outside and sniffing leaves and growing vegetables and cooking homemade pizzas on a fire. Tom was digging wild potatoes. She took up the punch. *Friend of Maatsuyker Island*.

She tried to imagine talking to Tessa and Sammie. Telling them of Tom. But this wasn't some holiday fling to be chalked up and gossiped over. There was no neutral space, no words for someone as indefinable as Tom. They were two people who'd shared something special and real. People fell in love at seventeen. Steph tried to muster energy for her old life, her friends. It would be easier to say nothing. She studied the plaque. She ran her fingers over the name punched in the tin. *Tom Forrest*. Who hadn't come back at New Year's to see her. Who hadn't called her on the radio. Perhaps it hadn't meant as much to him.

On the final afternoon her parents joined her and they hiked to the Light Keepers Tree, her mother constantly checking for leeches. Her father nailed the family plaque to the crowded trunk. 'Chosen somewhere for Tom?' he said quietly.

'Next to ours.'

The plaques were in place. No one spoke. It was just breeze through the crowns of trees, birds flitting and calling, the lushness of tree ferns, the dampness of shadows. Her mother knelt beside her father's plaque. 'Oh, Dad.' She rubbed at the graffiti scrawled across his name. 'That's a disgusting thing to do to someone's plaque.' She turned to Steph with new understanding. 'You knew.'

Steph nodded.

'You wanted to protect me.'

'I can make a new one. We have time.'

Her mother studied the plaque. 'No,' she said. 'This was our plaque. I know he was a good man. That's all that counts.'

★

The helicopter took off to the south. It flew them low around the Needles for a final view. Steph felt heady and strange, separate from her body. She wanted to go. She wanted to stay. Over the lighthouse whose prisms and windows threw back a piercing blue sky. The breath held in her chest felt tight enough to break her ribs. Leaving. Forever. Part of Steph was still down there, winding through the tea-tree, along the length of road. They flew over the cottage and weather station where the new caretakers stood with arms stretched toward the sky, their new fluoro jackets shining. Steph wanted to cry out, have them turn the helicopter around. She wanted to be set down among the green so she could race to the lighthouse—*her* lighthouse—and clamber up the stairs and look out across the ocean.

The island looked slender, velvet folds of green draped across its spine. Steph breathed. The cliffs dropped away to a ruffle of white, a chain of buoys; a small fleet of working boats sitting at rest. Across the way South West Cape tapered long and low. Land ended and the ocean ran on, assuaged and still.

26

Tom woke. His shoulder throbbed. He forced himself to swallow—
his mouth, the inside of his throat gravel dry. His head pounded.
His eyes adjusted to the dark. Was he dead? He squeezed sleep from
his eyes. He tried to rearrange the smell permeating his senses into
something recognisable. He sensed more than saw the shaft of light—
above him? behind?—a mosaic of leaves thrown like a hologram
upon a textured wall. The ground beneath him crunched like corn-
flakes. His stomach belched; even his bile tasted of starvation. Tom
raised himself to sitting and knocked his head hard. He shrank back
down, rubbed his wounded skull. His fingertips felt slimy: he licked
the taste of blood. Where was he? He ran his hand across a ceiling of
rock that rained grit upon his face and hair. He rubbed his watering
eyes, blinked, blew a string of gritty snot. He waited for the stinging
of his eyes to pass. He sniffed his finger. Old—no, ancient traces of
charcoal, tree sap. Others had used this place; he felt it with certainty. At the far corner of his memory he caught an image of a girl
with shaven hair, smeared with white, her heels cracked beyond their
years. *Tom*, she whispered—then she was gone. Tom drew his legs up
to his chest. His gumboots were gone. His pack. He searched around,
fingered at the texture thick and warm upon the ground. A downy
quilt of leaves, dried moss that crackled and crumbled on touch.

Tom turned. He winced. The glare. He raised his hand to shield his eyes. His focus sharpened. Sunlight. An opening. Daytime. Alive. Entombed inside a shallow cave.

He pushed feet first, angled his shoulders to slide through the curved exit of rock. From the outside you'd never know the cave was here. The air felt sharp. Tom's eyes smarted with light; the day felt onion raw. He stumbled through scrub—his soles tender and tingling, his stockinged feet not lifting properly though his eyes registered the obstacles. He reached an outcrop of rock and stopped to rest. His breath was laboured, his fingers coated in soot, a smear of blood. He followed the line of the ridge until he found the track. He panted with each step, light-headed with weakness. A saddle. An open plain. The air was still. He stopped at a planked bridge and a creek that he'd seen once before. Nothing made sense. Behind his eyes the light throbbed. He knelt at the water and slurped handfuls of liquid so icy it hurt to swallow. Tom drank and drank but no amount of liquid quenched his thirst. His belly felt distended—a waterlogged buoy that gurgled and sloshed with each intake of air. He thought he might be sick. He moved back up the track, out into the open. He found a slab of rock. Sun warmed his back, heat spread through his clothes. He didn't feel inclined to move. He imagined himself as a lizard basking in the sun. He needed sleep. He wanted food and heat. He curled foetal on the rock, his hands tucked beneath his groin, his back angled to the sun.

★

Mighty. Hey. Mighty. Wakie, wakie. A voice nudged through Tom's dream clips of boat, lighthouse, his mother knitting, Stephanie's laugh, a small dark girl. Mighty?

Tom opened his eyes. Sunlight. A glare of sky. A silhouette hovering. 'Frank?'

'You scared me there. Thought you were a goner.'

'Frank?'

William, the voice might have said, though it sounded more like *Willem*. 'Let's get you upright, get a brew into you. Where's your pack, boy? Your boots? You whacked your head?'

Tom watched wordlessly as the old man pulled a thermos from his pack and poured tea in jerky movements. As much steaming liquid spilled on the dirt as in the cup. 'Which way you headed, mighty?' *Matey*, he was saying with an accent. He sounded European.

Tom slurped warm sweet tea. He downed the remainder. 'Cockle Creek. Hobart.'

'Have some of this.' William handed him a plastic bag with chocolate, nuts, a rainbow of dried fruit and boiled lollies. The lining of Tom's mouth drooled in anticipation. 'At least you're a few days ahead of the swarm. The rain's held them back. The old days you wouldn't see a soul along this track.'

Tom's senses drowned in an aroma of flavours. He had to stop himself from shovelling chocolate and lollies and dried fruit into his mouth all at once. William watched. His eyes shifted to Tom's socks, his mud-caked jeans. Tom bit into a licorice coin. His face puckered.

'Double salt.' William spilled more tea. 'Acquired taste.' The old man's shake was fierce.

'You walked the track before?' Tom said. His voice sounded brittle, like old netting you could put your hand through.

'I come down this way in summer. Look on it as a bit of a pilgrimage.'

Tom spoke with his mouth full. 'Why?'

'Part of it's the challenge. The weather. The mud. The first time you do it you swear you'll never step foot on it again. Half an hour later you're not so sure.' William gestured to the path. 'This is the crux of it. Down the other side you've got a lovely stretch of coast ahead of you. That's the reward.'

Tom looked past the creek, past the outcrop of rocks, the ridge, the world shifting back in kilter. This landscape, full of primal wilderness. He surveyed the coast. The ocean flooded back to him and with it a disdain for Frank, a poison that burned beneath the shoulder of his sleeve, the pulse of it white hot. 'My things.' Tom looked back up the track. 'They must be at the camp.'

William motioned. 'Other way, mighty. High Camp's further along, beside the stream.'

'The cave, I meant.'

'Cave?'

Tom pointed to a knoll.

William looked at him dubiously. 'You been on the silly weed?'

'No.'

'No caves around here, not that I know of. Caves back down along the coast that the old people used. Before us whities.'

None of it made sense to Tom.

'Never mind,' said William. 'We'll find your gear. Another cuppa first. Take your time. Always time for a brew.'

*

'Travelling light,' William said when they found Tom's pack lying on grass at High Camp. No gumboots to be found. Tom pulled his Blundstones from his pack, thankful he hadn't turfed them along the way. His daypack and torn plastic sheet looked comical beside William's oversized pack. The old man must be hauling thirty kilos on his back. 'What happened to you?' William said.

'Nothing.'

'They've been searching for some fellas out at South West Cape. A group came through as I was leaving Melaleuca.'

'Nothing to do with me.' There was no getting out of it. 'I had a falling-out. Decided to walk home on my own.'

'Without gear? How much food are you carrying?'

Tom felt himself withdraw. 'I'll be all right.'

'You didn't look too all right when I found you.'

His tone reminded Tom of Frank. 'When I get down to the coast I'll find some fishing line, catch a feed. I know better than most what to do.'

'Mighty, it's none of my beeswax but anyone can see that at this present point in time you're in a tight spot. Walk down together, share a meal or two. No questions asked. Scout's honour.' The old man's fingers knocked a shaky salute against the brim of his hat.

William was offering help, offering his food to Tom, a stranger. Tom hadn't even shared his name. Resistance rippled through him. 'Why would you do that? I could be some bad arse for all you know.'

'Right thing to do. Simple as that.'

Frank would shun William's offer of help. Even Tom's mother, though not as bluntly. In Tom's family it always came down to saving face: they were above anybody's *charity*. Frank measured his worth—his whole identity—with self-sufficiency, an ability to provide. Yet, in that, something was awry. In an odd inverted way, between the bullying and boasting, through every reminder of benevolence, it felt to Tom that Frank was seeking his regard; that

Tom's approval mattered in the same way that an insistent sinner needs redemption from the Church.

'The river crossing down at Prion,' William went on. 'Those two dinghies weigh a ton on your lonesome.' As if to convince Tom, the older man held out trembling hands. 'You never imagine the day will come when you can't manage on your own.'

Something melted in Tom. He put his hand in William's. 'Name's Tom. I hope I can keep up with you.' That brought a smile.

★

The wind had dropped away, the morning sun intense. Tom was far taller than William but each step down the Ironbounds measured a full stride. At times Tom stepped in a slurry of mud and found a firm footing. As often he sank past his knees in a quagmire. His feet slid inside his short leather boots. His toenails felt soft and bruised, the pads of his toes were chafing into blisters. Tom felt weak and feverish, his limbs, his insides, everything aflame. He stopped to catch his breath, wipe his cuff across his brow. 'Good old Tassie,' William said. 'Frostbite for breakfast, burned to toast by lunch.'

Tom let his mind wander. He tripped on a root and fell hard. Pain tore through his arm. His shoulder throbbed. He picked himself up. 'That's usually my trick.' William offered Tom one of his hiking sticks. Tom shook his head. Let William think he was proud. The old man was nuggety and tough, never mind his two strapped knees. He wasn't quick but each step was efficient—he kept at it, unfazed by mud and effort. The Master of Zen.

The rainforest petered out to sclerophyll, to tall leatherwoods and myrtle, to brilliant coloured fungi, to an understorey of cutting grass too sharp to grab for support. Its long reeds lay as a woven mat across the track, catching one boot, tripping the other. The change in vegetation did little to reduce the mud. They sank to their knees, slogged over exposed roots, crawled beneath fallen trees. Tom's jeans and William's bare legs looked moulded from clay. Tom forced himself to concentrate, to place his feet with intent, to block out boredom and weariness and a pulsing heat that pinched his shoulder with the slightest motion of his arm.

A change in the air. A whiff of kelp. They were nearing ocean. He caught a glimpse of blue. The path flattened, dense forest and tall trees thinned to stands of tea-tree, to open coastal scrub. To a view across the ocean.

William halted, he cocked his ear. 'Chopper.' He searched the sky.

Tom saw a gleam of red, sun sparking off glass as the machine tooled its way from the direction of Maatsuyker, a load slung beneath. His skin smarted. Stephanie. They were leaving for home. A well of emotions threatened to spill. For weeks Tom had steeled himself, afraid he might unravel if he let thoughts of her slide in. It was the same mind game he used to get through weeks of working on the boat. But seeing Stephanie leave, the thought of Maatsuyker without her, was a severing of magnitude. Everything he knew of Stephanie, of the part of himself that had finally found the nerve to stand up to his brother, stemmed from that small island and this stretch of coast. Another wash of feelings overcame him. His steps slowed. Until a week ago this whole corner of coast was Tom's patch. By leaving the boat he'd relinquished his rights to a place, to knowledge and skill. He couldn't now define himself as the deckie who could trace every cove and bay in his mind, who knew the cliffs and beaches better than Frank, who recognised a storm sky and loved the night sky, who'd served an apprenticeship long enough to anticipate the changes in dawn and evening light across the seasons. This sudden pining; a pathetic kind of grief that made no sense to Tom.

The rotor noise grew urgent, the helicopter passed by close enough that he could see floats strapped to skids, the sling load crammed with plastic boxes. Tom faced the ocean, imagining Stephanie belonging to another place, continuing on, her future mapped out along self-assured lines of navigation. He begrudged her that certainty, her privileged position in life. When she flew over she might look down upon this coast, upon tannin streams and button grass plains, see scraggy stands of paperbark and tea-tree and leatherwoods. She might register this craggy mountain range, make out stretches of the track. She'd see the crowns of trees but she wouldn't see the twisted trunks or fallen logs cling-wrapped in moss, moist in the chill of the shadows. She wouldn't sense Tom, or comprehend his turmoil.

The noise of the helicopter receded. Native bees droned. Tom filled his mind with the taste of Leatherwood honey, inextricably linked to his sense of home. He felt a stab of irritation at William standing, waiting, at this meaningless track that people chose to be a slave to. Pilgrimage? Get a life, man. Tom cast him a glare. He scratched at beads of sweat running down his neck, felt a gnawing ache and put it down to hunger. From his backpack he fished the bag of chocolate William had given him. He didn't care that he'd broken his resolve to save what was left. He filled his mouth, caught sight of William looking on, the old man's silence at odds with the jerk of his limbs, the tremor of his hands. His whole body seemed to quiver, as if there was nothing of weight to keep him grounded. William was past it. A good gust could take him out. He must be pushing seventy.

'If you've got something to say, say it,' Tom said. William gave a wounded blink. Listen to yourself, Tom, as foul-mouthed as your brother. 'Sorry,' Tom muttered. 'I'm over mud.' William nodded to move on.

They reached Little Deadman's Bay. Tom couldn't see Maatsuyker. The track had taken on a different feel. He was spent. 'Aren't we stopping here?'

'Next beach along. Forty minutes tops,' William claimed. It took Tom, trailing behind, one hour and a half.

The beach squeaked. The crust of sand broke beneath his weight. Tom pulled off his boots and revelled in scuffing barefoot through dry sand after kilometres of mud. Tannin water from a creek poured down to the ocean in shallow rivulets—burnt toffee, the creek bed like patterned curls of salted butter. The creek was flanked by cobbled stones warmed from the sun. Tom drank from the creek, wet his hair and face. He adjusted to this landlocked point of view. He gazed out to a sparkly ocean frilled with wavelets that rolled across the shallows. The only way Tom knew the coastline was from the vantage of the boat.

William was naked, his torso and buttocks stark against his skinny suntanned legs. He waded thigh deep in water, *oohing* and *aahing* at the cold, splashing water at his armpits like a wren in a birdbath. Tom felt heady and odd. His flannel shirt was soaked with sweat. He thought he might throw up. He removed his beanie, unbuttoned his shirt, pulled off his T-shirt. The ocean felt sharp, the wet sand soothing on his feet. Tom's jeans dragged off when he dived. He gathered them up, dunked them in the ocean, squeezed mud from the denim and plunged them through water with the vigour his mother used to prewash his fishing clothes. The water clouded with clay and mud. Tom felt dizzy with the effort. His shoulder was on fire. He threw his jeans up on the rocks and dived in again, savouring the cold, the feel of water on his face and streaming through his hair. He surfaced near William.

Tom followed the old man's gaze to the skin of his shoulder. A ragged flap, the skin pulled loose; Tom's tattoo was open flesh, raw and inflamed.

'Did someone put a knife to you?' William was serious.

'I don't know.' Tom didn't. William looked at him awry. 'It's the truth, man. All I remember is weird stuff, dreams.'

William inspected it. 'It's infected. No wonder you're out of sorts. We need to get it seen to. Give it a good rinse in the salt water.'

William spread the contents of his first-aid kit across the rocks, an array of bandages and strips, a worn foil sachet of capsules. 'Get a couple of these into you. Past their best but better than a kick in the pants.'

Antibiotics. Tom grinned. William had as much gear in his backpack as you'd find in the galley cupboard. 'Good thing I met a scout.'

'The way you look after yourself, you're more in need of an undertaker.'

Tom's laugh was cut short by the swab of antiseptic that William manically dabbed with his jittery hand. Tom clenched against the pain. 'Hey, William?'

'Hey, what.'

'Promise me you don't have a suture kit you're planning on using.'

'Don't tempt me, boy.'

★

They lit a fire on the beach. Tom proudly produced his last packet of pasta with creamy bacon sauce. 'Tried this?' William hadn't. 'Mate, you haven't lived.'

William didn't look convinced. 'What happened to the mighty hunter? I was led to believe we'd be tucking into fresh seafood.'

'All in good time.'

William laid out the makings for risotto. Tom could barely wait for it to cook. William added stock powder and dried herbs to rice, garlic flakes and onion, dried tomatoes, a medley of coloured curls and chips that drew up water and blossomed into zucchini, mushroom, red and green capsicum.

The rainbow colour of the vegetables took Tom back to crunching on peas snapped from the vine, to carrot thinnings smudged with dirt, to running the big sprinkler in summer when he got home from school, spraying the greens for slugs and bugs. His mother still brewed an eye-smarting concoction from onion, garlic, chilli and soap flakes. When Tom was small it hadn't been called organic: she'd made her own pesticide because they couldn't afford the bought stuff.

William shaved off slices of cheese and served himself a modest bowlful. He handed Tom the pot.

'You get enough?' Tom said.

'I'm watching my figure.'

It tasted wondrous. Better than wondrous. 'You dried all this stuff?'

'And grew a fair deal of it. The gardening keeps me out of mischief.' William finished his meal with a mug of tea and a cocktail of tablets. 'Don't grow old, Tom.'

Tom couldn't think of a better way to ask: 'What's the matter with you?'

'Parkinson's, I'm told.'

A *sorry* sounded lame. Tom settled on a nod.

'You stick around long enough, something's going to grab you,' William said. He tipped his mug of tea at Tom. 'I wish at your age I'd known the things I know now.'

'What would you have done different?'

'Taken a few more opportunities when they presented them-selves. Pursued a certain girl when I still had the chance.'

'Never too late, they say.'

'On the contrary.' William didn't expand.

William lived on the Mid North Coast of New South Wales, had a stake in a community garden with others in his neighbourhood. The old man could put away his share of tea. He poured himself another cup and took a big slurp. 'Haah.' Tom held an image of his mother's swollen feet rising like scones above the rim of her work shoes. She'd give that same satisfying *Haah* when she prised them loose and stepped into worn-down slippers. She'd take off her glasses and rub her eyes and listen to Tom's prattle as she chopped the things for dinner. She'd suddenly halt. *Will you look at you?* She'd rinse her hands and wipe them down her apron—the touch of damp fingers combing his stick-ing-up hair as dreamy as their aroma of freshly chopped onion. *Have you done your homework, Tom?* He'd sag. He'd bump against her. The best kind of homework was gathering vegetable seeds, spreading them out like seashells, drying and storing them for next year.

The night was still, the sky enormous. A great swathe of con-stellations glittered through the sky, brighter, stronger as darkness deepened, like someone winding up the volume. The fire felt warm. Tom's belly was taut with food. He'd taken paracetamol and the pain of his shoulder had eased. He blinked to keep awake.

'How about we stay put tomorrow?' William said. 'I don't know about you but I could do with a bit of resting up.'

It was for Tom's benefit, not William's. 'I haven't much food to share,' Tom said. 'A few Iced Vo Vos.'

'I expect we'll make do,' William said. His mother's favourite saying. A rest day sounded good to Tom. 'Who's Frank?'

'Why?'

'Up there,' William nodded to the mountain. 'In your delirium you called me Frank.'

'I wasn't delirious.'

'Might, you were off your bloody rocker.'

'That's a matter of opinion.'

'It's a matter of fact. You were in a bad way. Thought you were either dead or on the drugs.'

'Nah.' The ocean hummed. Breeze flounced the skirts of she-oaks. 'Frank's my brother. I work—used to work—on his cray boat.'

'You liked the fishing?'

'Not much.'

'One door closes,' William said.

'It's the door that needs to open that's my problem.'

'Come up our way. Mountains, rivers, beaches, farms. Best climate in Australia.'

'Any mud up your way?'

William smiled. 'Streets are sprinkled with fairy dust. Tracks are lined with gold.'

'You always been there?'

'Came out from Holland in the seventies. Settled near Laurieton. Nice a place as you could find.'

William reminded Tom of Peter Cundall from the TV gardening show—the old codger's enthusiasm fuelling his own, gardening tips so timely that each Sunday night of Tom's growing up, Peter Cundall spoke directly to him. Tom had gone to see him at the Hobart Show. He'd waited until all the other people had left before stepping forward to ask his questions. The old man had given Tom his first proper lesson in soil. He'd spoken to Tom man-to-man. The right kind of compost, the right pH, adding nitrogen, rotating crops, drainage and aeration. Tom did have skills. He did have things to offer.

'You have family?' William said. 'Other than Frank?'

'Just Mum.' Tom gathered the dinner things to rinse in the stream. 'Hey, William?'

'Hey, what.'

'I owe you.'

'You owe me nothing, boy-o. One day you do the same for some other scruff.'

*

The flotsam along the shoreline changed from buoys and fishing rope to domestic rubbish, the remains of a television, beer bottles, toys, unpaired rubber thongs. They passed two groups of hikers walking east to west, raucous with chatter, their gear pristine.

Wilderness eased to an undulating track free of mud, to mountain peppers laden with red berries, to sheltered beaches and sweeping views, to long easy stretches of boardwalk. Tom walked without having to study every step; he looked around thinking, *This is good*, a wedge-tailed eagle circled above.

An old misshapen conifer, wooden shacks, a white painted bridge across a lazy creek. The South Coast Track ended and a gravel road began.

Tom used the public toilet and caught sight of his wild bushman reflection in the mirror. Hardened and coarse: he bore the look of Frank. His stubble had grown to a charcoal beard, his hair looked grimy. He felt older, hollow-eyed, his underarms stank. He'd lost a heap of weight; William had given him a length of cord to thread through his belt loops to stop his jeans sliding to his ankles.

William had the bus timetable already figured out. When Tom followed him onto the coach and pulled out a wallet stuffed with notes, he felt the driver's wariness. He paid his fare to Hobart and watched the way the driver counted out the change with nervous concentration. None of the easy friendliness he afforded others on the coach.

Tom stretched along the back seats and slept the three hours into town. He woke groggy as the coach jerked forward, down Macquarie Street then around to the Davey Street lights. He propped himself to sitting at the sight of Constitution Dock, the *Perlita Lee* tied up in her usual berth. He didn't want to think about his brother, he didn't want to arrive home to Frank perched at the kitchen table with a stubby in his hand. He thought about his mother. She'd be worried sick.

He and William walked from the bus stop, Tom weary and stiff-kneed, the old man's hiking sticks still tapping out their rhythmic gait. Tom waited until William's airport bus arrived, until the hiss of doors forged a clasp of hands and a clumsy hug. There was something tender and sad in William's palm pressed against the glass as his bus drew away.

Tom walked home from town. He breathed out when he rounded the corner to their street: Frank's car wasn't in the driveway. Tom unlocked the gate—his mother should have been home by now. Tom paced down the side of the house. He stopped at the garden—everything looked parched. He marched to the glass-house. Withered blooms, sagged leaves; his mother's African Violets, her pride and glory, dead.

Tom unlocked the kitchen door. He called. He checked his mother's room. Rosary beads, potpourri, Jesus in His rightful place, melting from His cross. The house smelled old and sad.

Tom opened the bread bin and took out the few stale crusts. Lift your game, Mother. He inspected the fridge—the shelves almost bare. She must have snagged a cheap flight and gone to Melbourne to his aunt's. Tom sniffed the carton of milk and drank what was left. He slathered peanut butter on the crusts and layered them with cheese. He opened the cupboard and pulled down a packet of biscotti. He changed his mind and imagined takeaway chicken and salted chips—a whole barbecued chicken—Tom could taste it. He threw his clothes in the laundry tub and ran the shower. The odd sensation of warm running water, the concentrated scent of soap. He found the nailbrush and cleaned a layer of grime from his hands and feet. He wrapped himself in a towel, trimmed his beard then shaved.

He found his mother's first-aid Tupperware box and returned to the mirror to re-dress his wound. All that remained of Frank was a single fluke of anchor. His shoulder no longer looked angry and inflamed. When Tom pressed on the wound it throbbed— something tender that if knocked or scraped could flare again—but somewhere on the track a healing had begun, though such an injury would never be expunged. Tom knew that for the remainder of his life a puckered scar, a broken anchor, would brand his skin to remind him of his choices: Tom Forrest would never let himself be entwined with anyone again.

Tom dressed in shorts, a lightweight shirt to conceal the wound from his mother. The lemony smell of laundered clothes, the precision of her ironing. He walked into the living room. He halted. Cards on the mantlepiece as cluttered as Christmas. Cards with doves, butterflies, crosses and angels, mournful cards with lilies and roses. Blood drained from Tom's brain. *In Deepest Sympathy. Blessed Are They That Mourn. In Remembrance. At This Sad Time.*

Tom's hands shook when he opened a card. *Your beloved sons.* He couldn't focus. He fumbled. He opened another. *Our deepest condolences on the tragic loss of Tom and Frank—Jeannie and John (Bluey) MacIntyre.* Part of him wanted to laugh. Tom felt dizzy. Nothing made sense. He sat on the coffee table his mother forbade him from sitting on because it wouldn't take his weight. A search party, William had said. South West Cape. *South West Cape.* Where Frank had dumped him. The click of the gate, familiar steps along the path. Tom tried to stand but his legs wouldn't hold him. The back door, plastic shopping bags set upon the kitchen table. 'Mum?' Tom's voice warbled. He sounded like a boy.

She didn't answer. Everything went still. He heard the ragged whimper, he heard her take a step. Tom breathed the tainted air that was different from the old stale grief that infiltrated curtains and elevated his father's recliner to a monument of loss. Tom's mind flicked to an image of Frank. He saw his brother turn the dinghy and not look back to Tom abandoned on New Harbour's shore. The dinghy motoring out through fog, the sight and sound swallowed by the pall. No bearings. No GPS. No line of sight to lead his brother safely to the larger boat.

The lounge room, the walls and curtains, a knitted sleeve unravelled from its needle—everything began to spin. Tom blinked, he pulled air into his lungs but he couldn't slow the vortex in his head. His mother filled the doorway, her body stooped. She looked so frail. Her pale face a crumpling of fear, a giddy disbelief. He saw her close her eyes in communion with her Saviour. Then she gazed upon Tom with a look that caused his eyes to swim. Something precious and maternal, something raw and shameful passed between his mother and himself: if a lifetime of abiding faith had earned the chance for even one son to be spared, she had prayed that it be him.

27

2015

The slide toward emptiness is upon her. 'When will I see you?' Steph asks, watching him dress. She knows this part, is attuned to the note that creeps into her voice, a neediness that has her lover pause. He studies her with measured patience. Acknowledgment, perhaps, of this small breach between them, the inevitable chafing that comes from talk about the future. In the lamplight his gaze seems parental. 'I'll call you.' He leans down to the bed to kiss her, traces his thumb in a downward arc across her lips. 'Soon.'

Her. Him. Two years of this. Does it even rate as love?

Steph hears the back door close, hears the key he keeps catch the lock. He parks in the darkened lane behind her condo. She waits for the engine to thrum. In minutes he'll be merging with evening traffic on St Francis Drive. One more commuter heading home from Santa Fe.

If he ever were to leave his wife, would Steph become the woman waiting?

It isn't meant to feel this way.

★

Steph paces the glass studio, her senses jarred by reflective noise as she readies herself for work. On these public open days the feel of the hot shop transforms from a foundry to a performance. She's never been much good at theatre.

Bryn, on the other hand, gathers up the microphone with gusto, looks to Steph to check that she's ready. Bryn loves to talk. He knows glass. He is her oldest friend in Santa Fe.

He roves the floor, Mister Affable chatting easily with art students and customers who visit the studio gallery and stay awhile to watch the co-op of glass artists at work. Five years they've been managing this studio.

Her two assistants wear standard foundry attire: leather boots and shorts, faded black tops. With their tattoos and piercings they remind Steph of theatre nurse goths, anticipating the right instrument to pass her, where on the floor to stand without getting in her way. They may still be students but they're on the same journey as she is, all apprentices to glass.

Voices fall away. Bryn introduces Steph and her team. 'Hot glass,' she hears him say, 'or glassblowing, as we often call it, is something of a misnomer for a craft in which very little actual blowing is required.'

The piece she's working on glimmers beside the bench, her drawing plans on show. The glass canes she's made are lined together like a tin of colour pencils. People remark on her oceanic greens and blues—a hemisphere removed from New Mexico's high-altitude juniper and pinyon, from arroyos milky with snowmelt.

Bryn calls this unfinished piece her fisherwoman's basket. Its woven twists and curves remind Steph of tea-tree: an arbor, a craypot. Oceans removed from this landlocked state.

Bryn runs through the hot shop tools: jacks, pincers, diamond shears. He could be pointing out the workings of a forge. There's nothing delicate or glamorous in the furnaces around her, in working in heat, her hands perpetually rough, stripes of skin scarred from burns.

'This steel bench we call the marver, used for rolling the molten glass across its surface. The marver, rather than the blowpipe, is the precision tool for shaping glass. The top tool in the hot shop and by far the most difficult to master.'

The other piece Steph has on display belies the effort and hours she's put into it: hand-ground prisms and orbits that fit one into the other, planetary beneath the spotlight. She turns to begin, but something in the way those prisms spear light through the dark grips her mind and curls her in a wave. She's sixteen again, standing beside the lighthouse lens, her whole life ahead of her. Island and ocean still pour through her glass.

She takes a heated pipe and rests it on the furnace sill. Steadily, she rotates the pipe and angles it down. 'Stephanie starts by gathering a measure of molten glass onto the end of the blowpipe. This we call the gather.'

The liquid is as blinding as staring at the sun. Steph calculates the distance through dead reckoning and feel—a dipper touching honey. Down too far and the weight of molten glass will sit too high, lopsided on the pipe. Heat scorches her fingers. She wheels the pipe once, twice, through a viscous sea of glass. She tilts the far end of the pipe to raise it free. She turns the molten liquid bulbous at its end until spindly trails of glass fall free. 'A step that may look quick and effortless but one that takes years to perfect.' Steph paces carefully toward the bench, skirts around the bucket of pipes, her blowpipe angled to the floor. She readies to work the shape, craving the moment when consciousness of self will slide away and she can lose herself to glass.

Bryn walks before the crowd. A spruiker, holding out a laden tray for all to see and touch. 'Silica—this simple mineral we know of as sand—is the main ingredient of glass. We use a recipe of silica and chemical ingredients melted in the furnace at 2150° Fahrenheit. Add a mineral such as cobalt and what do we get? That's right: blue glass. Gold? Red. Those of us in the hot shop still think of it as a special kind of alchemy.'

A magic that has held Steph in its grip since her student days.

These hours in the hot shop are all she can name to fill this strange persistent emptiness. At home on her own she'll picture waking up with someone, walking together across the crowded plaza. In two years they've never sat together at a cafe over Sunday breakfast. Never held hands in public. Good things. Normal things. Not this worn-out swaddling of privacy she wraps around her— she's lost track of the excuses she spins to friends.

'Making a glass sculpture in the hot shop requires a team effort,' Bryn says to the onlookers. 'It takes trust, time and expertise.' Steph pays her assistants a nod. Without their help, none of this would happen.

Concentrate, Steph. Focus. The times she's been seared when her thoughts dared to flutter.

She turns the blowpipe in a steady motion, the gather rolling away across the marver, back, away. She hears Bryn, the musicality of his voice, she thinks about the email waiting in her inbox. A residency. Her old school in Canberra. An invitation she ought to seize. Her mistake was in telling Bryn when they opened up this morning.

Name one thing to stop you, Bryn had snapped at her reluctance. It was out of character to see him exasperated with her. He shook his head at her silence. *But what would I know? Why would you ever want to take up a marvellous opportunity when here in Santa Fe you have a douche bag with a wife and kid to make you perpetually anxious and unhappy?*

She'd felt her face flame. All this time he knew?

Steph lifts the pipe, turns to make her way toward the glory hole. She catches Bryn—a flicker in his gaze she can't interpret—and feels a sting that curves toward shame. She steps awkwardly, stumbles, she fails to right herself. *Oof.* Hard on a buttock amid a clatter of steel, a wounded cry from onlookers. The foundry spins. She feels drunk. What is wrong with her?

Her assistants retrieve the pipe, the ruined molten glob. Bryn helps her to her feet. 'Are you hurt? What happened?'

She grips his hand. She doesn't want to let it go. She's exhausted by the woman she's become.

28

Slack-jawed, panting, a life-loving grin that defines a border collie. Tom cups his dog's chin and she blinks at him adoringly. 'Zulu.' He only has to say her name; she knows whose dog she is. He scratches her neck, her body propped against his legs. She balances on three paws, her fourth scratching stupidly at air, sharp little nails catching her side. 'Shall we get the paper? Shall we, girl?'

Tom loves the dawn. He savours this break-of-day ritual, he and Zulu pacing the gravel road—two kilometres from house to gate and back—a pot of coffee and breakfast on his deck with the paper and the call of birds.

The road from his house looks down upon the elbow of the Camden River. A kayak rests on the old wooden landing, beside it a new outdoor setting and matching tan brolly—a step up from the old hand-me-down from William. Not tan, Tom corrects himself. *Latte*, he's informed.

Over the second rise a row of greenhouses and sheds set back from the road, vast to his own eye, a new dam semi-excavated. He's done with seventy-hour weeks and years of scraping by, selling organic vegetables from a tin shed at his front gate, giving boxfuls away when all the time the reward stared him in the eye, finally coming into focus during a community college business course that his neighbour Annie coerced him into. It was such basic common sense it embarrasses Tom to think he'd been ready to wipe his hands and walk away. Value-adding. A mountain of overripe, blemished and unsold produce that no longer had to be discarded. Relish and chutney recipes, old-fashioned *Tomato Sauce for Bottling* that he found in a Country Women's cookbook. Basic recipes, good unto themselves but that lacked an edge until sharpened with his own mix of herbs and spices: home-ground ras el hanout, baharat, an array of Moroccan and Turkish flavours from plants he'd learned to grow and harvest.

If Tom had known back then all there was to see and learn, he could have made better choices. Frank might still be alive. Habib, unemployed, had urged him to leave, to find something new. He had helped Tom get Frank's boat ready for sale, the boat keys handed to a sister-in-law Tom would never see again. Leave? He'd been trapped in no-man's-land. For weeks he drifted without purpose or direction, trying to make sense of what had happened, reliving endless runs of the lead-up to his brother's death. Tom's head had pounded. He woke in the night heaving for air, wondering if this was his punishment. He couldn't even face his mother's garden. Finally he summoned the gumption to go down to the wharf. He hadn't seen Bluey MacIntyre or others from the fleet since the funeral. All those fishermen Frank had been a prick to there at the church paying their respects.

Bluey looked at the testimonial Tom had written: *A1 Deck Hand.* He gave Tom a look he couldn't translate. *I'm not here for me,* Tom quickened to say. *I don't want anything for myself.*

Bluey read over it, said he'd speak with the others. Between them they'd find something for Hab. *You?* Bluey looked at him hard. *What's your next move?*

The way Bluey said it brought to mind a chess game, the big pieces sweeping across the board, the pawns shuffling one square at a time, next to no use but not to be trusted. He needed Bluey to know he had a clear path. A future of his making. The words spewed out from nowhere. *I head off in a few weeks. Fresh start. Do it properly this time,* he added.

That same inexplicable look. Then a broad freckled hand. *I wish you well, young fella.* A handshake that gripped like a pardon.

That it could be that swift and easy.

Twenty years old with a backpack, a Lonely Planet guide and a taped-together map, through Spain to Tangier, Algiers, Tunisia, back up to Turkey, staying longer than intended with Habib's cousins and cousins of cousins, sharing wash days and meals and special ceremonies. Tom hadn't understood most of what they'd said, yet somehow the important stuff had been imparted. Tom soaked up hours in the kitchen with Habib's elderly *Nine* who punched out flat bread at an impossible rate, who whacked his arm each time he got it wrong, whacked it harder when he finally got it right. Helping out, paying back, was a harder gig than fishing: months of three a.m. starts and in the field to pick produce for drying, the rest driven into market. Exotic patterns, hand-dyed robes, community and culture in forms he'd never been exposed to. He'd filled his days with work; left no room to remember.

★

The sliding doors of his house catch the morning sun, an ultra-modern Queenslander designed from corrugated iron and a wall of tinted glass, elevated on steel girders. Tom stands on the deck, pours the last slug of coffee. On a clear day, from the top of the hill, a half-moon of ocean shines back. From nothing to now, a life not so much planned as stumbled upon.

He leaves his breakfast bowl in the sink, cleans his teeth. He can hear Zulu pacing outside, issuing small yelps. She knows the drill. On the front step every morning, *c'mon girl*, airborne and on the back tray, ears folded down and on alert as his Hilux burbles down toward the sheds and greenhouses. Give her half a chance she'd be over the bridge and onto Annie's place to round up her goats. But dare Tom whisper *bath*, take up the garden hose, try coaxing Zulu toward the river on a stinking day of summer: watch her scarper for a mile.

Tom has the gates and shed doors open before the horticultural crew begins their day. He watches the roof of the first greenhouse slide back. He has a manager he trusts, a good team, but still he gravitates here to walk each row, keep a lookout for disease. He inspects rows of zucchini, chokos, cucumber, spinach, weird-shaped gourds and pumpkins he feels the urge to pat. Randomly he tests the moisture in the planted bags of soil. He's been around long enough to harbour a perpetual mistrust of automated irrigation. Mister Leave Nothing To Chance, they call him at the showroom to wind him up.

The largest greenhouse is given to a sea of tomatoes—vines winding up trusses toward exposed strips of sky, rows of leafy tendrils bejewelled with shiny baubles. Tom inhales the stringent smell of fruit ripening on the vine, the cloistered warmth of greenhouse air. Dozens of species of tomato grow elevated along these gridded plat-forms. Tradiro, Trinidad, Nisha, Oxhearts. A suite of flavours. Tom knows them all. Countless forms and colours, some as fine as sculp-tures. The old mainstay, Tommy Toe, the nation's benchmark since before he was born, a perpetual judging favourite. The showroom is packed with crates of fresh produce, packets of organic seeds, display shelves with jars of relishes and chutneys, vinegars and marinades, bottled sauces of a range he's losing track of. Above, the walls are festooned with ribbons and plaques from agricultural shows. Three years running his sweet and savoury preserves have taken out trophies, won fine food awards as far away as Hobart.

Too many hard memories to settle back there. When Tom came home from travelling he helped his mother sell up and shift to Melbourne. He drove up here to Camden Haven, tracked down old William whose bushwalking days were behind him. William drove him out here, a sale sign nailed to the gate. They parked on the rise beyond a derelict timber cottage with a rusted-out tank. William pulled out his thermos to *share a brew.* Where they sat overlooked rolling pasture, a winding river, swathes of unlogged bush. *What someone like you could do with a place as fine as this.* Tainted money from working on the boat that Tom had never touched. Money that could be changed to something good.

Tom once believed that if a person clocked up enough good then maybe, just maybe, it could cancel out the past. But his brother lingers, ghostly as a shadow. Some nights he slides into Tom's dreams, steals air from his lungs. *Unfinished business,* William liked to say.

Tom snaps off a Tiger Green. He pares it open with his pocketknife. He prides himself on the heirloom varieties he's championing around the markets—species not groomed for some citified mode of perfection, but tomatoes that taste the way tomatoes were intended. The heirlooms are a different league to the sorry specimens that line supermarket shelves, chameleons selected for their staying power—forget goodness and taste. Tom catches himself. As forthright as William was, banging on about the virtues of organic.

The old man grew frail before Tom's eyes. He was chairbound by the time Tom pegged out the foundations for the house. Propped beneath the old canvas brolly doing his utmost to supervise. In that final year, afternoons together at the hospice, their talk held an intimacy. Plenty of well-worn stories, yes, but moments of William's life Tom had never been privy to. *The trouble with memories is they can work against you,* the old man said. *People you cared about, things you've lost.*

They spoke of Frank. Tom begrudged Stephanie for some of what had happened. She would have known of Frank's death, he told William. She must have heard talk on the radio among the fishermen. She left that island and never once contacted him. Just pissed off and got on with her future.

Tom could have predicted the old man's response. *We don't get all we want in life, Tom. No one's to blame.*

Not that long ago he typed the name on the web. The world teemed with Stephanie Wests: attorney, movie producer, project manager, embezzler, ophthalmologist, realtor, an obituary for a grandmother, a scholar in Bristol, a designer in Fort Worth, a glass artist in Santa Fe, New Mexico ... the bristle at the sight of her. Blue jeans, long hair. Skinny still, wearing an armful of silver bangles. He looked over the studio's web page, clicked her portfolio, he read of her studies at the Canberra glass school, the move to America, workshops she ran for Bullseye Glass. He looked through photos, installations, high-end galleries with work that sold for thousands. He closed off the page and returned to his business, newly determined to focus on his own wellbeing. The good things. The big new deal with Qantas. Gourmet outlets. Internet sales that had tripled in eighteen months. New enquiries each and every week.

Vehicles crunch over gravel. Tom hears voices, laughter, his dog being made a fuss of.

'Morning, Tom.'

'Morning.'

'Hello, Mr Forrest,' spouts the new work experience kid.

Sheesh. 'Tom is good,' he tells the kid. He whistles his dog. She bounds ahead of him, sits rigid at the gate, her tail sweeping gravel, while Tom slides the sign to Open. The old metal honesty box he fashioned from salvaged bits of tin still sits nailed to a post. A measure of the distance he's come, he likes to think of it. For the less informed, a mailbox. He fishes out an advert for chopped firewood, for someone's lost cat—a shifty-looking beast with a knotted face, *answers to the name of Satan*. Good luck with that one. Tom nods to Yvette driving in, her back windscreen sporting a line of My Family stickers: a zany Mum, Dad with his surfboard, an unruly assortment of kids, pets and geese.

They're as good as family, his team, solid friends amongst them. Tom's made it this far without having wronged anyone. Strong prospects for the future, a decent house, the world's best dog, a girl who'd quit her job tomorrow and move up here for good. Tom slows, slides his boot across the gravel. A girl antsy for him to say the word.

He makes his way back toward the sheds. Zulu blasts ahead to round up Yvette and chaperone her to the showroom. He wishes William were still around to set him straight.

29

A twinkling of lights from some tiny Pacific island, barely discernible from this great height. Had Steph turned a moment later to look out the cabin window she would not have known it was there. Perhaps we navigate life that way. Perhaps we change course at precisely the wrong moment, blink and miss landfall. Perhaps returning is a bad idea. But Santa Fe is behind her, too late now to change her mind, her apartment rented for the year, farewell drinks and a cake decorated with a map of Australia.

She reclines her seat, tucks the doona around her feet. Her thoughts drift to that other farewell, a spill of pledges that could have swayed her to stay. Steph had moved beyond herself, had risen through the night and looked down upon the pair of them, the strange turnabout of roles. She'd felt disdain, a momentary surge of pity, not for him or her but for all of them. She'd looked to herself, the wasted time, months of wretchedness she'd brought upon herself. She'd taken a step away, shrugged off the woollen coat he'd gifted her last birthday and laid it on the plaza bench. A silent declaration shored up by her refusal to shiver with the sharpness of the air.

The cover of the inflight magazine. Glass vessels the colour of the ocean. She raises her seat, riffles through the pages. *Harvest from the Haven*. She halts at the photo of a man, jeans and jacket, his arm resting on a wooden crate of produce. The likeness is uncanny. Mid thirties, even the age is right. Oceans more worldly than the boy she once knew. Steph studies his hands. She skims the text. *Organic dressings and condiments served in our first-class cabins and Qantas lounges.* A name shimmies off the page.

★

Sydney. International Arrivals. A wall of waiting faces. Lydia!

On her cousin's hip a toddler in pyjamas and a dressing-gown, holding up a monkey balloon. His nose, the shape of his chin: little jigsaw pieces of Callam. 'Crazy woman.' Steph hugs her. She strokes the boy's fine hair. 'I would have caught the train and got a taxi up to your place.'

Lydia snorts. 'You have an accent. You even look American.'

'Not true.'

'You do. Squeaky clean, in a hip kind of way. Way too glam for the likes of us, isn't she, Nicky?' Nic buries his face in his mother's neck.

Lydia lives north of Forty Baskets Beach. They drive across the Harbour Bridge on a spring-filled morning. Steph is transfixed by cobalt water and the pulsing brilliance of the sky. The light makes her squint. She looks down at coloured spinnakers as ballooned as blown glass, at the Manly ferry trundling across to Circular Quay, a constant through her girlhood. A lone paddler glides in the glassy green that edges the shore. Steph wishes she could gather every artist from Santa Fe, portal them here to witness this magic.

For years she has distanced herself. Left Australia for her art and in the doing fell for New Mexico: *Land of Enchantment.* She feels the first tug of everything she's left behind.

Sydney's air feels maritime, moistened warmth against her skin. She peels off to a T-shirt, glass foundry attire as worn as her boots. She wears Santa Fe old: denim jeans, old pueblo turquoise and silver. Too glam?

Nic is out to it, slumped in his car seat. Lydia's eyes rhythmically glance at the rear-view mirror. Motherhood. Her cousin looks serene, radiates contentment, everything in Lyd's world is proper and right.

'So,' her cousin says. 'Ready for Canberra?'

'I am. I'm excited about it. Heard from Gran?'

'She's slowing down. She says she still gardens every day. She's over the moon about having you back to stay. She's asked us all down for Christmas. Your mum and dad are flying over from the west.'

'I can't remember the last time we were all together.' Steph looks from the waterway to a shiny, shiny headland verdant with green. 'If ever I forget how beautiful this is, remind me of this moment.'

Lydia smiles. 'My mission is to never let you go.'

The morning light, the first flush of lilac painting leaf-bare jacarandas, children playing in the park as the car weaves around the water's edge. The smell and feel of oceanic air washes through Steph with childish squeals from summers at Forty Baskets Beach. Mum and Callam, Dad and Steph: never-again lives through a pungent gauze of memory. The words spill before she can stop them: 'Can we drive past my old house?' To punish herself? Can home ever be more than a catalogue of loss?

★

'It makes no sense.' Lydia puts down the Qantas magazine, pours her tea. 'If Tom Forrest survived—returned from the dead, whatever— you'd have heard about it, read it in the papers.'

Steph has no explanation. She spent the last half of the flight in a light-headed whirl, reeling between the present and the past. She couldn't get warm, she couldn't sleep, her mind scrambling for answers to questions Lydia now asks. 'Perhaps it never made the news in Sydney,' she tells her cousin. 'Perhaps we missed it. When we came back from Maatsuyker everything was manic. The house sold in the first week. Dad flew off to his new job in Western Australia. I left for Canberra to start at the glass school.'

'Stephie, if this is Tom . . .'

'It is. There's no mistake.'

'Have you told your parents?'

'Not yet. When they get back from their trip. I need to come to terms with it myself.'

'What now?'

'I have eight days before Canberra. I could go up there if I wanted.'

Lydia studies her. 'To what end, exactly?'

'He and I—we were kids back then. I was so confused. I didn't know how to deal with things. Nothing got resolved. I always regretted that we never had the chance to talk.'

Lydia turns to the photo. 'He's not nineteen, Steph. He has a new life. He could be married with a family. Imagine how I'd feel if some old girlfriend knocked on the door asking after my husband. Perhaps you should ask yourself what you hope to gain. Weigh up the consequences.'

Consequences. She hasn't paid much heed to those in recent times. But how can she deny the past? How can she brush off a person and the memories of a time and place that meant so much? 'Tom was the first man I loved. I've gone through my adult

259

life believing he was dead. It's like a weight, a longing deep inside me that's never gone away. It feels monumental, Lydia. Something I need to face, not shut away.' Steph studies her coffee. 'What do I hope to gain? I want to see him, talk to him. Set things straight. I *want* to know he's happy. No agenda. Nothing more than that.'

Her cousin throws her a look Steph knows from their girlhood: *I don't buy that.*

★

Camden Head Pilot Station: Retreat accommodation, short or long term. She clicks through photos. A refurbished timber cottage, an historic signal shed that sits on a headland of rolling lawns and bushland, that overlooks the ocean. Steph keys in her credit card number. Her fingers hover above the keyboard. *You can't relive the past,* her father's trusty saying. She makes the payment and closes the screen.

30

The tight arses stake out their route. Tom recognises the woman, hair the colour of bruised potato, a serial sampler who brazenly snacks her way through the Sunday markets without giving up a coin. She makes her way to his stall, rubbing his neighbour's sun cream into her liver-spotted arms.

Tom opens a jar of salsa and hands the woman a plastic spoon. 'Tomatillo and roasted jalapeño chilli. From our new range.'

She screws her nose. 'Not too hot is it?'

'Most manage.'

She spoons the salsa across a lavash cracker and studs the surface with marinated feta. 'In for a penny.' She crunches and swallows, grunts an appraisal. 'Wouldn't say it's my favourite.' She ignores the tongs and helps herself to a stack of extra crackers. Off she totters toward Annie's homeopathic balms.

Why suffer this gig for a paltry handful of sales? A day of the weekend when Tom could be doing better things. The money is in contracts. The exposure from the Qantas deal alone has been worth trialling new recipes, forking out for fancy jars and custom-ised labels he's come to better understand as *branding*.

The woman moves on. She'd be given short shrift in Annie's mild-mannered way. Perhaps Tom does know why he puts up with

261

this caper. For all the things you can never put a ticket value on. Musings with Annie over a *your turn to buy the coffee* and a slice of her homemade cake, a chinwag with the mayor, talk of a fundraiser locomotive ride to Kempsey, a barbecue, a working bee, an invite to someone's house for dinner. The woman from twelve months ago he pegged as just another tourist—which she was until she tasted the first sampler, and then another and another, purchased one of each and asked for a price list and quizzed him with a volley of astute questions. She riffled through her handbag, pulled out a card. *I'm on holiday until next week. Give me a call after that.* Qantas Q-Catering. A chance meeting with someone who could just change your life.

Tom takes a deep breath, pushes against the tightness strapped around his chest. He hasn't slept. His gut's been churning since he left the house this morning. He checks his watch. If only he could gauge the difference between anticipation and dread. Tom heels his boot into the grass beneath the trestle. How do you begin to fathom the obscure trail of dots that reconnects a person with your life? She was Stephanie's friend first, a small girl who scored a stack of unwanted signal flags. Love flags, she chose to think of them. She claims destiny reconnects people, that some overarching guardian has the whole thing figured out.

Destiny, no. A trip down to Hobart the year before last, a new line of preserves that took out trophies in the Fine Foods Fair. A stranger tapped him on the shoulder. A small woman. Red hair. *It's Marcie,* she said expectantly. Tom drew a blank. *Maatsuyker Island,* she blurted, undeterred. *I was there with Stephanie. You drove me back to school. The signal flags.*

Marcie. The name was gone but the day thudded into place. *That was a lifetime ago*, he said. She asked him out for coffee and as she talked, Tom felt oddly buoyant by the line she cast back to his past. She was wholesome, sweet, a reminder that there'd been moments of good amongst the bad. One small untarnished link. When they went their separate ways Tom found himself walking to the docks, past fishing boats tied up at their berths. If the *Perlita Lee* was still around she was nowhere to be seen. He found Bluey's boat and slowed. The new owner, a man Tom didn't know, refused to look up from his work. It was he, Tom, who was the stranger, one more gawking tourist to be ignored.

Marcie invited him to lunch the day he flew home. He found her pretty, vivacious, he felt bolstered by her energy and was taken by the way she enthused about Maatsuyker—the thousand details she remembered. Several of the signal flags lined her hallway. A single day on that island that she carried like an amulet. She made it known to Tom that she was unencumbered, good riddance to a worn-out relationship. Tom breathed in all that zest and chatter, smitten enough to phone her when he got home.

Easters. Long weekends. January. Visits in July to escape the winter chill. He's grown accustomed to Marcie's comings and goings, the whirlwind of her presence, bursts of chatter and ideas for jazzing up his house. He likes showing her around, a drive up to South West Rocks to her favourite place for lunch. Mostly he likes the everydayness: preparing a meal for someone other than himself, the curve of her body against his in the bed. On his birthday last she arrived with a puppy from her father's farm. Named and registered. *You'd never have decided if I'd consulted with you first.* The world's biggest ditherer, she called him. Now Tom can't imagine his day beginning or ending without that crazy hound. He tries to assemble a My Family sticker. Tom. Marcie. Zulu. Her hints at children waiting at the end. He draws a ragged breath, checks his watch again. Marcie's not good at being made to wait.

Finally Yvette arrives to take over the stall. 'Have I made you late?' Yvette states the blinking obvious. Tom peels off plastic gloves, kneels down to Zulu tethered to the marquee pole, laid out in a sulk. 'You look after Yvette. Just a few days.' A picture of abject misery. You'd think she was being banished to the vet.

'The boys had tennis and halfway there Tyler discovers he's left his racquet at home. Kids. Anyway, never mind. A flight to meet. Drive carefully. Have fun. Go, Tom. Go.' She shoos him away. 'And don't even think about work,' she bellows after him.

Crunch time.

★

Steph wanders the markets. Only a small part of herself is attuned to marquees emanating a potpourri of goat milk soaps and scented candles, the glitter of restorative crystals. An elderly man shows off his turned wooden bowls; a bearded greenie sells pump packs of lemon myrtle moisturiser with utilitarian labels. All around her is local produce—even jalapeño chilli that makes her forget this is spring and swamps her with longings for fall. You're here, Steph. Be in the now.

Her accommodation at the old pilot station is a five-minute drive to this tidy town. Cottage roofs reflect banks of photovoltaics alongside old-fashioned chimneys. People walk at a leisurely place, they smile unguardedly. *You wouldn't be dead for quids*, the rental car man bragged about the sunshine when he met Steph at the train.

A community contained by three tall-timbered coastal mountains—the Three Brothers, named by no less than Captain Cook—by
a lazy winding river home to oyster farms and flat-bottomed run-
abouts, to boys fishing after school in crumpled school shirts, a
shoreline of pelicans pink-pouched and gawky, impatient to scoop
up picnickers' fish and chips discards. Steph sees how the Tom she
knew would be drawn to this place. Even with the photo from the
inflight magazine folded in her bag, her senses are primed for the
profile of a face, an intonation of voice, a stance that matches her
image of a nineteen-year-old boy.

How to impart years of innocent misunderstanding.

Steph spent a day in Sydney's reference library before coming
here. She trawled back through old Sydney newspapers without
finding a mention. Finally she uncovered the story through digit-
ised clippings in Tasmanian papers.

The abandoned *Perlita Lee*, the land and air search, the upturned
dinghy fouled by line that issued a plummeting of hopes of finding
the brothers alive. These things she had known. But Steph saw,
as she couldn't back then, the anguish Tom's mother would have
suffered at the finding of a coat with a name, a body that Steph,
like all of them, assumed to be Tom. Steph imagined her despair
when the search was scaled down, her other son unlikely to be
found. Steph balked at the coroner's report, at grisly testimonials of
a faceless carcass afloat in the water. *A Mother's Miracle*, the Hobart
paper read—*Missing Son Walks Home*. But not until Steph read
of Frank's tattoo—entwined anchors identical to Tom's—did the
pieces finally fit.

Everything back then had been in disarray: mourning for Tom,
despairing at her parents for selling off the house and packing to

move away. Steph could barely focus on the glass school. No one lingered over television news, leafed through morning papers. Even after months on Maatsuyker, friends and relatives would not have connected them with the crew of a fishing boat in south-west Tasmania.

Could Steph have unearthed the story if she'd had the wherewithal to search? Was *Google* even part of the vocabulary? She'd just turned seventeen, too raw, after Callam, to face another death. When she returned from Maatsuyker she'd not spoken of Tom to her friends, not to Gran in any detail, not to anyone but Lydia, and even then a long time after.

In Canberra—a new city, new friends—she boxed up her feelings, sealed away loss, not seeing then the cost that such denial would have on her life, on her willingness to take another chance at love. Callous, it would seem to Tom, as if she hadn't cared. She discovered soon enough that a glass foundry had no compassion for any plane of time beyond the present. She let herself be owned by glass, physically, emotionally, entirely.

She could share with Tom the letter of condolence that she wrote to his mother months later, believing Tom was dead. A singular, heartfelt bow to loss, a declaration of her feelings, a testament she laboured over for days. What good could come from that admission? Steph still sees the biro line crossed through the front of the envelope, *Return To Sender* in his mother's handwriting she recognised from Tom's house. The letter had been opened, read, resealed with tape. Had his mother withheld it from her son? Or had Tom been offered it and shaken his head: all done with the past.

At seventeen, that rejection from his mother delivered a stinging slap across her face: *Keep away*, her words on the envelope might as easily have read. *Your kind brings nothing but trouble.*

Your kind. It grew into a silent incantation Steph carried deep within her, concealed behind the luminosity she strived for with glass. Prospects with good men, honourable men, she sabotaged and walked away from, denying them a chance for fear they'd fail. Safe haven had been a lover who was taken. A man she knew would never leave his wife.

Did Tom ever try to find her? God, what would he make of the woman she's become?

Her kind? Tom's mother had known a thing or two.

★

'All natural ingredients,' says the bubbly woman from the homeopathic stall. An earth mother with long-flowing hair and a lilting voice. 'Care to try something?'

Steph pushes back her bangles, turns over her hands. 'Are these a lost cause?' Dry skin, scars from glass burns, violet tattoos from the ink jar of her childhood.

'Not by a long shot.' The woman dabs a tester of cream on each. 'The most interesting hands are the ones that tell a story.'

She rubs cream into her hands. It feels wholesome and good.

'A small dab, morning and night. A jar will last a good six months.'

'Sold.' Steph pulls out her purse.

The woman looks through her stock. 'Sorry. I should have checked. I must have sold the last one. I have more at home. I can put one aside for next weekend.'

'I'm only here for a couple of days.'

'I do postal orders.' The woman hands Steph a brochure and a card. 'Or if you're out and about, I'm twenty minutes up the road. Call in anytime.'

On a whim. 'Do you know a Tom Forrest?'

'You bet,' she chirps. 'He has a place on the opposite side of the river. You're a friend?'

'I haven't seen him for a very long time.'

'Then head down thataway and surprise him. His stall's at the end. Blue tarp roof.'

Not Tom but a woman sorting tomatoes, weighing them into paper bags. 'You missed him by half an hour. He's raced off to the airport. Won't be back today.'

'Does he have a mobile? I'm a friend. I'm just visiting.'

The woman looks wary. She passes Steph a brochure. 'This has the shop details. He won't be around. They're having time away.'

Steph curbs the urge to ask. She kneels down to the border collie stretched on her lead beneath the trestle. 'You're a sweet girl.' She strokes her ears. The dog licks Steph's hand, looks at her pleadingly. 'Is she still a puppy?'

'About a year old, I'd say. She's Tom's dog. Spoiled rotten. An overgrown puppy that likes to think she's a person. Don't you, Zulu?'

The dog nuzzles Steph's hand. 'He called you Zulu?' The one signal flag from Maatsuyker. Zulu blinks at her.

'I believe Marcie took charge of the naming,' the woman says. 'Brought her up from Tassie as a puppy.'

Marcie? Steph tightens. 'Marcie with red hair?'

'That's her. Can talk underwater,' the woman adds, none too kindly.

'They're married?' The question is out before she can stop it.

'If one of them has their way,' the woman says. She busies herself bagging tomatoes.

How? When? Steph catches herself. He owes her nothing. How they came to be together is not her business. And yet this graze of betrayal. She slips the brochure in her bag, feels compelled to make a purchase. 'You choose. Whichever one you think is good.'

'They're all good.' The woman sets her straight. 'All Tom's recipes.' The woman packs a jar in a carry bag. 'Try this one from the new range.' She passes Steph her change. 'We're expecting them back Wednesday, if you're still around.'

She hears Lydia's caution. *Consequences.* She hasn't left the far side of the world to overturn a new round of lives. 'Ships in the night,' she says to the woman.

'How did you say you knew Tom?'

She didn't. 'It was years ago.' She was silly to waltz up here unannounced. She's been freewheeling through some jumbled, jet-lagged time warp. Did she really imagine she could pick up where she left off?

'Tell him hello. Tell both of them hello. Tell them all the best from Stephanie.'

31

Tom stands on the balcony of Smoky Cape Lighthouse—painted stonework, brass railings, the whole sweep of ocean ruffled with dusk. To the north, beyond the former keepers' cottages, hill after hill of rainforest. This would have been something in the old days, living and working out here on your own. Eighteen ninety-one. A new age. A coastline of lights giving ships their bearings.

Down the hill, Marcie naps, the old light keepers' cottages converted to upscale accommodation. She's had this retreat planned for months. It feels churlish to think it, but Tom is thankful for this quiet reverie, just birdsong and bush, the sun tracked low enough behind the hills that the shallows of the ocean are cast indigo with shadow. He'd almost forgotten the sensation of sea salt heavy in the air, the trace of seaweed.

You're lucky to snag a week without other bookings. Marcie thanked the caretaker sweetly for giving them their choice of cottage. *Back tomorrow arvo.* The man entrusted Tom with the keys as if complicit with Marcie's yearning for time on their own. Breeze curls around Tom's legs.

He circles the balcony, this solid footing anchored to the earth. He's far above the ocean, his reflection in the glass, a place where a person could look down upon their life. Beyond the ridge of bush the crescent moon of North Smoky Beach.

*

Roo time. A mob of eastern grays moves across the empty car park, their tails pulling at shadows thrown across the asphalt. The roos gather on grass that lustres with evening sun. Thick tan coats, soft pale bellies, a female with her pouch distended. A large buck stands tall, giving Tom the eye.

'See you down there,' he calls to Marcie in the bathroom, her hair dryer shrill. He grabs his jacket from the verandah, plucks a box of matches from the glove box of his car, paces down the boardwalk to the beach.

Waves pull back on sand. The ocean soughs. Tom stands near the water, looking out to sea, the beach chill with shadow. Perhaps he'll never grow accustomed to the setting sun being eaten by the land; a limitless horizon is the legacy of a fisherman's time at sea.

Near the rocks he scoops a hollow in the sand a safe distance from the bush. He sets dried seaweed, leaves and branches, drift-wood he's dragged along the beach. Tom strikes a match and hears a crackle of leaves. He crosses smaller bits of wood on the flames. He shields his eyes from smoke, waiting for the fire to burst to life, for sparks and smoke to spiral through the air.

Marcie jumps from the boardwalk and strides along the beach with a basket and rug, her red hair lifting like a sail in the breeze. She's a beautiful woman. Childlike, he sometimes thinks. *Am I what you want, Tom?*

The wooded headland stands buttery with flower, above it the dome of lighthouse. He could be back at Maat, setting pots beneath the cliff with Frank.

'Are we allowed a fire?'

Tom gives a sheepish shrug.

'My,' she teases. 'Next you'll be out there skinny dipping.'

'Don't hold your breath.'

He pours Marcie a glass of her champagne and digs the bottle in the sand. He chugs back on a beer. She has cheeses, crackers, olives, a jar of his salsa. Daylight is vanishing, the sky a quiet train of velvet sequinned with tiny sparks of light. An amphitheatre waiting for night to wind it up.

'We should come back here.' Marcie pours herself a second glass. 'You're relaxed here, away from work.'

Tom sets another log, the breeze falling away like a slow exhalation. Waves scrabble at the sand. He rests on the rug beside Marcie, his head on his elbow. It's hardly cold enough for a fire, but he savours the feel of it.

'Look,' Marcie cries. 'The light's on.' She points to the headland. 'The top of the lighthouse could be Maatsuyker. Twin lights.'

The same year as Maatsuyker. The only light along this stretch you could even draw a likeness to. 'A distant cousin, perhaps.' Tom counts the beams one through nine. He draws in the night damp of salt air.

'Tomorrow,' she declares, 'I'll get up early, watch the sunrise with you.' Tom nods. He ought to encourage her, he ought to say, *I'd love that*. 'Do you ever miss your old life?' she says. 'Being at sea?'

He pulls his jacket close. 'The skies, I miss. The seasons. Changes in the light.' He doesn't speak to Marcie about shooting pots at South West Cape, the cliffs aflame. Mornings when the Mewstone floated on a sky burning like a pyre. A different time. A different life.

'When are you going to decommission this?' She tugs at his sleeve. 'You've had this daggy old jacket for as long as I've known you. It's fit for the bin.'

'Excuse me.' He pulls his sleeve free. 'Past its best, it may be. Which makes it an ideal fishing jacket.'

She scoffs. 'Pardon me for pointing out the obvious. You don't fish. You don't even put your big toe in the water.'

'This,' he ignores her and pats his jacket, 'I have to thank for keeping me alive. Put that in your pipe and smoke it.'

Marcie runs her fingers through his hair. 'Alive, how?'

'When I decided I'd walk one hundred ks home without gear or a stove, no food to speak of, this was about the only thing of sense I had to keep me warm.'

'Unlike the Tom Forrest I know.'

'I was younger. Impetuous. Trying to prove some point or other.'

'You never had a tent?'

'I had bugger-all. I slept on bare ground. A plastic tarp I found along the way.'

'Were you doing a Bear Grylls? Wrestling wombats. Eating raw grubs. Did you drink the blood of leeches?' She walks her fingers across his forehead.

'I ate out of an old tin. Made a fire at night—or tried to with a useless box of matches. Luckily for me I met William halfway along. He had everything strapped to his back except the kitchen sink.'

'I wish I could have met him.'

'He was one of a kind.'

Marcie pours herself another glass. She passes Tom a second beer. He closes his eyes, listens to the ocean.

Marcie bumps him. 'Keep talking. You never talk about back then. What else?'

'Nothing. Just days of being wet and cold, feeling pissed off with myself.' Tom shakes the box of matches in his hand. 'What I would have given for a decent box of these. One night I was down to my last matches, hadn't a hope of finding anything dry to get a fire started. I dug around in my pockets of *this jacket.*' He pauses for emphasis. 'Hey presto.'

'I'm waiting.'

'Paper, a sprig of dry twig. I can still see it, clear as day. Carefully tearing this small sheet of yellow graph paper into strips, delicately lacing it over the twigs, trying to shield the whole thing from the rain.'

Marcie gives a shrug.

'It may sound meagre to you,' Tom sets her straight. 'Back then it felt like a gift from the heavens. Enough to get a fire started, warm up some packet food. I believe I had a guardian angel looking over me during that time.'

Marcie sits in silence, staring at the flames. 'Maybe your guardian angel is closer than you think. I was the one who brought your jacket back from Maatsuyker Island.'

Tom rubs her knee. 'Your big day on the island. I'd forgotten. Thank you.'

'Did you meet Stephanie's mum?'

'A couple of times.'

'She took care of me like a daughter. She was so kind to me.'

'They were nice.'

'Her father was a light keeper, way back.' Marcie guzzles her drink. 'You see her after that?'

Tom blinks. 'Why would I see Gretchen?'

'Stephanie. Did you get in touch with her?'

'No.' He's told her that before.

'She never called you?' Tom takes a breath. This old road. Marcie changes shape if another woman so much as smiles in his direction. She even puts the ladies at the showroom on edge. 'After the tragedy,' Marcie clucks. 'After everything that happened with your brother. Not much compassion.'

'She was someone I crossed paths with a very long time ago. I'm sure she had her reasons.' Tom closes his eyes to the crackle of the fire, the ocean stirring.

'Last night. You sang out in your sleep.'

'Did I?'

'You know you did, babe. You called your brother's name.' She loops her arm around his chest. 'I think it would help if you opened up. Stop bottling things up. You hear about soldiers who come back from combat and they hold it all in and hide it from their loved ones and then years and years later they begin to unravel—'

'Hush.' He squeezes her hand. 'I've never been to war. I'm not wounded. I have a few bad dreams. End of story.' He doesn't mean to sound sharp. He sees her chest rise, hears her breath change. This constant withholding on his part. This shabby imbalance. He reaches for her. 'Don't go getting upset.'

She pushes him away. Wine spills across his jacket. 'You always keep me at a distance. You don't talk to me.'

'What are we doing now?'

'Why don't you say you love me?'

'Marcie. You're lovely. I tell you all the time. I care for you. Very much.'

The beam from the tower cuts the sky, nine prisms, nine sweeps of light. A burning log tumbles in a whoosh of sparks. The Milky Way strewn across the sky.

'Do I make you happy?'

This wariness he feels, headlong toward a trap. 'Yes.'

'Then let me move up here. Let's give it a try. I could help you at home, with the business. What do we have to lose?' She's been angling toward this all year, impatient for the world's worst ditherer to get his act together.

How to put into words something he can't fathom for himself? 'It's a big step. It would mean you giving up your job. Your apartment.'

'I don't care about my job.'

'I'm not sure we're quite ready.'

Marcie sighs. 'When will we be ready? How long will *we* wait?'

'You're free to make your own choices.' Heartless, Tom. She drains her glass, moves to pack the things away. 'Don't go. Let's enjoy tonight. Here. Together.'

She cogitates. 'You have a good business. A nice house. You have me. Zulu. Why can't all that be enough?'

'What do you want me to say?' Any answer will be wrong.

'I want to know what you want from your life that you don't already have. I'm serious, Tom. Name one thing.'

Tom turns to the ocean, sees lines of phosphorescence, waves snapping at the sand. He listens hard and hears the ocean cackle. 'I want peace. I want to be at peace.'

★

Tom wakes on the beach, stiff-necked, pins and needles in the arm crooked beneath his head. Sun drills his back. He stretches, scratches sand from his hair, he clears away the remnants of the fire. He gathers up the rug, a row of empty stubbies.

The cottage stands empty, the covers of the bed thrown back. He sees Marcie at the lighthouse, her hair aflame in morning sun. He dumps his jacket on a post, climbs the hill.

A magazine rests on her lap. 'You're up early,' he says.

'Couldn't sleep.'

He slides down beside her. 'You okay?'

She shakes her head. He loops his arm around her shoulder, she rests her head against him. She starts to cry. 'Last night. I'm sorry.'

He pulls her in. 'You have no reason to apologise.'

'I drank too much.'

They could keep going, coast along for months, years. 'What you said was honest. It was real.'

She looks to him expectantly.

'Marcie, you deserve someone who will give you what you want.'

He sees her face deflate. 'I don't want someone. I want you. I'm happy to wait.'

'It isn't fair to make you wait. You said it yourself.'

'It's fine. I'm happy. It wasn't fair rushing you, putting pressure on you.'

Tom stands at a precipice. 'It isn't about needing more time.' The truth of it shears off as he speaks. 'It doesn't feel right. Not the way it should to build a life together.'

He feels her tremble. Her voice remains resolute. 'We're meant to be together, Tom. I've known that from day one. The day you drove me home. The signal flags.'

Togetherness staked on a haphazard gift. 'Listen. When I gave you those flags I was happy for you to have them. I was. But that gift was not intended for you, at least not to begin with. You need to understand that. I was nineteen. You were a kid. It was not some grand offering of love.'

'It was for someone,' she says.

He doesn't dare respond.

'You think that because I was younger than you I didn't see or understand?'

'I wasn't saying that—'

'I knew the flags were for her. To put in the lighthouse. I knew back then.'

He scratches at his head. 'Then I don't get it. You made out they were some kind of cosmic sign. The universe throwing us together.'

Marcie collects her magazine, rolls it up. For a moment he thinks she's going to swat him. A florid mottling creeps like tide across her throat. 'You have blinkers on. All you see when you look at me is a stand-in for some idealised concept.'

'I see more than you give me credit for.'

She gives a quiet scoff. 'Do you? Back then? Before you lit that match?'

'You've lost me.'

'It pays to be observant, Tom.'

Nothing slips by Marcie. 'Enlighten me.'

'I saw her write it. I watched her fold it up and put it in your pocket. A note you tore into pieces and put a match to.'

'Stephanie? A note that said what?'

Marcie stands to leave. 'I wouldn't know,' she says, the blade of triumph turning. 'It wasn't meant for me.'

32

Tom hammers down the highway, his brain grappling with the sequence of events. Last night they were sitting happily by a fire on a beach. This morning he had his arm around her on a lighthouse balcony. This afternoon she's gone, a goodbye at the airport that arced into tears and accusation. Tom pulls in through his gate—one day early. He wants to shut himself inside his house, bunker down, write off this fucked-up day.

His Hilux climbs the second rise toward the house, slowing and meandering to avoid the worst potholes. Tom catches a movement in the rear vision, Zulu bounding up from the sheds in pursuit, an escape artist with her collar and lead somewhere back down the hill. He pulls in beneath the house and readies himself for the onslaught. No second-guessing with a dog. When he pulls his keys from the ignition he sees the second pair clipped to the ring. Smoky Cape. The caretaker's keys. Good one, Tom.

Zulu licks his face, tail beating, quivering with exhilaration. All grievances absolved. Tom dumps the esky, a box of uneaten food, slings his bag on the verandah.

He grabs the spare lead and shakes his car keys. 'C'mon, girl.' Zulu looks momentarily confused. 'Hup.' She leaps from the step onto the vehicle tray.

Down the hill, past the sheds where Yvette and the horticultural boys stand in a pocket of shade, slugging on coffee and cigarettes. Tom gives a half-wave. He's in no mood to stop and chitchat. He turns the car north, back to Smoky Cape.

He apologises to the caretaker. *Not a problem, just drove in myself.* Tom makes his way back down the path. It's late enough in the day that the same long shadows stretch across the car park, the same family of kangaroos grazes on the grass, careless of Zulu tethered to the tray. They scarper when a youth with dreadlocks appears from the beach track and slinks toward Tom's car, the only vehicle remaining in the car park. Tom pats his pocket to check his wallet. The boy stands in conversation with his dog whose tongue laps at air. 'You picked yourself a dodgy saviour,' Tom mutters to the air. The boy catches sight of Tom and saunters off along the road.

Tom feels wired, onion-raw, unready to climb back in his car and face the long drive home. His brain is tired of slapping around the failures of his life. He pokes around the old light keepers' stables adorned with signal flags and information signs: historic photos of the lighthouse, pictures of Dunghutti women and their dark-eyed daughters digging pipis from the beach.

A memory: being led by the hand by a small Aboriginal girl—strong for her size. When Tom first moved to Camden Haven, he talked to old William about that spirit girl, about waking in a cave atop the Ironbounds. *When I found you, mighty, you were off with the pixies, you didn't know which way was up.* Why then this knotted scar on his shoulder, this remnant scrap of anchor? Tom had held a blade to his arm in his effort to expunge his brother. He remembers that small girl crying, *No, Tom.* She called him by his name.

He's had a gutful of his head. He pulls a ziplock from the glove box and locks the car behind him. He leads Zulu down the beach track, unclips her lead. Tom kicks off boots and socks and dumps them on the boardwalk. The air smells floral with spring pollen, thick with sea salt. Tom sets off across the sand while Zulu races in the opposite direction, rounding up seagulls, regularly diverting up the beach lest her paws be wetted by the smallest lapping wave.

Beyond the point a reef break, a haunt for surfers when the swell is right. A runabout fangs north across the ocean, home to South West Rocks, the day of fishing done. Above the headland, the light-house gazes down.

No one up here would credit the swells he and Frank worked in. Not a skipper to compare to his brother behind the wheel, a sorcerer's magic against a witch of an ocean. Tom paces over sand the same buff colour as New Harbour, as Louisa Bay, as any stretch of beach along that wild angry coast. For his whole time on the boat Tom lived in fear of a malevolent ocean. He dreamed and dreamed again of swallowing the sea. Tom it had spat onto a beach. All the while it had lain in wait for Frank.

He's spent years questioning why he, Tom—destined to be taken—should be the brother spared. His mother's answers came straight from books in her Bible; Corinthians, John, the Book of Revelation: she cherrypicked them all. Tom wants someone—anyone—to acknowledge that he was a player in his brother's death. He's never again set foot in the ocean. Never swum, never kayaked on the river with Marcie. Just hung back on the old wooden landing, his toes dragging in the water. His brother would be the first to say it: *Too much a coward to let the ocean take another bite at you.*

No one left to call him *Tom-Tom* now.

Tom rolls up his jeans, makes his way across shallows to the rocks beneath the headland. Another time this ocean would pound around the corner, laden with weed, sending up spindrift.

At the northern end of the beach, Zulu plays out a cycle of run, stop, squat, bark. Squawks from irritated gulls.

The water is clear, a bed of rippled sand. A school of fish zigzags by. Lettuce seaweed turns and folds as delicate as tissue. Tom thinks on Marcie, Stephanie. A note he never saw, torn to strips. Too late now for might-have-beens.

He feels a churning in his gut, his mind sliding into feckless gear. He hasn't smoked a reefer in years but keeps a small stash in the glove box. Call it a tribute to his youth, a small rebellion against the upright citizen he claims to have become. The cigarette paper feels fragile from heat and age, weed and seed heads dry as desiccated coconut. In its prime a joint like this would have worked some magic. Now it probably won't hold a kick.

At the touch of the match it sizzles and flares, burns down too fast. Tom draws smoke into his lungs, takes a long deep breath, the heat cloying on his throat. He coughs, puffs through to the end, thumps his chest to clear his throat.

Squat.

He rolls another, draws it deep into his chest.

He searches out to sea, his body sliding with the drift.

Tom sways toward Marcie, trawls through ripples of red hair and regret. Was he hasty? Did he make the right decision? He sees her walking naked to the ocean, trying, trying to lure him in. He shakes his head. She played him. All that time she knew about the note. The signal flags he gave her—a kind of coveting, wanting someone else's life.

He fixes his focus on ocean. He rocks toward the rhythm of a dislocated dare knocking at his groin. His body grows urgent with desire. He pictures a woman naked in the water, tall, slender, turning and laughing, reaching for his hands and pulling him in. The two of them pressed together, their skin yellow through a river of black tea. Everything he's lost is in the water. Tom pulls his belt loose, looks down at his jeans and underwear pushed down around his ankles. He tears at the snaps of his shirt and hears them pop. He hears himself snicker. *Butt naked. Tom-Tom goes the ocean.*

Tom dives, the crown of his head bruising sand. He surfaces and heaves at air, waiting for a numbing sting of cold. Warm water envelopes him, silky as a robe. He swims toward the deep, stopping once to check that he can touch the bottom. He angles out across the bay, his arms leaden as sinkers. He turns to watch the lighthouse, sees a slender figure standing on the balcony. Stephanie? He gives a manic wave, feels to be grinning like a clown. No one waves back. Tom turns, swims on.

He stops to catch his breath. He floats on his back to rest, his ears immersed in water. He can hear each intake of air, his heart thudding in his ears: *Brother. Brother. Brother.* The old people filled the Three Brothers with legend. Each brother taken by a witch, buried where each mountain stands. Tom's Brother. Stephanie's Brother. A witch of an ocean; one Brother spare.

Tom closes his eyes against the moment when sun slides across his face. This is where he wants to be: far enough from shore to escape the shadow of land. He hears submarine trills of moving water, terrestrial squawks of gulls. A dog barking, far, far away. He feels Frank close by. *Hup you come.* The pair of them together in the dinghy, bobbing in a sea of fog. Tom sees the prop fouled with tangled line torn from pots. He feels Frank shiver from the dampness of the air. His brother steels himself against the press of cold. He watches Frank pull on Tom's red float coat and try to work the faulty zip. Good luck with that, matey. Too tight to fork out for a new one. But look, Frank. In the bottom of the boat: Tom's orange knife. Another handy discard. He hears Frank cackle with relief. Frank takes the knife from its sheath and here is his chance, sawing at those loops of rope, forged on by indignation at this unwarranted predicament, abandoned by a shit of a kid brother to whom Frank Forrest had given all but his life, shortly to settle the balance. Tom feels the set through the fog and tries to warn Frank, *Look out! Sit tight!* A triple, a quintet rolling through in quick succession, overturning the dinghy and upending Frank into the water. Frank, Frankie, hold the dinghy's keel. Don't waste your lungs cursing your good-for-nothing little brother who wasn't there to render assistance the one and only time he was required.

Brother mine, the cold would have got you first, it wouldn't give a rat's arse for how tough and nuggety you were within that fiefdom of a wheelhouse. Wooden fingers. No amount of bullying would stop your grip loosening from the boat. Frank Forrest cast adrift like all the craypot buoys he'd ordered cut. A surrender to the whimsy of the ocean. His brother bobbing in a dirty undone float coat labelled with his useless brother's name.

Tom rolls in the water, onto his front, he forges forward, pushing back tears in his throat and the burning in his arms. He savours a mouthful of salt, the tanginess of ocean. He stops to purge the next. With each new wave of shuffled thoughts Tom slows to rest. He is partway to an island glistering with sunlight—a perfect place, a perfect girl, all beyond his reach. He feels to be a vast way out from shore, his dog a moving, barking blur on a scalloped frill of beach. Zulu. She'll be fretting something awful. I'm sorry, little dog.

A life for a life. His dues to the ocean. Tom floats on his back, ready, now, for sleep to pull him down. 'I'm sorry, Frank.' Tom's voice warbles through the water. 'I'm so sorry.' Across his face a lapping wash of peace. His debt to Frank made payable in full.

*

Tom gasps awake. A flash of black cuts through water at his side. He inhales ocean, retches in a fit of coughing. Pain slashes at his back. He can hear panicked cries, around him the water inking violet with his blood. Tom's arms flail, he thrashes to escape the tearing at his back. He swings to face the set of razored teeth. Instead a dog, a billowing of black and white.

Zulu's eyes bulge, her shrill cries the pitch of a terrorised woman. Her legs thrash in frenzy, her nails tear his throat and shoulders, he feels razors down his sides. She swims in desperate circles, her coat a skirt of bull kelp fanned across the surface. She tries repeatedly to board his back as if he were a raft. Tom fends her off. All this way from shore. 'You idiot dog,' he growls. She seems to calm at the reprimand. His dog looks to breathe again. She turns toward the shore, whimpers, looks across to check that he is there. Tom pictures the scene from above: a thrashing dog, a wounded master, a berley of freshly pumped blood. There is the definition of panic. There is the will to go on. 'In we go, girl. In we go.'

*

Steph takes a last wander along Wash House Beach and Pilot Beach before locking up the pilot station. She carries her bags to the car, slows beneath the grove of casuarina to watch a nesting pair of tawny frogmouths, still and quiet in the branches. Empty, worse than if she'd never come at all. She drives into town to leave the keys. Tuesday. She has a whole day to fill.

Her map shows a coastline of lighthouses from New South Wales to Queensland's border. She drives past convivial seaside towns with charming names: Lake Cathie, Bonny Hills. The signboard at a community hall makes her look again and smile: *Spring Into Song Weekend*; *USB Thumb Drive Found*.

Holiday homes punctuate forested hills and towering timber country, the bush tinted and lush with flower. Rolling pastures, contented cattle, gardens an impossible green after years of living in a landlocked desert. The world feels off kilter, as if only the outline of her has arrived, the rest far behind in no-man's-land.

Tacking Point Lighthouse stands proud at the end of the road, set upon a cleared nub of headland. A family seated on a bench looks out to froths of white kicking up the ocean. 'Humpbacks,' says the woman. 'They're breaching.' She hands Steph her binoculars. 'It's a mother and a calf.'

The lighthouse is newly painted with accents of blue, brilliant in the light. It could as easily watch over the Aegean Sea, its short tower offset by a low arched roof: more Greek Orthodox chapel. She tries the door. Locked. Eighteen seventy-nine. It's nothing like Maatsuyker. *You can't wind back the clock.*

Steph finds her way into Port Macquarie, her eagerness to look around subdued. She eats a sandwich at a cafe, messages Lydia: *Lost cause. Back in Sydney in the morning. Could only get on late night train.* All this way for nothing. She hasn't even gained a proper sense of Tom.

She drives north, deliberates on whether to take the dirt road all the way in to Smoky Cape. She strums the steering wheel. She has hours before the train.

She parks beside a Hilux ute, the only other vehicle in the car park. Kangaroos graze on the grass. They raise their heads, chewing as they watch her.

A red quad bike sits outside the cottages, its makeshift trailer piled with linen, a vac pack and mops. The caretaker hauls a tub of laundry on the back. 'Sorry, love,' he tells her. 'Not today. Mondays, Wednesdays and Fridays we run the tours.'

The top door to the lighthouse is open. 'Would it be possible for me to take a look? I won't be too long.'

He thinks a moment. 'Close the bottom door behind you so others don't follow you up.'

She passes by a worn old jacket slung over a post. Something about it makes her think of Tom.

A fresnel lens, a working lighthouse. Newly painted. Not a skerrick of rust. That would please her mother. She and Dad are somewhere in the Kimberley, celebrating her father's retirement from the ABC. Steph has to work to imagine the time before he was a producer in WA, when he read the news on air. She keeps an old cassette recording, with no device to play it on, of when his voice was smooth. Steph texts them a photo. *Hi from Smoky Cape. How's the Kimberley?* The message fails. No signal. She climbs the spiral stairs, steps out through the upper doorway. She stands on the lighthouse balcony, unprepared for this giddiness of feeling. A sweep of wild beaches north and south. A pacific ocean faithful to its name.

She spends time gazing at the ocean. A long way out a movement. A whale? Dolphins? A raft of birds? She loses track of it. She scans the ocean. There. A ruffling. A swimmer, bold, alone, gliding through the water.

Steph moves around the balcony, the flat of her hand against brick and mortar—a texture that feels a part of her. She presses her ribs against the round of the wall, tilts her gaze to the catwalk's latticed steel, the windows of the lantern room. The platen murmurs, air curls around the lighthouse like a whisper. Place. Memory. Love. Loss. All the forces that shape a person—not into the neat, symmetrical vessel she thought her life would be, but this, the past pulling at the edges, knotted strands of that long-ago girl wound within the woman. Steph feels a ruffle of oceanic air, cool and clean. The scent of the bush. This. Her homeland. A future of her making stretching out before her. Through her hands and chest the humming of the lighthouse. A small, determined light warming her with readiness.

★

Steph punches numbers on her phone. 'It's not too late if I call by now?'

She has the address on the card, but dutifully scrawls down Annie's directions. 'Town side of the Camden River,' Annie says. 'One click on from Tom's. Hang a left as soon as you cross the bridge.'

Steph drives south, glad to leave the highway for meandering roads through tall timber forest, rolling hills of pasture.

She drives over a rise that looks down upon a bend of the river, a large array of greenhouses. She slows the car, pulls off to the gravel shoulder.

Steph stands against the padlocked gate. Acres of steel framework, multi-spanned greenhouses encased in heavy plastic. The leap between the boy back then and this. She hadn't pictured anything as grand. A rusted mailbox, belonging to a different time, sits nailed to a post beside the gate. *T. L. FORREST* punched from tin. Why would such a simple rustic thing seize her with emotion? Steph touches the roughened surface of the letters.

She turns to leave before anyone should catch her, like some skittish animal slinking off into the night. She changes her mind and pulls her sketchbook from her bag. She sits in the passenger seat and draws an outline at the corner of the page, adds a dotted beam of light. She writes the date. *Dear Tom.* A line thrown out.

Seeing this old tin box with your name brought to mind a plaque
I made when Mum and Dad and I left Maatsuyker, all those years
ago. Remember the Lighthouse Tree? (Remember the leeches!)
I expect the plaque is still nailed to that tree, rusting with age like
all the keepers' names and dates of service that surround it, only
this was a tribute to the memory of your life. If that makes no
sense, too mixed-up for words, perhaps you will begin to understand
my reaction to discover you here, alive and well.

I've been in two minds about whether to contact you. I do
not wish to intrude on your life, or cause you any problems. This
afternoon I stood on the balcony of Smoky Cape Lighthouse
and thought about Maatsuyker, how that
special place, that fragile time, shaped the
person I've become. I saw a ruffling in the
water, a long way out. It took a few moments
to even find it again and to realise the
movement was a person, completely on their
own, swimming across the bay. Surely the

*worst decision would be to catch sight of someone after all this time
and then to turn away.*

*I imagine a vastness of ocean between that long-ago time and
the lives we lead now, but should you ever feel inclined to talk,
without expectation or obligation, my contact is below.*

*Whichever path you take, whatever you do, I wish you love
and joy.*

In friendship,

Your Stephanie

★

Dusk when Tom walks the beach naked, the air no longer warm.
He finds his jeans snagged on a rock, his shirt and underwear
floating in a tidal pool. All but one snap is ripped from his shirt.
His body trembles as he dresses. Zulu stands dripping on the sand,
a paroxysm of shivering, too spent to shake down her coat. Tom
gathers his boots, carries his dog in his arms. He finds an old
towel behind the car seat and rubs her down as best he can. 'In
the front. There we go.'

She sits with her legs and bottom wedged against his leg, his
hand on her rump, the heater slowly pumping warmth into the cab.
The light will soon be gone, the road out slow and corrugated, the
hour when a kangaroo might leap out from the shadows. He tells
himself to stay awake.

He slows at a movement, a person at the edge of the road. Zulu
stands to look. Young Dreadlocks from the car park, a thumb stuck
out in last hopes of a ride. It's miles to the highway. Zulu comes
alive. She whimpers. 'No,' he tells his dog. She whines, she howls
through the open gap of window. 'For fuck's sake, Zulu.' Tom slows

the car. He winds down the window. He waits for the guy to saunter to the car. 'Here comes lightning,' he mutters to his dog. 'You right, matey? Needing a lift?'

'Where you headed?'

'South.'

The boy hesitates, wary, looks him up and down as if he, Tom, were the suspect party.

'Anywhere in Port would be good.'

Anyweir. A Kiwi. Matted hair as ratty as his pack. 'Get in if you're getting in. Move over, girl.' Tom catches himself. Surrendering his life to the ocean one minute, helping some scruffball the next. He's always been weird.

Zulu issues a grin. *And you?* Tom would very much like to tell her. *You're a piss weak judge of character.* They start up, the cab a stink of wet dog, heated air, the kid's unwashed body. Zulu presses against the boy's side, his arm finds its way around her neck, the rank odour of his armpits perfume to her nose. A tackle box of piercings through his nose and ears. The kid hardly looks seventeen.

'Travelling light,' Tom says for something to say. All quiet on the Western Front. 'Long way from home,' he tries again. 'What brings you up this way?'

The kid gives him a sideways look like he's been asked a hundred times before. 'Looking after my own business.'

Ungrateful little shit. 'Don't mind me,' Tom says. 'I'm just the schmuck helping you out.'

At least the kid has the decency to look contrite. 'Sorry. I'm looking for work. Heard it was a cool place.'

'You could do worse.'

The ute bumps across corrugations. Tom sits upright, stiff-backed, wincing from a crosshatch of raw wounds slashed across his side and back.

The kid eyes him. 'Rough day?'

'You could say that.' Tom catches his reflection in the mirror. Christ. Hair stiff with salt, fierce scratches down his chin and throat. His collar looks black with blood.

'You have a wipe-out on the reef?'

'Nup.' Tom shakes his head. 'An old score that needed settling.'

'Cripes,' the boy says. 'Who won?'

Tom gives a smile. 'More of a truce.' He turns down the heater. 'What kind of work you after?'

'Fruit picking, farm work. I can turn my hand to anything.'

'A man of many talents.'

'Enough to get by.' The boy scowls, wary that he's being mocked. 'Never been afraid of hard work. Ask anyone back home.'

Finally the kid dozes. Zulu's head stays slumped on his lap, his dog twitching in her sleep. The vehicle rumbles through the night, the high beam a ghostly arc through branches of the trees.

Tom rubs at his shoulder, a remnant fluke of anchor ragged on his skin. Once he claimed he'd never be entwined with anyone again, convinced that one more setback would knock him down for good. He was a kid back then, hardly older than this boy, still finding who he was and floundering to free himself of a bad situation. A brave kid, he turned out to be, a decent man who somehow found his way.

Gravel road gives way to bitumen, darkness to an orange glow of streetlights. The Hilux idles at the junction. The boy sleeps on.

Tom lowers his window, draws in the quiet cool of night, the ocean air a balm upon his skin. He flicks the indicator, turns south onto the highway. Home.

AUTHOR'S NOTE

Maatsuyker Island is home to Australia's most southerly light station, the last in Australia to have been de-manned. While the grand old lighthouse still stands, its structure is being ravaged by weather that gives the Roaring Forties its title. If you wish to learn more about Maatsuyker Island, and the valiant efforts to save the lighthouse, please visit:

    www.facebook.com/groups/FriendsOfMaatsuykerIsland
    or email: wildcaremaatsuyker@gmail.com

ACKNOWLEDGEMENTS

Thank you for choosing *Wildlight* to read and for supporting Australian literature.

I am indebted to the Australia Council for the Arts for a grant to research and write the early stages of *Wildlight*. As significant as the grant's practical support was the affirmation that the project was worth backing.

To the former Watermark Literary Society, and Varuna, the Writers House, thank you for a marvellous writing residency that catapulted this project into being. I am indebted to writing guide Ian Templeman AM for sage direction and friendship; to the Watermark Committee led by Elaine van Kempen and deserving of the collective title *The Goddesses*; and to Peta Simmons, Gordon Bennett and Tanya Newman of Bennett Steel for their generous hospitality at Camden Haven. The Varuna residency was further enriched by evening talks and readings with fellow writers.

Chapters of *Wildlight* were written during a postdoctoral fellowship and I am most grateful to Edith Cowan University South West and to retired Dean Robert Irvine OAM.

I could not have navigated this island story without two crucial life experiences. The first was living and working at Maatsuyker Island, with my partner Gary, as volunteer caretakers and weather observers. My thanks go to Parks and Wildlife Service Tasmania, who manage the role in conjunction with Hobart's Bureau of Meteorology, and the tireless efforts of Friends of Maatsuyker Island. My appreciation extends to 'Club Mud' hiking companion Tony Marshall for the second experience of walking the South Coast Track with me and for being blown over at the top of the Ironbounds.

Along the way, many generously shared knowledge, expertise and experiences. Thank you, Grant and Sallie Brockman, Marina Campbell, Susan Donovan, Gwen Egg, Greg Finlay, Michael Garner, Pip Gowen, Elizabeth Mavrick, Lilly McCallum, Charles Morgan, Margaret Mortimer, Claudia Samson, Anthony Sarks of Ricardoes Tomatoes & Strawberries, Vicki Samuel, John Sansom, Jenny Scott, and Tacoma's Museum of Glass Hot Shop. Thank you, Ailsa Fergusson, for the lighthouse sketch that appears in the novel.

For invaluable feedback on manuscript drafts my sincere gratitude goes to Amanda Curtin, Lynne Leonhardt, Richard Rossiter, Nicole Sinclair and Annabel Smith. Thanks also to Gus Henderson and Ali Jarvey.

To weigh a book in your hands and share a story with readers is a privilege for any writer. I am indebted to literary agent Fran Moore (with a hug to Alasdair McGregor), Picador publisher Alex Craig, and the fabulous team at Pan Macmillan: editors Julia Stiles and Libby Turner, and cover designer Josh Durham.

Gary Miller: your zing for adventure and love of nature gladden my heart.

Robyn Mundy